Penguin Science Fiction 2702
The Joyous Invasions

Marion, beautiful jet-tressed wife to Theodore
Sturgeon, maintains that the author *has* no
biography, he being born anew each morning.
He professes recollection of children, not less
than four nor more than six, aged not more than
24 nor less than 4. He is at times aware of
residence in an impulsively rambling house in a
village a hundred miles from New York City,
which latter he avoids as a species of unreality.
His recollections include brief glimpses of early
education in a half-dozen eastern U.S. cities and
a schoolship, an infinitely more educational
sojourn as a merchant mariner, a long and heady
love-affair with bulldozers and other heavy
equipment, and certain rewarding experiences as
salesman, mechanic, cook, teacher, advertising
man, copywriter, and incessant repair-man of
broken toys. He prefers, however, to remember
ahead instead of back, the future being much
more interesting to recall than the past.
More Than Human, Theodore Sturgeon's
prize-winning novel, is also in Penguins.

Theodore Sturgeon

The Joyous Invasions

Penguin Books

Penguin Books Ltd, Harmondsworth, Middlesex, England
Penguin Books Australia Ltd, Ringwood, Victoria, Australia

First published by Victor Gollancz 1965
Published in Penguin Books 1967
Copyright © Theodore Sturgeon, 1965

To Marry Medusa, copyright © 1958, by Galaxy Publishing Corp.
Published originally in *Galaxy Science Fiction*, August 1958.

The Comedian's Children, copyright © 1958, by Mercury Press Inc.
Published originally in *Venture Science
Fiction Magazine*, May 1958.

The [Widget], The [Wadget], and Boff, copyright © 1955,
by Fantasy House Inc.
Originally published in two parts in *The Magazine of Fantasy
and Science Fiction*, November and December 1955.

Made and printed in Great Britain by Cox and Wyman Ltd,
London, Reading and Fakenham
Set in Linotype Pilgrim

To John Pike
Non-beat bohemian

To Marry Medusa

'I'll bus' your face, Al,' said Gurlick. 'I gon' break your back. I gon' blow up your place, an' you with it, an' all your rotgut licker, who wants it? You hear me, Al?'

Al didn't hear him. Al was back of the bar in his place three blocks away, probably still indignantly red, still twitching his long bald head at the empty doorway through which Gurlick had fled, still repeating what all his customers had just witnessed: Gurlick cringing in from the slick raw night, fawning at Al, stretching his stubble in a ragged brown grin, tilting his head, half-closing his sick-green, muddy-whited eyes.

'Walkin' in here,' Al would be reporting for the fourth time in nine minutes, 'all full of good-ol'-Al this an' hiya-buddy that, an' you-know-me-Al, and hows' about a little you-know; an' all I says it I know you all right, Gurlick, shuck on out o' here, I wouldn't give you sand if I met you on the beach; an' him spittin' like that, right on the bar, an' runnin' out, an' stickin' his head back in an' callin' me a – '

Sanctimoniously, Al would not sully his lips with the word. And the rye-and-bitters by the door would be nodding wisely and saying, 'Man shouldn't mention a feller's mother, whatever,' while the long-term beer would be clasping his glass, warm as pablum and headless as Anne Boleyn, and intoning, 'You was right, Al, dead right.'

Gurlick, four blocks away now, glanced back over his shoulder and saw no pursuit. He slowed his scamper to a trot and then a soggy shuffle, hunching his shoulders against the blowing mist. He kept on cursing Al, and the beer, and the rye-and-bitters, announcing that he could take 'em one at a time or all together one-handed.

He could do nothing of the kind, of course. It wasn't in him. It would have been success of a sort, and it was too late in life for Gurlick, unassisted, to start anything as new and different as success. His very first breath had been ill-timed and poorly done, and from then on he had done nothing right. He begged badly and stole when it was absolutely safe, which was seldom, and he rolled drunks providing they were totally blacked out, alone and concealed. He slept in warehouses, boxcars, parked trucks. He worked only in the most extreme circumstances and had yet to last through the second week.

'I'll cut 'em,' he muttered. 'Smash their face for them ...'

He sidled into an alley and felt along the wall to a garbage can he knew about. It was a restaurant garbage can and sometimes ...

He lifted the lid and, as he did so, saw something pale slide away and fall to the ground. It looked like a bun, and he snatched at it and missed. He stooped for it, and part of the misted wall beside him seemed to detach itself and become solid and hairy; it scrabbled past his legs. He gasped and kicked out, a vicious, ratlike spasm.

His foot connected solidly and the creature rose in the air and fell heavily at the base of the fence, in the dim wet light from the street. It was a small white dog, three-quarters starved. It yipped twice, faintly, tried to rise and could not.

When Gurlick saw it was helpless, he laughed aloud and kicked it and stamped on it until it was dead, and with each blow his vengeance became more mighty. There went Al, and there the two barflies, and one for the cops, and one for all judges and jailers, and a good one for everyone in the world who owned anything, and to top it, one for the rain.

He was a pretty big man by the time he was finished.

Out of breath, he wheezed back to the garbage can and felt around until he found the bun. It was sodden and slippery, but it was half a hamburger which some profligate had left unfinished, and that was all that mattered. He wiped it on his sleeve, which made no appreciable difference to sleeve or bun, and crammed it into his mouth.

He stepped out into the light and looked up through the mist at the square shoulders of the buildings that stood around to watch him. He was a man who had fought and killed for what was rightfully his.

'Don't mess with me,' he growled at the city.

A kind of intoxication flooded him. He felt the way he did at the beginning of that dream he was always having, where he would walk down a dirt path beside a lake, feeling good, feeling strong and expectant, knowing he was about to come to the pile of clothes on the bank. He wasn't having the dream just then, he knew; he was too cold and too wet, but he squared his shoulders anyway. He began to walk, looking up. He told the world to look out. He said he was going to shake it up and dump it and stamp on its fat face.

'You gon' to know Dan Gurlick passed this way,' he said.

He was perfectly right this time, because it was in him now.

It had been in the hamburger and before that in the horse from which most of the hamburger had been made, and before that in two birds, one after the other, which had mistaken it for a berry. Before that . . . it's hard to say.

When the first bird ate it, it sensed it was in the wrong place, and did nothing, and the same thing with the second. When the horse's blunt club of a tongue scooped it up with a clutch of meadow-grass, it had hopes for a while. It straightened itself out after the horse's teeth flattened it, and left the digestive tract early, to shoulder its way between cells and fibres until it rested in a ganglion.

There it sensed another disappointment, and high time too – once it penetrated into the neurone-chains, its nature would be irreversibly changed, and it would have been with the horse for the rest of his life. As, in fact, it was, but after the butcher's blade missed it, and the meat-grinder wrung it, pinched it, stretched it (but in no way separated any part of it from any other), it could still go on about its job when the time came.

Eight months in the deep-freeze affected it not at all, nor did hot fat. The boy who bit into the resulting hamburger was the only human being who ever saw it. It looked like a boiled raisin, or worse. The boy said so and got another free and it was dumped atop the garbage can, to be found and fought for by Gurlick.

The rain came down hard. Gurlick's exaltation faded, his shoulders hunched, his head went down. He slogged through the wet and soon sank to his usual level of feral misery. And there he stayed for a while.

This girl's name was Charlotte Dunsay and she worked in Accounting. She was open and sunny and she was a dish. She had rich brown hair with ruby lights in it, and the kind of topaz eyes that usually belong to a special kind of blonde. She had a figure that Paul Sanders, who was in Pharmaceuticals, considered a waste when viewed in the light of the information that her husband was a Merchant Marine officer on the Australia run. It was a matter of hours after she caught the attention of the entire plant (which was a matter of minutes after she got there) that news went around of her cheerful but unshakeable 'Thanks, but no, thanks.'

Paul took this as an outright challenge, but he kept his distance and bided his time. When the water-cooler reported that her husband's ship had come off second best in a bout with the Great Barrier Reef and had limped to Hobart, Tasmania, for repairs, Paul decided that the day was upon him. He stated as much in the locker room and got good odds – 11 to 2 – and somebody to hold the money – one of the suckers who gave him the cue for the single strategic detail which so far had escaped him.

He had the time (Saturday night), the place (obviously her apartment, since she wouldn't go out), and the girl. All he had to figure out was how to put himself on the scene, and when one of the suckers said, 'Nobody gets into that place but a for-real husband or a sick kitten,' he had the answer.

This girl had cried when one of the boss's tropical fish was found belly-up one morning. She had rescued a praying mantis from an accountant who was flailing it against the window with the morning *Times*, and after she let the little green monster out, she had rescued the accountant's opinion of himself with a comforting word and a smile that put dazzle-spots all over his work for the rest of the afternoon.

So on Saturday night, late enough so he would meet few people in the halls, but early enough so she wouldn't be in bed yet, Paul Sanders stopped for a moment by a mirror in the hallway of her apartment house, regarded his rather startling appearance approvingly, winked at it, and then went to her door and began rapping softly and excitedly. He heard soft hurrying footsteps behind the door and began to breathe noisily, like someone trying not to sob.

'Who is it? What's the matter?'

'Please,' he moaned against the panel, 'please, please, Mrs Dunsay, help me!'

She immediately opened the door a peering inch. 'Oh, thank God,' he breathed and pushed hard. She sprang back with her hands on her mouth and he slid in and closed the door with his back. She was ready for bed, as he had hardly dared to hope. The robe was a little on the sensible side, but what he could see of the gown was fine, just fine.

He said hoarsely, 'Don't let them get me!'

'Mr Sanders!' Then she came closer, comforting, cheering. 'No one's going to get you. You come on in and sit down until it's safe for you. Oh!' she gasped as he let his coat fall open, to reveal the shaggy rip and the bloodstain. 'You're hurt!'

He gazed dully at the scarlet stain. Then he flung up his head and set his features in an approximation of those of the Spartan boy who denied all knowledge of a stolen fox while the fox, hidden under his toga, ate his entrails. He pulled his coat straight and buttoned it and smiled and said, 'Just a scratch.' Then he sagged, caught the doorknob behind him, straightened up, and again smiled. It was devastating.

'Oh – oh, come and sit down,' she cried.

He leaned heavily on her but kept his hands decent, and she got him to the sofa. She helped him off with his coat and his shirt. It was indeed only a scratch, and she didn't seem to find the amount of blood too remarkable. A couple of cc swiped from the plasma lab. goes a long way on a white sport shirt.

He lay back limp and breathing shallowly while she flew to get scissors and bandages and warm water in a bowl, and averted his face from the light until she considerately turned it out in favour of a dim end-table lamp, and then he started the routine of not telling her his story because he was not fit to be here . . . she shouldn't know about such things . . . he'd been such a fool . . . and so on until she insisted that he could tell her anything, anything at all if it made him feel better.

So he asked her to drink with him before he told her because she surely wouldn't afterwards, and she didn't have anything but some sherry, and he said that was fine. He emptied a vial from his pocket into his drink and managed to switch glasses with her, and when she tasted it, she frowned slightly and looked down into the glass, but by then he was talking a sub-dued, dark blue, convoluted streak that she must strain to hear and puzzle to follow.

In twenty minutes, he let it dwindle away to silence. She said nothing, but sat with slightly glazed eyes on her glass, which she held with both hands like a child afraid of spilling. He took it away from her and set it on the end table and took her pulse. It was slower than normal and a good deal stronger. He looked at the glass. It wasn't empty, but she'd had enough. He moved over close to her.

'How do you feel?'

She took seconds to answer, and then said slowly, 'I feel . . .' Her lips opened and closed twice, and she shook her head slightly and was silent, staring out at him from topaz eyes gone all black.

'Charlotte . . . Lottie . . . lonely little Lottie. You're lonesome. You've been so alone. You need me, li'l Lottie,' he crooned, watching her carefully.

When she did not move or speak, he took the sleeve of her robe in one hand and, moving steadily and slowly, tugged at it until her hand slipped inside. He untied the sash with his free hand and took her arm and drew it out of the robe.

'You don't need this now,' he murmured. 'You are warm,

so warm ...' He dropped the robe behind her and freed her other hand. She seemed not to understand what he was doing. The gown was nylon tricot.

He drew her slowly into his arms. She raised her hands to his chest as if to push him away but there seemed to be no strength in them. Her head came forward until her cheek rested softly against his. She spoke into his ear quietly, without any particular force or expression.

'I mustn't do this with you, Paul. Don't let me. Harry is the ... there's never been anyone but him. There never must be. I'm ... something's happened to me. Help me, Paul. Help me. If I do it with you, I can't live any more. I'm going to have to die if you don't help me now.'

She didn't accuse him in any way.

Not once.

The carcass of the old truck stood forgotten in the never visited back edge of a junkyard. Gurlick didn't visit it; he lived in it, more often than not. Sometimes the weather was too bitterly cold for it to serve him, and in the hottest part of the summer he stayed away from it for weeks at a time. But most of the time it served him well. It broke the wind and it kept out most of the rain; it was dirty and dark and cost-free, which three items made it pure to Gurlick.

It was in this truck, two days after his encounter with the dog and the hamburger, that he was awakened from a deep sleep by ... call it the Medusa.

He had not been having his dream of the pile of clothes by the bank of the pool, and of how he would sit by them and wait, and then of how *she* would appear out there in the water, splashing and humming and not knowing he was there. Yet, this morning there seemed not to be room in his head for the dream nor for anything else, including its usual contents.

He made some grunts and a moan, and ground his stubby yellow teeth together, and rolled up to a sitting position and tried to squeeze his pressured head back into shape from the outside. It didn't help. He bent double and used his knees against his temples to squeeze even harder, and that didn't help either.

The head didn't hurt, exactly. And it wasn't what Gurlick occasionally called a 'crazy' head. On the contrary, it seemed to contain a spacious, frigid and meticulous balance, a thing lying like a metrical lesion on the inner surface of his mind.

He felt himself almost capable of looking at the thing, but, for all that it was in his head, it existed in a frightening *direction*, and at first he couldn't bring himself to look that way.

But then the thing began to spread and grow, and in a few rocking, groaning moments there wasn't anything in his head *but* the new illumination, this opening casement which looked out upon two galaxies and part of a third, through the eyes and minds of countless billions of individuals, cultures, hives, gaggles, prides, bevies, braces, herds, races, flocks and other kinds and quantities of sets and groupings, complexes, systems and pairings for which the language has as yet no terms; living in states liquid, solid, gaseous and a good many others with combinations and permutations among and between; swimming, flying, crawling, burrowing, pelagic, rooted, awash; and variously belegged, ciliated and bewinged; with consciousness which could be called the skulk-mind, the crash-mind, the paddle-, exaltation-, spring-, or murmuration-mind, and other minds too numerous, too difficult or too outrageous to mention.

And, over all, the central consciousness of the creature itself (though 'central' is misleading; the hive mind is permeative) – the Medusa, the galactic man o' war, the superconscious of the illimitable beast, of which the people of a planet were here a nerve and there an organ, where entire cultures were specialized ganglia; the creature of which Gurlick was now a member and a part, for all that he was a minor atom in a simple molecule of a primitive cell – this mighty consciousness became aware of Gurlick and he of it.

He let himself regard it just long enough to know it was there, and then blanked ten elevenths of his mind away from the very idea. If you set before Gurlick a page of the writings of Immanuel Kant, he would see it; he might even be able to read a number of the words. But he wouldn't spend any time or effort over it. He would see it and discard it from his attention, and if you left it in front of him, or held it there, he would see without looking and wait for it to go away.

Now, in its seedings, the Medusa had dropped its wrinkled milt into many a fantastic fossa. And if one of those scattered spores survived at all, it survived in, and linked with, the person and the species in which it found itself.

If the host-integer was a fish, then a fish it would remain, acting as a fish, thinking as a fish; and when it became a 'person' (which is what biologists call the individual polyps which make up the incredible colonies we call hydromedusae), it would *not* put away fishly things. On the contrary; it was to the interest of the Medusa that it keep its manifold parts specialized in the media in which they had evolved; the fish not only remained a fish, but in many cases might become much more so.

Therefore, in inducting Gurlick into itself, in the unequal interflow of itself into Gurlick and Gurlick into itself, he remained – just Gurlick.

What Gurlick saw of the Medusa's environment(s), he would not look at. What the Medusa sensed was only what Gurlick could sense, and (regrettably for our pride of species) Gurlick himself. It could not, as might be supposed, snatch out every particle of Gurlick's information and experience, nor could it observe Gurlick's world in any other way than through the man's own eye and mind. Answers there might be, in that rotted repository, to the questions the Medusa asked, but they were unavailable until Gurlick himself formulated them.

This had always been a slow process with him. He thought verbally, and his constructions were put together at approximately oral speed. The end effect was extraordinary; the irresistible demands came arrowing into him from immensity, crossing light-years with considerably less difficulty than it found in traversing Gurlick's thin, tough layer of subjective soft-focus, of not-caring, not-understanding-nor-wanting-to-understand. But reach him they did, the mighty unison of voice

with which the super-creature conveyed ideas ... and were
answered in Gurlick's own time, in his own way, and aloud in
his own words.

And so it was that this scrubby, greasy, rotten-toothed near-
illiterate in the filthy clothes raised his face to the dim light,
and responded to the demand-for-audience of the most majes-
tic, complex, resourceful and potent intellect in all the known
universe: 'Okay, *okay*. So whaddaya want?'

Gurlick was not afraid. Incredible as this might seem, it must
be realized that he was now a member, a person of the creature;
part of it. He no more thought to fear it than a finger might
fear a rib. But at the same time his essential Gurlickness was
intact – or, as has been pointed out, possibly more so. So he
knew that something he could not comprehend wanted to do
something through him of which he was incapable, and would
unquestionably berate him because it had not been done. ...

But this was *Gurlick*! This kind of thing could hold no fears
and no surprises for Gurlick. Bosses, cops, young drunks and
barkeeps had done just this to Gurlick all his life! And 'Okay,
okay! So whaddaya want?' was his invariable response, not
only to a simple call, but also, and infuriatingly, to detailed
orders. They had then to repeat their orders, or perhaps they
would throw up their hands and walk away, or kick him and
walk away. More often than not, the demand was disposed of,
whatever it was, at this point, and that was worth a kick any
time.

The Medusa would not give up. Gurlick would not listen,
and would not listen, and ... had to listen, and took the easiest
way out, and subsided to resentful seething – as always, as ever
for him. It is doubtful that anyone else on Earth could have
found himself so quickly at home with the invader. In this
very moment of initial contact, he was aware of the old
familiar response of anyone to a first encounter with him – a
disgusted astonishment, a surge of unbelief, annoyance and
dawning frustration.

'So whaddaya want?'

The Medusa told him what it wanted, incredulously, as one

explaining the utter and absolute obvious, and drew a blank from Gurlick. There was a moment of disbelief and then a forceful repetition of the demand.

And Gurlick still did not understand. Few humans would, for not many have made the effort to comprehend the nature of the hive-mind – what it must be like to have such a mind, and further, to be totally ignorant of the fact that any other kind of mind could exist.

For in all its eons of being, across and back and through and through the immensities of space it occupied, the Medusa had never encountered intelligence except as a phenomenon of the group. It was aware of the almost infinite variations in kind and quality of the *gestalt* psyche, but so fused in its experience and comprehension were the concepts 'intelligence' and 'group' that it was genuinely incapable of regarding them as separable things. That a single entity of any species was capable of so much as lucid thought without the operation of group mechanisms was outside its experience and beyond its otherwise near-omniscience. To contact any individual of a species was – or had been until now – to contact the entire species.

Now it pressed against Gurlick, changed its angle and pressed again, paused to ponder, came back again and, puzzling, yet again to do the exploratory, bewildered things a man .might do, faced with the opening of and penetration through some artifact he did not understand.

There were tappings and listenings, and (analogously) pressures this way and that, as if to find a left-hand thread. There were scrapings as for samples to analyze, proddings and pricks as for hardness tests, polarized rayings as if to determine lattice structures. And in the end there was a – call it a pressure test, the procedure one applies to clogged tubing or to oxide-shorts on shielded wire: blow it out. Take what's supposed to be going through and cram an excess down it.

Gurlick sat on the floor of the abandoned truck, disinterestedly aware of the distant cerebration, computation, discussion and conjecture. A lot of gabble by someone who knew more than he did about things he didn't understand. Like always.

Uh!

It had been a thing without sight or sound or touch, but it struck like all three, suffused him for a moment with some unbearable tension, and then receded and left him limp and shaken. Some mighty generator somewhere had shunted in and poured its product to him, and it did a great many things inside him somehow; and all of them hurt, and none was what was wanted.

He was simply not the right conduit for such a force. He was a solid bar fitted into a plumbing system, a jet of air tied into an electrical circuit; he was the wrong material in the wrong place and the output end wasn't hooked up to anything at all.

Spectacular, the degree of mystification which now suffused the Medusa. For ages untold, there had always been some segment somewhere which could come up with an answer to anything; now there was not.

That particular jolt of that particular force ought to have exploded into the psyche of every rational being on Earth, forming a network of intangible, unbreakable threads leading to Gurlick and through him to Medusa itself. It had always happened that way – not almost always, but always. This was how the creature expanded, Not by campaign, attack, siege, consolidation, conquest, but by contact and influx. Its 'spores', if they encountered any life-form which the Medusa could not control, simply did not function. If they functioned, the Medusa flowed in. *Always.*

From methane swamp to airless rock, from sun to sun through two galaxies and part of a third flickered the messages, sorting, combing, test-hypothesizing, calculating, extrapolating. And these flickering began to take on the hue of fear. The Medusa had never known fear before.

To be thus checked meant that the irresistible force was resisted, the indefensible was guarded. Earth had a shield, and a shield is the very next thing to a weapon. It *was* a weapon, in the Medusa's lexicon; for expansion was a factor as basic to its existence as Deity to the religious, as breath or heartbeat to a single animal; such a factor may not, must not be checked.

Earth suddenly became a good deal more than just another berry for the mammoth to sweep in. Humanity now had to be absorbed, by every measure of principle, of gross ethic, of life.

And it must be done through Gurlick, for the action of the 'spore' within him was irreversible, and no other human could be affected by it. The chances of another being in the same sector at the same time were too remote to justify waiting, and Earth was physically too remote from the nearest Medusa-dominated planet to allow for an attack in force or even an exploratory expedition, whereby expert mind might put expert hands (or palps or claws or tentacles or cilia or mandibles) to work in the field.

No, it had to be done through Gurlick, who might be – must be – manipulated by thought emanations, which are non-physical and thereby exempt from physical laws, capable of skipping across a galaxy and back before a light-ray can travel a hundred yards.

Even while, after that blast of force, Gurlick slumped and scrabbled dazedly after his staggering consciousness, and as he slowly rolled over and got to his knees, grunting and pressing his head, the Medusa was making a thousand simultaneous computations and setting up ten thousand more. From the considerations of a space-travelling culture deep in the Coalsack Nebula came a thought in the form of a speculative analogy:

As a defence against thick concentrations of cosmic dust, these creatures had designed spaceships which, on approaching a cloud, broke up into hundreds of small streamlined parts which would come together and reunite when the danger was past. Could that be what humanity had done? Had they a built-in mechanism, like the chipmunk's tail, the sea-cucumber's ejectible intestines, which would fragment the hive-mind on contact from outside, break it up into two and a half billion specimens like this Gurlick?

It seemed reasonable. In its isolation as the only logical hypothesis conceivable by the Medusa, it seemed so reasonable as to be a certainty.

How could it be undone then and humanity's total mind restored? Therein lay the Medusa's answer. Unify humanity (it thought: re-unify humanity) and the only problem left would be that influx. If that influx could not be done through Gurlick directly, other ways might be found; it had never met a hive-mind yet that it couldn't enter.

Gasping, Gurlick grated, 'Try that again, you gon' kill me, you hear?'

Coldly examining what it could of the mists of his mind, the Medusa weighed that statement and doubted it. On the other hand, Gurlick was, at the moment, infinitely valuable. It now knew that he could be hurt, and organisms which can be hurt can be driven. It realized also that Gurlick might be more useful, however, if he could be enlisted.

To enlist an organism, you find out what it wants and give it a little in a way that indicates promise of more. It asked Gurlick then what he wanted.

'Lea'me alone,' Gurlick said.

The response to that was a flat negative, with a faint stirring of that wrenching, explosive force it had already used. Gurlick whimpered, and the Medusa asked him again.

'What do I want?' whispered Gurlick. He ceased, for the moment, to use words, but the concepts were there. They were hate and smashed faces, and the taste of liquor, and a pile of clothes by the bank of a pond; she saw him sitting there and was startled; then she smiled and said, Hello, Handsome. What did he *want?* ...

The Medusa at this point had some considerable trouble interrupting. Gurlick, on the subject of what Gurlick wanted, could go on with surprising force for a very long time. The Medusa found it possible to understand this resentment, surely the tropistic flailing of something amputated, something denied full function, robbed, deprived. And, of course, insane.

Deftly, the Medusa began making promises. The rewards were described vividly indeed, and in detail that enchanted Gurlick. They were subtly implanted feed-back circuits from his own imaginings and they dazzled him. And from time to time there was a faint prod from that which had hurt him, just to remind him that it was still there.

At last, 'Oh, sure, sure,' Gurlick said. 'I'll find out about that, about how people can get put together again. An' then, boy, I gon' step on their face.'

So it was, chuckling, that Daniel Gurlick went forth from his wrecked truck to conquer the world.

Dimity Carmichael sat back and smiled at the weeping girl. 'Sex,' she told Caroline, 'is, after all, so *unnecessary.*'

Caroline knelt on the rug with her face hidden in the couch cushion, her nape bright red from weeping, the end strands of her hair wet with tears.

She had come unexpectedly, in mid-afternoon, and Dimity Carmichael had opened the door and almost screamed. She had caught the girl before she could fall, led her to the couch. When Caroline could speak, she muttered about a dentist, about how it had hurt, how she had been so sure she could make it home but was just too sick, and, finding herself here, had hoped Dimity would let her lie down for a few minutes . . .

Dimity had made her comfortable and then, with a few sharp unanswerable questions ('What dentist? What is his name? Why couldn't you lie down in his office? He wanted you out of there as soon as he'd finished, didn't he? In fact, he wasn't a dentist and he didn't do the kind of operation dentists do, isn't that so?') she had reduced the pale girl to this sodden, sobbing thing huddled against the couch. 'I've known for a long time how you were carrying on. And you finally got caught.' It was at that point, after thinking it out in grim, self-satisfied silence, that Dimity Carmichael said sex was, after all, so unnecessary. 'It certainly has done you no good. Why did you give in, Caroline? You didn't have to.'

'I did, I did . . .'

'Nonsense. Say you wanted to and we'd be closer to the truth. No one *has* to.'

Caroline said something –'I love [or loved] him so,' or some such. Dimity sniffed. 'Love, Caroline, isn't *that.* Love is everything else there can be between a man and a woman, without *that*.'

Caroline sobbed.

'That's your test, you see,' explained Dimity Carmichael. 'We are human beings because there are communions between us which are not experienced by – by rabbits, we'll say. If a man is willing to make some great sacrifice for a woman, it might be a proof of love. Consideration, chivalry, kindness, patience, the sharing of great books and fine music – these are the things that prove a *man*. It is hardly a demonstration of manhood for a man to prove himself merely as capable as a rabbit.'

Caroline shuddered. Dimity Carmichael smiled tightly. Caroline spoke.

'What? What's that?'

Caroline turned her cheek to rest it in her clenching hand. Her eyes were squeezed closed. 'I said . . . I just can't see it the way you do. I can't.'

'You'd be a lot happier if you did.'

'I know, I know . . .' Caroline sobbed.

Dimity Carmichael leaned forward. 'You can, if you like. Even after the kind of life you've lived – oh, I know how you were playing with the boys from the time you were twelve years old – but that can all be wiped away, and this will never bother you again. If you'll let me help you.'

Caroline shook her head exhaustedly. It was not a refusal, but instead doubt, despair.

'Of course I can,' said Dimity, as if Caroline had spoke her doubts aloud. 'You just do as I say.'

She waited until the girl's shoulders were still, until she lifted her head away from the couch, turned to sit on her calves, looked sideways up at Dimity from the corners of her long eyes. 'Do what?' Caroline asked forlornly.

'Tell me what happened – everything.'

'You know what happened.'

'You don't understand. I don't mean this afternoon – that was a consequence and we needn't dwell on it. I want the cause.

I want to know exactly what happened to get you into this.'

'I won't tell you his name.'

'His name,' said Dimity Carmichael, 'is legion. I don't care about that. What I want you to do is to describe to me exactly what happened, in every last detail, to bring you to *this*,' and she waved a hand at the girl, and her 'dentist', and all the parts of her predicament.

'Oh,' said Caroline faintly. Suddenly she blushed. 'I – I can't be sure just wh-which time it was.'

'That doesn't matter either,' said Dimity flatly. 'Pick your own. For example, the first time with this latest one. All right? Now tell me what happened – every last little detail, from second to second.'

Caroline turned her face into the upholstery again. 'Oh . . . why?'

'You'll see.' She waited for a time, and then said, 'Well?' and again, 'Look, Caroline, we'll peel away the sentiment, the bad judgement, the illusions and delusions, and leave you free. As I am free. You will see for yourself what it is to be that free.'

Caroline closed her eyes, making two red welts where the lids met. 'I don't know where to begin . . .'

'At the beginning. You had been somewhere – a dance, a club?'

'A . . . a drive-in.'

'And then he took you –'

'Home. His house.'

'Go on.'

'We got there and had another drink and – it happened, that's all.'

'*What* happened?'

'Oh, I can't, I can't talk about it! Don't you see?'

'I don't see. This is an emergency, Caroline. You do as I tell you. Just talk.' She paused and then said quietly, 'You got to his house.'

The girl looked up at her with one searching, pleading look, and, staring down at her hands, began speaking rapidly. Dimity

Carmichael bent close to listen, and let her go on for a minute, then stopped her. 'You have to say exactly how it was. Now – this was in the parlour.'

'L-living room.'

'Living room. You have to see it again – drapes, pictures, everything. The sofa was in front of the fireplace, is that right?'

Caroline haltingly described the room, with Dimity repeating, expanding, insisting. Sofa here, fireplace there, table with drinks, window, door, easy-chair. How warm, how large, what do you mean red, *what* red were the drapes? 'Begin again so I can see it.'

More swift, soft speech, more interruption. 'You wore what?'

'The black faille with the velvet trim and that neckline, you know – '

'Which has the zipper – '

'In the back.'

'Go on.'

After a time, Dimity stopped her with a hand on her back. 'Get up off the floor. I can't hear you. Get up, girl.' Caroline rose and sat on the couch. 'No, no; lie down. Lie down,' Dimity whispered.

Caroline lay down and put her forearms across her eyes. It took a while to get started again, but at last she did. Dimity drew up an ottoman and sat on it, close, watching the girl's mouth.

'Don't say *it*,' she said at one point. 'There are names for these things. Use them.'

'Oh, I – just *couldn't*.'

'Use them.'

Caroline used them.

'But what were you feeling all this time?'

'F-feeling?'

'Exactly.'

Caroline tried.

'And did you say anything while this was going on?'

'No, nothing. Except – '

'Well?'

'Just at first,' whispered the girl. She moved and was still again, and her concealing arms clamped visibly tighter against her eyes. 'I think I went . . .' and her teeth met, her lips curled back, her breath hissed in sharply.

Dimity Carmichael's lips curled back and she clenched her teeth and sharply drew in her breath. 'Like that?'

'Yes.'

'Go on. Did he say anything?'

'No. Yes. Yes, he said, "Caroline, Caroline, Caroline," ' she crooned.

'Go on.'

She went on. Dimity listened, watching. She saw the girl smiling and the tears that pressed out through the juncture of forearm and cheek. She watched the faint flickering of white-edged nostrils. She watched the breast in its rapid motion, not quite like that which would result from running up stairs, because of the shallow shiver each long inhalation carried, the second's catch and hold, the gasping release.

'Ah-h-h-h-h!' Caroline screamed suddenly, softly. 'Ahhh . . . I thought he loved me! I did think he loved me!' She wept. 'That's all . . .'

'No, it isn't. You had to leave, get ready to leave. Hm? What did he say? What did you say?'

Finally, when Caroline said, '. . . and that's all,' there were no questions to ask. Dimity Carmichael rose and picked up the ottoman and placed it carefully where it belonged by the easy-chair, and sat down. The girl had not moved.

'Now how do you feel?'

Slowly the girl took down her arms and lay looking at the ceiling. She wet her lips and let her head fall to the side so she could look at Dimity Carmichael, composed in the easy-chair – a chair not too easy, but comfortable for one who liked a flat seat and a straight back. The girl searched Dimity Carmichael's face, looking apparently for shock, confusion, anger, disgust. She found none of these, nothing but thin lips, dry skin, cool eyes.

Answering at last, she said, 'I feel . . . awful.' She waited but Dimity Carmichael had nothing to say. She sat up painfully and covered her face with her hands. She said, 'Telling it was making it happen all over again, almost real. But –'

Again a silence.

'– but it was like . . . doing it in front of somebody else. In front of – '

'In front of me?'

'Yes, but not exactly.'

'You did do it in front of someone – yourself. You will never be in such a situation again,' Dimity Carmichael intoned, her voice returning and returning to the same note like some soft insistent buzzer, 'without hearing yourself tell it, every detail, every sight and sound of it, to someone else. Except that the happening and the telling won't be weeks apart, like this time. They'll be simultaneous.'

'But the telling makes it all so . . . cheap, almost . . . funny!'

'It isn't the telling that makes it that way. The act is itself ridiculous, ungraceful, altogether too trivial for the terrible price one pays for it. Now you can see it as I see it; now you will be unable to see it any other way. Go wash your face.'

She did, and came back looking much better, with her hair combed and the furrows gone from her brows and the corners of her long eyes. With the last of her makeup gone, she looked even younger than usual; to think she was actually two years older than Dimity Carmichael was incredible, incredible . . .

She slipped on her jacket and took up her topcoat and handbag. 'I'm going. I – I feel a lot better. I mean about . . . things.'

'It's just that you're beginning to feel as I do about . . . things.'

'Oh!' Caroline cried from the door, from the depths of her troubles, her physical and mental agonies, the hopeless complexity of simply trying to live through what life presented. 'Oh, I wish I was like you! I wish I'd always been like you!' And she went out.

Dimity Carmichael sat for a long time in the not-quite-easy chair with her eyes closed. Then she rose and went into the bedroom and began to take off her clothes. She needed a bath;

she felt proud. She had a sudden recollection of her father's face showing a pride like this. He had gone down into the cesspool to remove a blockage when nobody else would do it. It had made him quite sick, but when he came up, unspeakably filthy and every nerve screaming for a scalding bath, it had been with that kind of pride.

Mama had not understood that nor liked it. She would have borne the unmentionable discomforts of the blocked sewer indefinitely rather than have it known, even within the family, that Daddy had been so soiled. Well, that's the way Daddy was. That's the way Mama was. The episode somehow crystallized the great differences between them, and why Mama had been so glad when he died, and how it was that Dimity's given name – given by him – was one which reflected all the luminance of wickedness and sin, and why Salome Carmichael came to be known as Dimity from the day he died. No cesspools for her. Clean, crisp was little Dimity, decent, pleated, skirted and cosy all her life.

To get from her bedroom into the adjoining bath – seven steps – she bundled up in the long robe. Once the shower was adjusted to he rliking, she hung up the robe and stepped under the cleansing flood. She kept her gaze, like her thoughts, directed upwards as she soaped.

The detailed revelation she had extracted from Caroline flashed through her mind, all of it, in a second, but with no detail missing. She smiled at the whole disgusting affair with a cool detachment. In the glass door of the shower stall, she saw the ghost-reflection of her face, the coarse-fleshed, broad nose, the heavy chin with its random scattering of hairs, the strong square clean yellow teeth.

I wish I was like you! I wish I'd always been like you! Caroline had said that, slim-waisted, full-breasted Caroline, Caroline with the mouth which, in relaxation, pouted to *kiss me*, Caroline with the skin of a peach, whose eyes were long jewels of a rare cut, whose hair was fine and glossy and inwardly ember-radiant. *I wish I was like you.*

Could Caroline had known that Dimity Carmichael had

yearned all her life for those words spoken that way by Caroline's kind of woman? For were they not the words Dimity herself repressed as she turned the pages of magazines, watched the phantoms on the stereophonic, Technicolored, wide deep unbearable screen?

It was time now for the best part of the shower, the part Dimity looked forward to most. She put her hand on the control and let it rest there, ecstatically delaying the transcendent moment.

... *be like you* ... perhaps Caroline would, one day, with luck. How good not to *need* all that, how fine and clear everything was without it! How laughingly revolting, to have a man prove the power of a rabbit's preoccupations with his animal strugglings and his breathy croonings of one's name, 'Salome, Salome, Salome ...' (I mean, she corrected herself suddenly and with a shade of panic, Caroline, Caroline, Caroline.)

In part because it was time, and part because of a swift suspicion that her thoughts were gaining a momentum beyond her control and a direction past her choice, she threw the control hard over to *Cold*, and braced her whole mind and body for that clean (surely sexless) moment of total sensation by which she punctuated her entire existence.

As the liquid fire of cold enveloped her, the lips of Dimity Carmichael turned back the teeth met, the breath was drawn in with a sharp, explosive hiss.

Gurlick sank his chin into his collarbones, hunched his shoulders, and shuffled. 'I'll find out,' he promised, muttering. 'You jus' let me know what you want, I'll find out f'ya. Then, boy, look out.'

At the corner, sprawled out on the steps of an abandoned candy store, he encountered what at first glance seemed to be an odorous bundle of rags. He was about to pass it when he stopped. Or was stopped.

'It's only Freddy,' he said disgustedly. 'He don't know nothin', hardly.'

'Gah dime bo?' asked the bundle, stirring feebly, and extending a filthy hand which flowered on the stem of an impossibly thin wrist.

'Well, sure I said somebody oughta know,' growled Gurlick, 'but not him, f'godsakes.'

'Gah dime bo? Oh . . . It's Danny. Got a dime on ya, Danny?'

'All right, all right, I'll ast 'im!' said Gurlick angrily, and at last turned to Freddy. 'Shut up, Freddy. You know I ain't got no dime. Listen, I wanna ast you somethin'. How could we get all put together again?'

Freddy made an effort which he had apparently not considered worth while until now: he focused his eyes. 'Who – you and me? What you mean, put together?'

'I *tole* you!' said Gurlick, not speaking to Freddy; then, at the mingled pressure of threat and promise, he whimpered in exasperation and said, 'Just tell me can we do it or not, Freddy.'

'What's the matter with you, Danny?'

'You gon' tell me or aincha?'

Freddy blinked palely and seemed on the verge of making a mental effort. Finally he said, 'I'm cold. I been cold for three years. You got a drink on you, Danny?'

There wasn't anybody around, so Gurlick kicked him. 'Jerk,' he said, tucked his chin down, and shuffled away. Freddy watched him for a while, until his gritty lids got too heavy to hold up.

Two blocks farther, Gurlick saw somebody else and tried to cross the street. He was not permitted to. 'No!' he begged. 'No, no, no! You can't ast every single one you see.' Whatever he was told, it was said in no uncertain terms, because he whined, 'You gon' get me in big trouble, jus' you wait.'

Ask he must; ask he did. The plumber's wife, who stood a head taller than he and weighed twice as much, stopped sweeping her stone steps as he shuffled towards her, head still down but eyes up, and obviously not going to scuttle past as his kind usually did.

He stopped before her, looking up. She would tower over him if he stood on a box; as it was, he was on the sidewalk and she was on the second step. He regarded her like a country cousin examining a monument. She looked down at him with the nauseated avidity of a witness to an automobile accident.

He put a hand on the side of his head and screwed up his eyes. The hand fell away; he gazed at her and croaked, 'How can we get put together again?'

It seemed a long noisy while before the immense capacity of her lungs was exhausted by her first great ring of laughter, but when it was over, it brought her face down again, which served only to grant her another glimpse of Gurlick's anxious filthy face, and caused another paroxysm.

He left her laughing and headed for the park. Numbly he cursed the woman and all women, and all their husbands, and all their forebears and descendants.

Into the park the young spring had brought slim grass, tree-buds, dogs, children, old people and a hopeful ice-cream vendor. The peace of these beings was leavened by a scattering of adolescents who had found the park on such a day more attractive than school and it was three of these who swarmed into Gurlick's irresolution as he stood just inside the park, trying to find an easy way to still the demand inside his head.

'Dig the creep,' said the one with HEROES on the back of his jacket, and another: 'Or-*bit!*' and the three began to circle Gurlick, capering like stage Indians, holding fingers out from their heads and shrilling 'Bee-beep! Bee-beep' satellite signals.

Gurlick turned back and forth for a moment like a weather-vane in a williwaw, trying to sort them out. 'Giddada year,' he growled.

'Bee-beep!' screamed one of the satellites. 'Stand by fer re-*yentry!*' The capering became a gallop as the orbits closed, swirled around him in a shouting blur, and at the signal 'Burn-out!' they stopped abruptly and the one behind Gurlick dropped to his hands and knees while the other two pushed. Gurlick hit the ground with a whoosh, flat on his back with his arms and legs in the air. Around the scene, one woman cried out indignantly, one old man's mouth popped open with shock, and everyone else, everyone else, laughed and laughed.

'Giddada year,' gasped Gurlick, trying to roll over and get his knees under him.

One of the boys solicitously helped him to his feet, saying to another, 'Now, Rocky, ya shoonta. Ya shoonta.' When the trembling Gurlick was upright and the second of the trio – the 'Hero' – down on hands and knees behind him again, the solicitous one gave another push and down went Gurlick again. Gurlick, now dropping his muffled pretences of threat and counterattack, lay whimpering without trying to rise. Everybody laughed and laughed, all but two, and they didn't do anything. Except move closer, which attracted more laughers.

'Space Patrol! Space Patrol,' yelled Rocky, pointing at the approaching blue uniform. 'Four o'clock high!'

'Ess-*cape* velocity!' one of them barked; and with their antennae-fingers clamped to their heads and a chorus of shrill *bee-beeps*, they snaked through the crowd and were gone.

'Bastits. Lousy bastits. I'll killum, the lousy bastits,' Gurlick wept.

'Ah right. *Ah* right! Break it up. Move along. Ah right,' said the policeman. The crowd broke it up immediately ahead of him and moved along sufficiently to close the gap behind, craning in gap-mouthed anticipation of another laugh ... laughter makes folks feel good.

The policeman found Gurlick on all fours and jerked him to his feet, a good deal more roughly than Rocky had done. 'Ah right, you, what's the matter with you?'

The indignant lady pushed through and said something about hoodlums. 'Oh,' said the policeman, 'hoodlum, are ye?'

'Lousy bastits,' Gurlick sobbed.

The policeman quelled the indignant lady in mid-protest with a bland, 'Ah right, don't get excited, lady; I'll handle this. What you got to say about it?' he demanded of Gurlick.

Gurlick, half suspended from the policeman's hard fist, whimpered and put his hands to his head. Suddenly nothing around him, no sound, no face, pressed upon him more than that insistence inside. 'I don't care there *is* lotsa people, don't make me ast now!'

'What'd you say?' demanded the policeman truculently.

'Okay, okay!' Gurlick cried to the Medusa, and to the policeman: 'All I want is, tell me how we c'n get put together again.'

'What?'

'All of us,' said Gurlick. 'Everybody in the world.'

'He's talking about world peace,' said the indignant woman. There was laughter. Someone explained to someone else that the bum was afraid of the Communists. Someone else heard that and explained to the man behind him that Gurlick was a Communist. The policeman heard part of that and shook Gurlick. 'Don't you go shootin' your mouth off around here, or it's the cooler for you.'

Gurlick sniveled and mumbled, 'Yessir, yessir,' and sidled cringing away.

'Ah right. Move along. Show's over. Ah right, there . . .'

Gurlick ran. He was out of breath before he began to run, so his wind lasted him only to the edge of the park, where he reeled against the railing and clung there to whimper his breath back again. He stood with his hands over his face, his fingers trying to press back at that thing inside him, his mouth open and noisy with self-pity and anoxia. A hand fell on his shoulder and he jumped wildly.

'It's all right,' said the indignant woman. 'I just wanted to let you know everybody in the whole world isn't cruel and mean.'

Gurlick looked at her, working his mouth. She was in her fifties, round-shouldered, bespectacled and most earnest. She said, 'You go right on thinking about world peace. Talking about it, too.'

He was not yet capable of speaking. He gulped air.

'You poor man.' She fumbled in an edge-flaked patent leather pocketbook and found a quarter. She held it and sighed as if it were an heirloom, and handed it to him. He took it unnoticing and put it away. He did not thank her. He asked, 'Do you know?' He pressed his temples in that newly developed compulsive gesture. 'I got to find out, see? I got to.'

'Find out what?'

'How people can get put back together again.'

'Oh,' she said. 'Oh, dear.' She mulled it over. 'I'm afraid I don't know just what you mean.'

'Y'see?' he informed his inner tormentor, agonized. 'Ain't nobody knows – nobody!'

'Please explain it a little,' the woman begged. 'Maybe there's someone who can help you, if I can't.'

Gurlick said hopelessly, 'It's about people's brains, see what I mean, how to make all the brains go together again.'

'Oh, you poor man ...' She looked at him pityingly, clearly certain that his brains indeed needed putting together again, and Well, at least he realizes it, which is a sight more than most of us do. 'I know! Dr Langley's the man for you. I clean for him once a week, and believe me, if you want to know somebody who knows about the brain, he's the one. He has a machine that draws wiggly lines and he can read them and tell what you're thinking.'

Gurlick's vague visualization of such a device flashed out to the stars, where it had an electrifying effect. 'Where's it at?'

'The machine? Right there in his office. He'll tell you all about it; he's such a dear, kind man. He told me all about it, though I'm afraid I didn't quite – '

'Where's it at?'

'Why, in his office. Oh, you mean where. Well, it's 13 Deak Street, on the second floor. Look, you can almost see it from here. Right there where the house with the – '

Without another word, Gurlick put down his chin and hunched his shoulders and scuttled off.

'Oh dear,' murmured the woman worriedly, 'I do hope he doesn't bother Dr Langley too much. But then he wouldn't; he does believe in peace.' She turned away from her good deed and started home.

Gurlick did not bother Dr Langley for long, and he did indeed bring him peace.

There was a mad boy in Rome, and an angry warrior in Africa whose yams were being stolen at night, and there was

T – T.J.I. – B

the thief who stole them. All over the world people, with all their hearts, did the difficult things they must do to be human beings, and learned what they had to learn, paying what it cost them. Two and three-quarter billions ... two and three-quarter billion subjective planets, some circling close to each other and to light, and others far out and cold in the lonely dark; but all separate, isolated, discrete. Commissar, peasant, potentate, the children, the old ones, the insane, the under privileged – each basically alone.

Guido, the boy in Rome, had been born during the fighting at Anzio, and was found by an UNRRA team a year and a half later, living with some wild children, maggoting the bones of the ruined town. He was full of music, to a degree notable even in a country full of music. Before he could talk, he could whistle, and he would whistle any music he heard after one hearing. In the shuffle of souls that followed, he was taken in by a Corfu shepherd who, in the next ten years, kicked the music out of the boy, or perhaps he kicked it down.

The shepherd was a smuggler, and though he needed the boy's strong back and hard hands, he wanted nothing near him which might attract attention. Guido dared not utter a phrase of music, not a note. The shepherd developed a high skill in detection; he could be aware of music welling up in the boy before Guido himself knew of it, and would knock him down and kick him and his unborn melodies. And when the association between music and punishment was strong enough, there was no more music from the boy – and too much unkillably, unquellably inside him.

After the shepherd died, Guido turned into something not quite human. He committed a series of ingenious nuisances which for a long time were lost in the seethe of the city, unconnected as they seemed to be with each other. He smashed some stained-glass windows, and he broke the leg of a beggar over a kerbstone; he took a toy from a child and threw it into the river; he vandalized a print shop.

And at last a detective with rather more sight, more insight than most found the thread upon which was strung these episodes; for the stained glass was one of the windows of the Chapel of the Annunciation, and choir practice was in session; the beggar was one who sang for his supper; the child's toy was a harmonica; the print shop was printing sheet music. The detective contrived to give Guido a violin, and there was, for Guido, a burst of light, and would be, in time, a very explosion of music from him ...

And the warrior, Mbala, began to guard his yam patch at night, which was by custom the duty of his dead father, as Mbala would one day die and then guard the yam patch of his sons. But Mbala's faith in this old belief was shaken, for all he could agree that his father was supposed to guard against devils, not against men, and it was manifestly a man who was stealing the yams.

The thief, Nuyu, had once had faith in such beliefs too, but he no longer believed in anything at all but his own clever hands.

They were, in their own theology, Mbala and Nuyu, backslider and atheist respectively.

And one night, while Mbala watched and Nuyu hid, waiting him out, there came from the sky a floating, glowing sphere. It sank to the edge of the yam patch and, not quite touching the ground, slowly circled the field; and where it had passed, the thick tangle of bush which surrounded the cultivated land was cleared away, and in its place a thin drift of white, cold material which changed to water in a minute or two.

Now it happened that the sphere was an untenanted and automatic machine, and that the weed it harvested and processed was astralagus vetch, which has a high affinity for selenium, and the builders of the machine needed all the selenium they could get.

But to Nuyu the thief, who was hiding in the vetch at the time, this was retribution not only for his current sins, but all his past ones, cast as it was in the strange figure of a spirit guarding the yams – shades of his childhood legends, so long laughed away!

And to Mbala, this was his father, not only discovering the thief (who came howling and gibbering to huddle in contrite terror against Mbala) but at the same time clearing more land for him.

After the sphere was gone, falling upwards and away to the north (where it had detected another stand of vetch), Mbala did not, as he had earlier intended, kill his thief. Instead, they returned to the village, companions in revelation, each at the peak of a species of that rare ecstasy, the religious experience: one confirmed, the other converted.

THESE WERE people, these are anecdotes dwelt upon for their element of the extraordinary. But each man alive has such a story, unique unto himself, of what is in him and of its moulding by the forces around him, and of his interpretations of those forces. Here a man sees a machine as a god, and there a man sees a god as a mere kind of angry argument; and another uses the angry argument of others quite as if it were a machine. Yet for all his ability to work in concert with his fellows, and to induce some sympathy in their vibrations, he remains isolated; no one knows exactly how another feels.

At the very climax of sensation, Man approaches unconsciousness . . . unconsciousness of what? Why, of all around him; never of himself.

'You Doctor Langley?'

The doctor said, 'Good God.'

Dear, kind man he might be to his cleaning lady, but to Gurlick he was just another clean man full of knowledges and affairs which Gurlick wouldn't understand, plus the usual, foreseeable anger, disgust and intolerance Gurlick stimulated wherever he went. In short, just another one of the bastits to hate.

Gurlick said, 'You know about brains.'

The doctor said, 'Who sent you here?'

'You know what to do to put people's brains together again.'

'What? Who are you? What do you want anyway?'

'Look,' said Gurlick, 'I got to find this out, see. You know how to do it or not?'

'I'm afraid,' said the doctor icily, 'that I can't answer a question I don't understand.'

'So ya *don't* know anything about brains.'

The doctor sat tall behind a wide desk. His face was tall and narrow, and in repose fell naturally into an expression of arrogance. No better example in all the world could have been found of the epitome of everything Gurlick hated in his fellow man. The doctor was archetype, coda, essence; and, in his presence, Gurlick was so unreasonably angry as almost to forget to cringe.

'I didn't say that,' said Langley.

He looked at Gurlick steadily for a moment, openly selecting a course of action: Throw him out? Humour him? Or study him? He observed the glaring eyes, the trembling mouth, the posture of fear-driven aggressiveness.

He said, 'Let's get something straight. I'm not a psychiatrist.' Aware that this creature didn't know a psychiatrist from an accountant, he explained, 'I mean I don't treat people who have problems. I'm a physiologist, specializing on the brain. I'm just interested in how brains do what they do. If the brain was a motor, you might say I am the man who writes the manual that the mechanic studies before he goes to work. That's all I am, so before you waste your own time and mine, get that straight. If you want me to recommend somebody who can help you with whatev –'

'You tell me,' Gurlick barked, 'you just tell me that one thing and that's all you got to do.'

'What one thing?'

Exasperated, adding his impatience with all his previous failures to his intense dislike of this new enemy, Gurlick growled, 'I tole ya.' When this got no response, and when he understood from the doctor's expression that it would get none, he blew angrily from his nostrils and explained, 'Once everybody in the world had just the one brain, see what I mean? Now they all took apart. All you got to tell me is how to stick 'em together again.'

'You seem to be pretty sure that everybody – how's that again? – had the same brain once.'

Gurlick listened to something inside him, then. 'Had to be like that,' he said.

'Why did it have to be?'

Gurlick waved a vague hand. 'All this. Buildin's, cars, tools, 'lectric, all like that. This don't git done without the people all think with like one head.'

'It did get done that way, though. People can work together without – thinking together. That is what you mean, isn't it – all thinking at once, like a hive of bees?'

'Bees, yeah.'

'It didn't happen that way with people. What made you think it did?'

A startled computation was made among the stars, and, given the axioms which had proved unalterably and invariably true heretofore, namely, that a species did not reach this high level of technology without the hive-mind to organize it, there was only one way to account for the doctor's incredible statement – providing he did not lie – and Gurlick, informed of this conclusion, did his best to phrase it. 'I guess what happened was everybody broke all apart, they on their own now, they just don't remember no more. I don't remember it, you don't remember it, that one time you and me and everybody was part of one great big brain.'

'I wouldn't believe that,' said the doctor, 'even if it was true.'

'Sure not,' Gurlick agreed, obviously and irritatingly taking the doctor's statement as a proof of his own. 'Well, I still got to find out how to stick 'em all together again.'

'You won't find it out from me. I don't know. So why don't you just go and – '

'You got a machine, it knows what you're thinkin',' said Gurlick suddenly.

'I have a machine which does nothing of the kind. Who told you about me, anyway?'

'You show me that machine.'

'Certainly not. Look, this has been very interesting, but I'm busy and I can't talk to you any more. Now be a good –'

'You *got* to show it to me,' said Gurlick in a terrifying whisper, for through his fogbound mind had shot his visions (she's in the water up to her neck, saying, Hello, Handsome, and he just grins, and she says, I'm coming out, and he says, Come on then, and slowly she starts up towards him, the water down her collarbone, to her chest, to –) and a smoky curl of his new agony. He had to get this information. He *must*.

The doctor pressed himself away from his desk a few inches in alarm. 'That's the machine over there. It won't make the slightest sense to you. I'm not trying to hide anything from you – it's just that you wouldn't understand it.'

Gurlick sidled over to the equipment the doctor had pointed to. He stood looking at it for a time, flashing a cautious ratlike glance towards the doctor from time to time, and pulling at his mouth. 'What you call this thing?'

'An electroencephalograph. Are you satisfied?'

'How's it know what you're thinkin'?'

'It doesn't. It picks up electrical impulses from a brain and turns them into wavy lines on a strip of paper.'

Watching Gurlick, the doctor saw clearly that, in some strange way, his visitor was not thinking of the next question; he was waiting for it. He could see it arrive.

'Open it up,' said Gurlick.

'What?'

'Open it. I got to look at the stuff inside it.'

'Now look here! –'

Again that frightening hiss: 'I got to see it.'

The doctor sighed in exasperation and pulled open the file drawer of his desk. He located a manual, slapped it down on the desk, leafed through and opened it. 'There's a picture of the machine. This is a wiring diagram. If it makes any sense to you, it'll tell you more than a look inside would tell you. I hope it tells you that the thing's far too complicated for a man without train –'

Gurlick snatched up the manual and stared at it. His eyes glazed and cleared. He put the manual down and pointed. 'These here lines is wires?'

'Yes . . .'

'This here?'

'A rectifier. It's a tube. You know what a tube is.'

'Like radio tubes. Electric is in these here wires?'

'This can't mean anyth –'

'Those little lines? Ground. Here, and here, and over here, the current goes to ground.'

Gurlick placed a grimy fingertip on the transformer symbol. 'This changes the electric. Right?'

Dumbfounded, Langley nodded.

Gurlick said, 'Regular electric comes in here. Some other kind comes in here. What comes in here, huh?'

'That's the detector. The input. The electrodes. I mean whatever brain the machine is hooked up to feeds current in there.'

'It ain't very much.'

'It ain't,' mimicked the doctor weakly, 'very much.'

'You got one of those strips with the wavy lines?'

Wordlessly, the doctor opened a drawer, found a trace and tossed it on top of the diagram. Gurlick pored over it for a long moment, referring twice to the wiring diagram, then threw it down. 'Okay. Now I found out.'

'You found out what?'

'What I wanted.'

'Will you be kind enough to tell me just what you found?'

'God,' said Gurlick disgustedly, 'how sh'd I know?'

Langley shook his head, ready to laugh at this mystifying and irritating visitation. 'Well, if you've found it, you don't have to stick around.'

'Shut up,' said Gurlick, cocking his head, closing his eyes. Langley waited.

It was like hearing one side of a phone conversation, but there was no phone. 'How the hell I'm supposed to do that?' Gurlick complained at one point, and, later, 'I gon' need money

for anything like that. No, I can't. I can't, I tell ya; you just gon'
git me in th' clink ... what you think he goin' be doin' while I
take it?'

'Who are you talking to?' Langley demanded.

'I dunno,' said Gurlick. 'Shut up now.' He fixed his gaze on
the doctor's face, and for seconds it was unseeing. Then, suddenly, it was not, and Gurlick spoke to him: 'I got to have
money.'

'I'm not giving any handouts this season. Now get out of
here.'

Gurlick, showing all the signs of an unwelcome internal
goading, came around the desk and repeated his demand. As
he did so, he saw for the very first time that Doctor Langley
sat in a wheelchair.

That made all the difference in the world to Gurlick.

Henry was tall. He stood tall and had a surprisingly adult
face, which made him all the more ridiculous as he sat through
school day after day, weeping. He did not cry piteously or
with bellows of rage and outrage, but almost silently, with a
series of widely spaced, soft, difficult sniffs. He did what he was
told (get in line ... move your chairs, it's story time ... fetch
the puzzles ... put away the paints), but he did not speak and
would not play or dance or sing or laugh. He would only sit,
stiff as a spike, and sniff. Henry was five and kindergarten was
tough for him. Life was tough for him.

'Life is tough,' his father was fond of saying, 'and the little
coward might as well learn.'

Henry's mother disagreed, but deviously. She lied to everyone concerned – to her husband, to Henry's teacher, to the
school psychologist and the principal and to Henry himself.
She told her husband she was shopping in the mornings, but
instead she was sitting in the corner of the kindergarten room
watching Henry crying. After two weeks of this, the psychologist and the principal corralled her and explained to her that
the reality of home involved having her at home, the reality
of school involved *not* having her at school, and Henry was not

going to face the reality of school until he could experience it without her.

She agreed immediately, because she always agreed with anyone who had a clear opinion about anything, went back to the room, told the stricken Henry that she would be waiting just outside, and marched out. She completely overlooked the fact that Henry could see her from the window, see her walk down the path and get into her car and drive away. If he had any composure left after that, it was destroyed a few minutes later when, having circled the block and concealed her car, she crept back past the *Keep off the Grass* sign and spent the rest of the morning peeping in the window.

Henry saw her right away, but the teacher and the principal didn't catch on to it for weeks. Henry continued to sit stiffly and hiss out his occasional sobs, wondering numbly what there was about school so terrifying as to make his mother go to such lengths to protect him, and, whatever it was, feeling silent horror of it.

Henry's father did what he could about Henry's cowardice. It pained him because, though he was certain it didn't come from his side, other people might not know that.

He told Henry ghost stories about sheeted phantasms which ate little boys, and then sent him up to bed in the dark, in a room where there was a hot air register opening directly into the ceiling of the room below. The father had troubled to spread a sheet over the register, and when he heard the boy's door open and close, he shoved a stick up through the register and moaned. The white form rising up out of the floor elicited no sound or movement from Henry, so the father went up-stairs laughing, to see the effect he had not heard.

As stiff as ever, straight and tall Henry stood motionless in the dark, so his father turned on the light and looked him over, and then gave him a good whaling.

'Five years old,' he told the mother when he got back down-stairs, 'and he wets his pants yet.'

He jumped out shouting at Henry from around corners and hid in closets and made animal noises and he gave him ruthless orders to go out and punch eight- and ten-year-olds in the nose and warmed his seat for him when he refused, but he just couldn't seem to make the little sissy into anything else.

'Blood will tell,' he used to say knowingly to the mother who had never stood up to anyone in her life and had manifestly tainted the boy. But he clung to the hope that he could do something about it, and he kept trying.

Henry was afraid when his parents quarrelled, because the father shouted and the mother wept; but he was afraid when they did not quarrel too. This was a special fear, raised to its peak on the occasions when the father spoke to him pleasantly, smiling. Undoubtedly the father himself did not realize it, but his pattern for punishing the boy was invariably of a soft-voiced, smiling approach and a sudden burst of brutality, and Henry had become incapable of discriminating between a genuine pleasantry and one of these cheerful precursors to punishment.

Meanwhile, his mother coddled and cuddled him secretly and unsystematically, secretly violated his father's deprivations by contrabanding to him too much cookies and candy, yet all the while turned a cold and unresponsive back to any real or tacit plea for help in the father's presence.

Henry's natural curiosity, along with his normal rebellious-ness, had been thoroughly excised when they first showed them-selves in his second and third years, and at five he was so trained that he would take nothing not actually handed to him by a recognized authority, go nowhere and do nothing unless and until clearly instructed to do so. Children should be seen and not heard. Do not speak unless spoken to.

'Why didn't you poke that kid right in the nose? Why? Why?' 'Daddy, I – ' 'Shaddup, you little yellow-belly. I don't want to hear excuses.'

So tall little, sad little Henry sat sniffing in kindergarten, and was numbly silent everywhere else.

After clubbing Dr Langley with the floor-lamp, Gurlick rum-maged around as ordered, and, bearing a bundle, went shopping.

The Medusa permitted him to shop for himself first, quite willing to concede that he knew the subtleties of his own matrix better than it did. He got a second-hand suit from a hockshop in the tenderloin district, and a shave and a trim at the barber college.

Aesthetically, the improvement was negligible; socially, it was enormous. He was able to get what he wanted, though none of it was easy, since he personally knew the names of none of the things he was compelled to buy.

Probably the metal samples were hardest of all to acquire; he had to go into an endless succession of glassy-eyed silences before a bewildered lab-supply clerk undertook to show him a periodic table of the elements. Once he had that, things moved more rapidly.

By pointing and mumbling and asking and trancing, he acquired lab-demonstration samples of nickel, aluminium, iron, copper, selenium, carbon and certain others. He asked for but could not afford deuterium, four-nines pure tantalum, and six-nines silver. The electrical-supply houses frustrated him deeply on the matter of small-gauge wire with a square cross-section, but someone directed him to a jewellery-findings store and he finally had what he wanted.

By now he was burdened with a wooden crate rigged, by an accommodating clerk, into something approximating a foot-locker in size and shape, with a rope handle to carry it by. His destination was decided after a painful prodding session by the Medusa, which dug out of Gurlick's unwilling brain a memory that Gurlick himself had long ago let vanish – a brief and un-profitable stab at prospecting, or rather at carrying the pack for a friend who was stabbing at it, years ago. The important facet of the memory was an abandoned shack miles from any-where, together with a rough idea of how to get there.

So Gurlick took a bus and another bus, and stole a jeep and abandoned it, and at last, cursing his tormentors, slavering for his dream, and wailing his discomfort, he walked.

Heavy woods, an upland of scrub pine and dwarf maple, then a jagged rock ridge – that was it; and the roofless remnant of the shack like a patch of decay between and against the stained tooth-roots of the snaggly ridge.

More than water, more than food or to be left alone, Gurlick wanted rest, but he was not allowed it. Panting and sniffing, he fell to his knees and began to fumble with the ropes on his burden. He took out the mercury cells and the metal slugs and the wire and tube-sockets, and began to jumble them together.

He didn't know what he was doing and he didn't have to. The work was being done by an aggregate of computing wills scattered across the heavens, partly by direct orders, partly by a semi-direct control, brain to neurone, bypassing that foggy swamp which comprised Gurlick's consciousness.

Gurlick disliked the whole thing mightily, but except for a lachrymose grumble, no protest was possible. So he blubbered and slaved, and did not, could not, let up until it was finished.

When it was finished, Gurlick was released. He stumbled away from it, as if a rope under tension had tied him and was suddenly cut. He dropped heavily, reared up on his elbows to blink at the thing, and then exhaustion overcame him and he slumped and slept.

When he fell asleep, the thing was a tangle of components, possessing (to any trained terrestrial eye) a certain compelling symmetry and an elaborate uselessness (but how useless would seem a variable frequency oscillator to a wise Bushman or a savage from Madison Avenue?); but when he awoke, the picture was different. Very different.

What Gurlick had built was not, in actuality, a matter receiver, although it acted as if such a thing were a possibility. It was, rather, a receiver and amplifier for a certain 'band' in the 'thought' 'spectrum' – each of these terms being analogous and general.

The first receiver, and its be-Gurlicked attachments, turned information into manipulation, and constructed, from the elemental samples Gurlick had supplied it, a second and much more efficient machine of far greater capacity. This in turn received and manipulated yet a third receiver and manipulator; and this one was a heavy-duty device. The process was, in essence, precisely that of the sailor who takes a heaving-line to draw in a rope which brings him a hawser.

In a brief span of hours, machines were making machines to use available matter to make machines which would scout out and procure locally unavailable matter, which was returned to the site and used by other machines to make yet others, all specialized, and certain of these in immense numbers.

Gurlick came unbidden out of that dream, where, as he sat on the bank on the piles of clothes, shiny black and red and an edge of lacy white, he was greeted (*Hello Handsome*) by her who so boldly (after he refused to go away) began to come up out of the water, slowly and gleaming in the sunlight, the water now down to her waist, and she was beginning to smile –

He awoke in the midst of an incredible clanking city. Around him were row upon row of huge blind machines, spewing forth more machines by the moment.

Tank-like things with long snake necks and heads surrounded by a circlet of trumpets; silver balls ten feet in diameter, which now and then would flick silently into the air, too fast to be believed, too silent; low, wide, massive devices which slid snail-like along roads of their own making, snouted with a projector which put out a strange beam which would have been like light if it were not cut off at the far end as if by an invisible wall; and with these, sniffing along the rocks, some of which trembled and slumped; and then there would be a movement up the beam to the machine, and from behind the machine, silvery ingots were laid like eggs which fine cold dust gouted off to the side.

Gurlick awoke surrounded by this, blinking and staring stupidly. It was some minutes later that he realized where he was – atop a column of earth, ten feet in diameter and perhaps thirty feet high. All around, for hundreds of yards, the ground had been excavated and . . . used.

At the edge of his little plateau was a small domed box which, when his eye fell on it, popped open and slid a flat bowl of hot, mushlike substance towards him. He picked it up and smelled it. He tasted it, shrugged, grunted, raised the bowl to his lips and dozed its contents into his mouth with the heel of his hand. Its warmth in his belly was soothing, then puzzling, then frightening, the way it grew. He put his hands to his belt-line and abruptly sat down, staring at his numb and disobedient legs.

Dazed, he looked out across the busy scape, and saw approaching him a stilted device with endless treads for feet and a turtle-like housing, perhaps a dozen feet in diameter. It straddled his imprisoning column of earth, achieving a sort of mechanical top-toe, and the carapace began to descend over him and all his perch, like a great slow candle-snuffer. He now could not speak, nor could he sit up any longer; he fell back and lay helpless, staring up and silently screaming. ...

But as the device, its underside alive with more wriggling tool-tipped limbs than has a horseshoe crab, slowly covered him, he was flooded with reassurance and promise, a special strength (its speciality: to make him feel strong but in no wise be strong) and the nearest thing to peace that he had ever known. He was informed that he was to undergo a simple operation, and that it was good, oh, good. He was informed why:

The spore, the 'raisin', had been life or its surrogate. It had traversed space physically, bodily, and it had finished its function and its capabilities with its invasion of Gurlick. But the transfer of the life-essence of all the Medusa into all of humanity was something that Earth-built machines – even alien-built machines – could not accomplish. Only life can transmit life. A very slight alteration indeed – an adjustment of isotopes in certain ionized elements in Gurlick's ductless glands – would make the membership of humanity in the corpus of the Medusa a certainty.

The machines now abuilding would effectively restore (the Medusa still unswervingly operated from a conviction that this was a restoration) the unity of the human species, its hive-mind, so that each 'person' could reach, and be reached by, all persons; but the fusion with the Medusa would be Gurlick's special chore and would take place on the instant that his seed married with the ovum of a human female, much like – he received two pictures: a pair of bees in nuptial flight, then a huge, busy, buzzing hive – with, of course, himself in the all-powerful tended centre. But with the difference, he was given to understand without understanding, that it would somehow be simultaneous.

As the machine slowly closed over him, its deft limbs already performing the first of a hundred delicate manipulations, it caught up his dream and congratulated him on it, and gave it detail and depth his creative poverty had never made possible to him before, so that he lived it realer than real, from the instant of approach (and a degree of anticipation which might have destroyed him had he felt it earlier) to the moments of consummation, so violent they shook the Earth and sent the sky itself acrinkle with ripples of delighted colour.

And more: for in these tactile inventions there was no human limitation, and it was given to him to proceed again, and yet again, without exhaustion or dulling familiarity, either through the entire episode or through any smallest part of it, whether it be the thrill of seeing the clothes (shiny black and scarlet, and the tumbled frosting of lace-edged white) or the pounding, fainting climax.

Always, too, was the laughing offhand promise that *any* conquest of Gurlick's would be such a peak, or a higher one; let him wallow in his dream because he loved it, but let him understand also that it was only one of many, the symbol of any, the quality of all.

So, while it built its machines to fuse ('again') the scattered psyche of humanity, it got Gurlick – good-and-ready.

If it isn't now, boy, Paul Sanders told himself, it never will be. Keeping one hand between the girl's gossamer-clad shoulder-blades, he slid gently off the sofa, stood, stopped, and lifted Charlotte Dunsay in his arms.

Dimity (*née* Salome) Carmichael had put in a long day. Full of her thoughts of it, she put her thoughts by; standing in her showerstall, she slipped into a delicious suspension, her hand resting on the chrome handle marked *Hot – Cold*.

In Rome, a mad boy walked, incapable of hate, no longer hunted, his pressured rebellions having been caught at the kindling point and flung into a violin case. There was nothing left in Guido, no room for anything in Guido, but a heady joy and a fierce passion for this hard-gleaming, carven miracle under his arm, waiting as sensitive as a naked nerve the hungry reach of his unshackled talent. No lover, no miser, no acolyte on Earth loved woman or money or Master more than Guido loved his violin; no whelping wolverine, no wounded water buffalo was quite so watchful for an enemy.

Henry, five years old, slept as usual flat on his back and face straight up, arms rigid, fists clenched under and pinned down by his buttocks, and his ankles together. He was having a nightmare, soundlessly, of being surrounded by gentle smiling fathers, some of whom wore the masks of the other kids in his class, and storekeepers, and passing puppy-dogs, but who were really just smiling fathers, dressed up and being gentle at the very verge of exploding in his face.

And between him and all the fathers was a loving goddess with soft hands full of forbidden lollipops and peanut-butter sandwiches to be passed to little boys in the dark when they had been sent to bed without their suppers because they were little cowards; this goddess was there to care for him and protect him, but when the explosion came, with this breath or the next or the one after, the puppies and children and grocers and fathers would whisk through to him as if the goddess weren't there at all; and while they did what they would do to him, she would still be there smiling and ready with guilty lollipops, not knowing what the fathers were doing to him. . . .

And under this nightmare was the colour of hopelessness, the absolute certainty that to awake from it would be to emerge into it; the dream and the world were one now, fused and identical.

They left the kraal, all of them, the infants carried dangling from headbands or piggyback, the toddlers awed and huddling together, the adults hushed and wondering; and, leading them, Mbala who had regained his faith and Nuyu who had found his. The village had not far to go, kraal to yam patch; and yet it was a pilgrimage of sorts, the devout fired by the transfigured, coming to witness the miracle of the cleared field.

These are motes among the millions, remarked upon for that about them which is remarkable, yet different only in so far as each is different *from*, or has a difference *of*, some quality, and pattern of qualities, repeated two and three-quarter billion living times under the sun. There is a place in this narrative for all those close enough to each of us to be called You, and for that far more limited and select company (for many can call a man You), the privileged who are entitled to call themselves 'I' (so few may do this, no two the same). *Peon*, peasant, *fellahin*, *jibaro*, mass-men with their hard hands: *matador*, mariner, apothecary, salesman, tilt-tongued with the special cants, canted each one to a special askew; this is their tale too.

Gurlick lay hooded and unaware, passive under the submicroscopic manipulations of the machine which brought his special membership in the Medusa to his seed. So he did not observe the change in the mighty operations around him, when the egg-laying snail-gaited miners drew in and darkened the snouts of light, and fell neatly apart to have their substance incorporated in other, more needed machines; and these in turn completed their special tasks and segmented and dispersed to others which still needed them, until at last there remained only the long-necked, tank-treaded, trumpet-headed ones, and enough silver spheres to carry them, in their multi-thousands, to their precisely mapped destinations.

There was no provision for failure, for there would be no failure. The nature of the electroencephalograph, and of its traces, clearly showed to the transcendent science of the Medusa exactly what was lacking in the average mind which kept it from being a common mind.

The net would be comparatively simple to cast and draw shut, for it found the potent base of the hive mentality alive and awaiting it, showing itself wherever humans blindly moved in the paths of other humans, purely because other humans so moved; wherever friends apart impulsively sat down to write one another simultaneous letters, wherever men in groups (cartels, committees, mobs, and nations) divided their intelligence by their numbers and let that incredible quotient chart their course.

The possible or probable nature of a human hive, once (re-) established, was a question hardly explored, because it was hardly important. Once united, humanity would join the Medusa, because the Medusa always (not almost, not 'in virtually every case', but *always*) infused the hives it touched.

So the factory area rumbled to silence, and the noiseless spheres swept over the storage yard and scooped up their clusters of long-necked projectors, fell away up with them, flashed away to all the corners of Earth, ready to place the projectors wherever their emanations (part sound, part something else) would reach masses of humans.

They could not reach all humans, but they would reach most, and the established hive would then draw in the rest. No human would escape; none could; none would want to.

Then, somewhere in this flawless, undivided, multi-skilled entity Gurlick would plant a tiny fleck of himself, and at the instant of fusion between it and a living ovum, the Medusa would spread through it like crystallization through a supersaturated solution.

Just another rash of saucer-sightings, thought the few observers, and recipients of their observations, in the brief minutes left to them to think as they had always thought.

Some of the military had, in these minutes, a harrowing perplexity. Anything tracked at such speeds as the radars reported must, with small variations, appear somewhere along an extrapolated path; the higher the speed, the finer the extrapolation.

The few recordings made of the flick and flash of these objects yielded flight-paths on which the objects simply did not appear. It was manifestly impossible for them to check and drop straight to their destinations at such velocities; they did, however, and before the theoreticians could finish their redefinition of 'impossible', they and all their co-workers, colleagues, acquaintances, cohabitants, heirs and assigns were relieved of the necessity to calculate.

It happened so quickly, one minute a heterogeneous mass of seething non-communicants, the next, the end of Babel.

He stood motionless with the girl in his arms, ready to put her down on the sofa; and then, without a start, without a word of wonderment, Paul Sanders set her on her feet and stood supporting her with a firm arm around her shoulders until her head cleared and she could stand alone.

There was nothing said, because there was in that moment nothing to be said. In a split second there was orientation of a transcendent nature – nothing as crude as mutual mind-reading, but an instant and permeating acknowledgement of relationships, I to you, we to the rest of the world; the nature of a final and overriding decision, and the clear necessity of instant and specific action.

Together, Paul Sanders and Charlotte Dunsay left her apartment. The hallway was full of people in all stages of dress – all moving wordlessly, purposefully. No one paid Charlotte, in her nylon nightgown, the slightest attention.

They walked to the elevator bank. She paused before it with a half-dozen other people, and he opened the door of the fire stairs and sprang up them two at a time. Emerging on the roof, he went to the kiosk which sheltered the elevator motor and cables, twisted off the light padlock with one easy motion, opened the door and entered. He had never been here before in his life; yet without hesitation he reached to the left and scooped up a five-foot slice bar which lay across the grating, and ran with it down the fire stairs.

Without glancing at floor numbers, he left the fire stairs on the fourth floor, turned left and ran down the hall. The last door on the right opened as he reached it; he did not glance at the old lady who held it for him, nor did she speak. He sped through a foyer, a living room, and a bedroom, opened the window at the far right and climbed out.

There was a narrow ledge on which he could barely keep his balance and carry the heavy bar as well, yet he managed it. The chief enemy of a balancing man is the poison of fear which permeates him: *I'll fall! I'll fall!* but Paul felt no fear at all. He made a rapid succession of two-inch sidewise shuffles until he reached the big eyebolt from which there hung, out and down, the huge chain supporting one end of a massive theatre marquee. Here he turned sidewise and squatted, brought his bar up over his shoulder and, reaching down, thrust the tip through the fourth link of the chain. Then he waited.

The street below – what he could see of it – seemed at first glance to be normally tenanted, with about as many people about as one might expect at this hour of a Saturday night. But then it could be seen that nobody *strolled* – everyone walked briskly and with purpose; one or two people ran, the way they ran indicating running to, not from anything. He saw Charlotte Dunsay cross the street, swinging along on her bare feet, and enter a showroom where computing machines were on display. Though the place had been closed since noon, it was now open and lighted, and full of people silently and rapidly working.

There came a sound, and more than a sound, a deep pervasive ululation which seemed at first to be born in all the air and under the Earth, sourceless. But as it grew louder, Paul heard it more from his left, and finally altogether from the corner of the building. Whatever was making that sound was crawling slowly up the street to take its place at the intersection, a major one where three avenues crossed.

Patiently, Paul Sanders waited.

From his soundless nightmare, Henry soundlessly awoke. He slid out of bed and trotted out of his room, past his parents' open door – they were awake, but he said nothing, and if they saw him, they said nothing either. Henry padded down the stairs and out into the warm night. He turned downtown at a dog-trot and ran for three blocks south, one west, and two south. He may or may not have noticed that while the traffic lights still operated, they were no longer obeyed by anyone, including himself. Uncannily, cars and pedestrians set their courses and their speeds and held them, regardless of blind corners, passing and repassing each other without incident and with no perceptible added effort.

Henry had been aware for some time of the all but subsonic hooting and of its rapid increase in volume as he ran. When he reached the big intersection, he saw the source of the sound on the same street he ran on, but past the corner where the theatre stood. It was a heavy tank-like machine, surmounted by a long flexible neck, on top of which four horns, like square megaphones or speakers, emitted the sound. The neck weaved back and forth, tilting the horns and changing their direction in an elaborate repetitive motion, which had the effect of adding a slow and disturbing vibrato to the sound.

Henry dashed across the street and under the side-street marquee. He came abreast of the thing just as it was about to enter the intersection.

Without once breaking stride, Henry turned and dived straight into the small space between the drive-spindle of the machine's tread and its carrier rollers. His blood spouted, and on it the spindle spun for a moment; the other track, till driving, caused the machine to swerve suddenly and bump up on the sidewalk under the marquee.

Paul Sanders, at the very instant the child had leaped, and before the small head and hands entered the machine's drive, leaned out and down and jammed the chisel point of his slice-bar hard through the fourth link of the chain. Plunging outwards, his momentum carried the bar around the chain and, as his weight came upon it, gave the chair a prodigious twist.

The eyebolt pulled out of the building wall with a screech, and the corner of the marquee sagged and then, as the weight of the chain came upon it, and Paul Sanders's muscular body with it, the marquee let go altogether and came hammering down on the machine.

In a welter of loose bricks, sheet-tin, movie-sign lettering and girders, the machine heaved mightily, its slipping treads grating and shrieking on the pavement. But it could not free itself. Its long neck and four-horned head twitched and slammed against the street for a moment, and then the deep howl faded and was gone, and the head slumped down and lay still.

Four men ran to the wreckage, two of them pushing a dolly on which rode an oxy-acetylene outfit. One man went instantly to work taking measurements with scale, micrometer and callipers. Two others had the torch going in seconds and fell to work testing for a portion of the machine which might be cut away. The fourth man, with abrasive rasps and a cold chisel, began investigating the dismantling of the thing.

And meanwhile, in unearthly silence and with steady determination, people passed and repassed, on foot, in cars, and went about their business. No crowd collected. Why should it? Everybody *knew*.

The entire village population, with Mbala and Nuyu at their head and the witch-doctor following, were within two hundred yards of Nbala's yam patch when the thing came down from the sky. It was broad daylight here, so the ghostly luminous moonlit effect was missing; but the shape of the projector as it dangled by invisible bands from the sphere was *outré* enough, unprecedented enough, to bring a gasp of astonishment and fear from the villagers. Mbala stopped and bowed down and called his father's name, and all the people followed suit.

The sphere dropped rapidly to the yam patch, which happened to be in a spot known locally as Giant's Voice – a flat area surrounded by four great ship's prow monoliths, the result of some ancient cataclysm which cleft the hill north and south, and again north-west by south-east. It was said that a man could shout here and be heard around the world. Exaggeration or no, it was, judging by the photograph taken by the selenium miner, an ideal position for a projector, and here it was.

The sphere set down its burden and started up again without pause, swift as a bouncing ball. The projector began its wavering bass hooting, which swept out through the echoing clefts of the Giant's Voice, rolled down upon the villagers, and silenced their chant as if it had blotted it up.

There was a moment – mere seconds – of frozen inaction, and then half the warriors turned as one man and plunged away through the jungle. The rest, and all the women and children, drew together, over four hundred of them, and poured swiftly up the slope towards the yam patch. No one said a word or made a sound, yet when they choked the space between two of the stone steeples, half the people ran into the clearing, skirting its edge, while half squatted where they were, blocking their avenue from side to side. The runners reached the north opening, filled it and also squatted, wordless and waiting.

Directly across from the first group, in the westward opening, there was movement, as one, two, a dozen, a hundred heads appeared, steadily and quietly approaching. It was the Ngubwe, neighbouring villagers with whom there was a tradition, now quiescent, of wife-stealing and warfare going back to the most ancient days. Mbala's people and the Ngubwe, though aware of each other at all times, were content to respect each other's privacy and each cultivate his own garden, and for the past thirty years or so, there had been room enough for everybody.

Now three openings to the rock-rimmed plateau were filled with squatting, patient natives. Even the babies were silent. For nearly an hour there was no sound but the penetrating, disturbing howl of the projector, no motion but its complex, hypnotic pattern of weavings and turnings. And then there was a new sound.

Blast after shrill blast, the angry sound approached, and the waiting people rose to their feet. The women tore their clothes to get bright rags, the men filled their lungs and emptied them, and filled them again, getting ready.

Through the open southern gateway, four warriors erupted, howling and capering. Hard on their heels came a herd of furious elephants, three, four, seven – nine in all, one old bull, two young ones, four cows and two calves, distraught, angry, goaded beyond bearing. The fleeing warriors separated, two to the right, two to the left, sprinted to and disappeared in the crowds waiting there.

The big bull trumpeted shrilly, wheeled, and charged to the

right, only to face nearly two hundred shrieking, capering people. He swerved away, his momentum carrying him along the rock wall and to the second opening, where he met the same startling cacophony. The other elephants, all but one young bull and one of the calves, thundered along behind him, and when he drew up as if to wheel and attack the second group, he was pounded and pressed from behind by his fellows.

By now quite out of his great fearless placid mind, he put up his trunk, turned his mighty shoulders against those who pressed him, and found himself glaring at this noisy, shining thing in the centre of the clearing.

He shrieked and made for it, followed by the bellowing herd. The noisy, shining thing moved on its endless treads, but not swiftly enough, nor far enough, nor in enough places at once to avoid the tons of hysteria which struck it. The elephants tore off its howling head and its neck, in three successive broken bits, and shouldered it over on its side and then on its back. The howling stopped with deafening suddenness when the head came off, but the tracks kept treading air for minutes.

Elephants were used in Berlin, too, on the machine which landed in the park near the famous zoo, though this was a more disciplined performance by trained animals who did exactly as they were told.

In China, a projector squatted in a cleft in the mountains, under a railroad trestle, and began hooting into the wind. An old nomad with arthritis hobbled out of the rocks and pulled two spikes, shifted one rail. A half-mile down the track, the engineer and fireman of a locomotive pulling a combination passenger-freight train with over four hundred people aboard wordlessly left their posts, climbed back over the tender and uncoupled the locomotive from the first car. There was, on the instant, a man at every handwheel on the train. It coasted to a stop, while far ahead the locomotive thundered over the edge of the trestle and was crushing the projector before the alien machine could move a foot.

In Baffin Land, a group of Eskimo hunters stood transfixed, watching a projector squatting comfortably on mounded and impassable pack ice, and, in the crisp air, blaring its message across the wastes to the ears of four and possibly five widely scattered settlements. The hunters had not long to wait; high above the atmosphere, a mighty Atlas missile approached, and, while still well below their horizon, released a comparatively tiny sliver, the redoubtable Hawk.

The little Hawk came shrieking out of the upper air, made a wide half-circle to kill some of its excess velocity, and then zeroed in on the projector with the kind of accuracy the old-time Navy bombardiers would brag about: 'I dropped it right down his stack.'

From then on, missiles got most of the projectors, though, in crowded areas, other means were found. In Bombay, a projector took its greatest toll – one hundred and thirty-six, when a mob simply overran one of the machines and tore it to pieces with their bare hands. And, in Rome, one man dispatched four of them and came out of it unscathed.

One *man*?

Unscathed?

A boy, rather, walking along the elevated section of the new highway over the hills just north of Rome, who paused for not more than three seconds in his steady walk, then wordlessly turned and entered the Lagonda which drifted up to the kerb just then. It was driven by a bright-eyed young woman, not excessively pretty, but of that unusual pure Italian type with pale red hair and green eyes. She had nothing to say, but drove the overpowered, scalded-cat Lagonda with a light touch and a sure hand.

As if on some unseen cue, the boy opened the door, slipped out on the running board, and inched forward to lodge himself firmly between the hood and the flaring fender, his knee hooked over the bracket which supports the great moon of a headlight.

Bent against the wind of their speed, he unclamped his arm from the violin case he had been clutching all this while, opened it and took out the violin, letting the case flap away like a misshapen bat. Stolidly he broke the violin in two, separating neck from sound-box, and with his teeth pulled the four pegs, freeing the strings. He let the soundbox flutter off and splinter on the steel-bound kerb, and with the fingerboard of the violin in his hand, its curled scroll uppermost, he unhooked his knee from the headlight brace and got his free hand on it instead. There he crouched, slit-eyed.

As the elevated road swept in a broad curve to the left, the girl tooled the car as far as she could into the left lane, then put on a burst of speed which made the boy Guido's muscles crack, and shot diagonally across the road and up on the sidewalk at the right. At the last possible instant, she wrenched the wheel and swerved away from the hard teeth of the railings, and Guido sprang up and out, soaring high over the sidehill, hurtling through the air at nearly eighty kilometres per hour.

For her velocity to the microsecond, for his altitude and trajectory to seven decimal places, the best computing minds on Earth had done their utmost, matching these factors to all the others: his height and weight and the strength of his legs, the fact that, of all pedestrians in the area at the time, he alone should possess such an object as the neck and carven scroll of a violin, which, it happened, was precisely the right size and curvature capable of disabling a vital membrane in the throat of the projectors at one blow; all matched with the observed trajectory of a descending sphere which carried, not one, but four projectors, obviously to a place in the City of Seven Hills where, by landing at the same place and moving apart a minimal distance, they could blanket a maximum area and number of people.

At the very peak of his parabola, and past it into the sharp descending curve, his free arm and both legs snapped like a trap around the intertwined necks of the four projectors. They were bound so that their heads were one atop the other. Guido shinnied upwards far enough to reach the topmost, and crammed his shaped and hardened club into its horn. He silenced it and, with three quick blows, the other three, striking the last just as the whole package touched Earth.

The sphere began its bounce skywards angrily, but fouled in

the coils of a giant steel-cored rope mat, one of those used to muffle blasting in built-up areas. The mat had been hung like a great curtain under the viaduct, and arranged to fall out and down as the sphere dipped low. A cluster of silent, sweating people waiting there caught the corner ropes and instantly anchored the mat to girders and concrete piers, and the sphere lunged and lunged upwards until suddenly it began to grow hot and then fell leadenly to the ground.

Guido helped take it apart to find out how it worked.

There she stands the water beading her bright body her head to one side the water sparkling off her hair, she smiles, says All Right Handsome What are You Going to Do About It?

A soft rumble and a glare of light: sky. Crash! A brighter, unbearable flash of light on light, a sharp smell of burning chemicals, a choking cloud of dust and smoke and the patter-patter of falling debris. Confusion, bewilderment, disorientation and growing anger at the deprivation of a dream.

The sharp command to every sentience, mechanical or not, on the entire hilltop: *Get Gurlick out of here!*

A flash of silver overhead, then a strange overall sticky, pore-choking sensation, like being coated with warm oil, and, underneath, the torn hill dwindles away. There are still hundreds of projectors left, row on row of them, but from the size of the terraces where they are parked, there must have been hundreds of thousands more.

Crash! A half-dozen of the projectors bulge skywards and fall back in shatters and shards. Look there, a flight of jets. See, two silver spheres, dodging, dancing; then the long curve of a seeking missile points one out, and the trail and the burst make a bright ball on a smoky string, painted across the sky. Crash! Crash! Even as the scarred hill disappears in swift distance, the parked projectors can be seen bursting skywards, a dozen and a dozen and a score of them, pressing upwards through the rain of pieces from those blasted a breath or a blink ago; and Cra –

No, not crash this time, but a point, a porthole, a bay-window looking into the core of hell, all the colours and all too bright, growing, growing, too, too big to be growing so fast, taking the hilltop, the hillside, the whole hill lost in the ball of brilliance.

And for minutes afterwards, hanging stickily by something invisible, frighteningly in mid-air under the silver sphere, but not feeling wind or acceleration or any of the impossible turns as the sphere whizzes along low, hedge-hopping, ground-hugging, back-tracking and hovering to hide; for minutes and minutes afterwards, through the drifting speckles of over-dazzled eyeballs, the pastel column can be seen rising and rising flatheaded over the land, thousands and thousands of feet, building a roof with eaves, the eaves curling and curling out, or are they the grasping fingers of rows and rows of what devils who have climbed up the inside of the spout, about to put up *what* hellish faces?

'Bastits,' Gurlick whimpered, 'tryin' to atom-bomb *me*. You tell 'em who I am?'

No response. The Medusa was calculating to capacity – to its immense, infinitely varied capacity. It had expected to succeed in unifying the mind of humanity. It had correctly predicted its certainty of success and the impossibility of failure.

But success like *this*?

Like this: In the first forty minutes, humanity destroyed seventy-one per cent of the projectors and forty-three per cent of the spheres. To do this, it used everything and anything that came to hand, regardless of the cost in lives or material:

It put out its fire by smothering it with its mink coat. It killed its rattlesnake by hitting it with the baby. It moved, reactive and accurate and almost in reflex, like a man holding a burning stick, and as the heat increases near one finger, it will release and withdraw and find another purchase while he thinks of other things. It threw a child into the drive of a projector because he fit, and because he contained the right amount of the right grade of lubricant for just that purpose at just that time. It could understand in microseconds that the nearest thing to the exact necessary tool for tearing the throat out of a projector would be the neck and scroll of a violin.

And like this: Beginning in the forty-first minute, humanity launched the first precision weapon against the projectors, having devised and produced a seeking mechanism which would infallibly find and destroy projectors (though they did not radiate in the electromagnetic spectrum, not even infra-red) and then made it compact enough to cram into the warhead of a Hawk, and, further, applied the Hawk to the powerful Atlas.

And this was only the first.

In the fifty-second minute – that is, less than an hour after the Medusa pushed the button to unify the mind of Man – humanity was using hasty makeshifts of appalling efficiency, devices which reversed the steering commands of the projectors (like the one which, under its own power, walked off the Hell Gate Bridge into eighty feet of water) and others that re-broadcast the projectors' signals 180° out of phase, nullifying them.

At the ninety-minute mark, humanity was knocking out two of every three flying spheres it saw, not by accurate aiming (because as yet humanity couldn't tool up to counter-measure inertialess turns at six miles per second) but by an ingenious application of the theory of random numbers, by which they placed proximity missiles where the sphere wasn't but almost certainly would be – and all too often was.

The Medusa had anticipated success. But to sum up: success like *this*? For hadn't humanity stamped out every operable instrument of the Medusa's invasion (save Gurlick, about whom they couldn't know) in just two hours and eight minutes?

This incredible species, uniquely possessed of a defence against the Medusa (the Medusa still stubbornly insisted) in its instant, total fragmentation at the invader's first touch, seemed uniquely to possess other qualities as well. It would be wise – more: it was imperative – that Earth be brought into the fold where it would have to take orders.

Hence –
Gurlick.

It swept Gurlick back into its confidence, told him that in spite of the abruptness of his awakening, he was now ready to go out on his own. It described to him his assignment, which made Gurlick snicker like an eight-year-old behind the barn, and assured him that it would set up for him the most perfect opportunity its mighty computers could devise. Speed, however, was of the essence – which was all right with Gurlick, who spat on his hands and made cluck-cluck noises from his back teeth and wrinkled up half his face with an obscene wink and snickered again to show his willingness.

The sphere hovered now at tree-top level over heavily wooded ground, keeping out of sight while awaiting the alien computation of the best conceivable circumstances for Gurlick's project. This might well have proved lengthy, based as it was on Gurlick's partial, mistaken, romantic, deluded and downright pornographic information, and might even have supplied some highly amusing conclusions, since they would have been based on logic, and Gurlick's most certainly were not.

These diverting computations were lost, however, and lost forever when the sphere dropped dizzyingly, released Gurlick so abruptly that he tumbled, and informed him that he was on his own – the sphere had been detected.

Growling and grumbling, Gurlick sprawled under the trees and watched the sphere bullet upwards and away, and a moment later, the appearance of a Hawk, or rather its trail, scoring the sky in a swift reach like the spread of a strain-crack in window glass.

He did not see the inevitable but heard it in due course, the faint distant thump against the roof of the world which marked the end of the sphere's existence – and very probably the end of all the Medusa's artifacts on Earth.

He said an unprintable syllable, rolled over and eyed the woodlands with disfavour. This wasn't going to be like flying

over it like a bug over a carpet, with some bigbrain doing all
your thinking for you. On the other hand ... this was the pay-
off. This was where Gurlick got his – where at long last he could
strike back at a whole world full of bastits.

He got to his feet and began walking.

Full of wonder, the human hive contemplated itself and its
works, its gains, its losses and its new nature.

First, there was the intercommunication – a thing so huge,
so different, that few minds could previously have imagined it.
No analogy could suffice; no concepts of infinite telephone
exchanges, or multi-sideband receivers, could hint at the
quality of that gigantic cognizance. To describe it in terms of
its complexity would be as impossible – and as purblind – as an
attempt to describe fine lace by a description of each of its
threads. It had, rather, *texture*. Your memory, and his and his,
and hers over the horizon's shoulder – all your memories are
mine.

More: your personal orientation in the framework of your
own experiences, your I-in-the-past, is also mine.

More: your skills remain your own (is great music made less
for being shared?) but your sensitivity to your special subject
is mine now, and your pride in your excellence is mine now.

More: though bound to the organism, mankind, as never
before, I am I as never before. When Man has demands on me,
I am totally dedicated to Man's purpose. Otherwise, within the
wide, wide limits of mankind's best interests, I am as never
before a free agent; I am I to a greater degree, and with less
obstruction from within and without, than ever before possible.

For gone, gone altogether, are individual man's hosts of pests
and devils, which in strange combinations have plagued us all
in the past: the They-don't-want-me devil, the Suppose-they-
find-out devil, the twin imps of They-are-lying-to-me and They-
are-trying-to-cheat-me; gone, gone is I'm-afraid-to-try, and
They-won't-let-me, and I-couldn't-be-loved-if-they-knew.

Along with the imps and devils, other things disappeared –

things regarded throughout human history as basic, thematic keys to the structures of lives and cultures.

Now if a real thing should disappear, a rock or a tree or a handful of water, there will be thunder and a wind and other violence, depending upon what form the vanished mass owned. Or if a great man disappears, there is almighty confusion in the rush to fill the vacuum of his functions.

But the things which disappeared now proved their unreality by the unruffled silence in which they disappeared. Tariffs, taxes, boundaries and frontiers, hatred and suspicion of humans by humans, and language itself (except as part of an art) with all the difficulties of communication between languages and within them.

In short, removed now was mankind's cess-gland, the secretions of which had poisoned its body since it was born, distorting decencies like survival and love into greed and lust, turning Achievement ('I have built') into Position ('I have power').

So much for humanity's new state-of-being. As to its abilities, they were simply based, straightforward. There are always many ways to accomplish anything, but only one of them is really best. Which of them is best – that is the source of all argument on the production of anything, the creator of factions among the designers, and the first enemy of speed and efficiency.

But when humanity became a hive and needed something – as, for example, the adaptation of the swift hunting missile Hawk to the giant carrier Atlas – the device was produced without consideration of pride or profit, without waste motion, and without interpersonal friction of any kind. The decision was made, the job was done.

In those heady first moments, anything and everything available was used – but with precision. Later (by minutes) fewer ingenious stopgaps were used, more perfect tools were shaped from the materials at hand. And still later (by hours) there was full production of new designs. Mankind now used exactly the right tool for the jobs it had to do. . . .

And within it, each individual flowed, finding freedoms

to be, to act, to take enrichment and pleasure as never before.

What were the things that Dimity (Salome?) Carmichael had always needed, wanted to do? She could do them now.

An Italian boy, Guido, packed taut with talent, awaited the arrival of the greatest living violinist from behind a now-collapsed Iron Curtain; they would hereafter spend their lives and do their work together.

The parents of a small stiff boy named Henry contemplated, as all the world contemplated, what had happened to him and why, and how totally impossible it would be for such a thing ever to happen again. Sacrifice there must be from time to time, even now; but never again a useless one. Everyone now knew, as if in personal memory, how fiercely Henry had wanted to live in that flash of agony which had eclipsed him.

All Earth shared the two kinds of religious experience discovered by the Africans Mbala and Nuyu, wherein one had become confirmed in his faith and the other had found it. What, specifically, it had brought to them was of no significance; the fact of their devotion was the important thing to be shared, for it is in the finest nature of humanity to worship, fight it as he sometimes may. The Universe being what it is, there is always *plus ultra*, *plus ultra* – powers and patterns beyond understanding, and more beyond these when these are understood. Out there is the call to which faith is the natural response and worship the natural approach.

Such was humanity when it became a hive – a beautiful entity, balanced and fine; self-sufficient and wondrously alive. A pity, in a way, that such a work of art was to exist in this form for so brief a time . . .

Gurlick, alone of humans insulated from the human hive, member of another, sensed none of this. Driven, hungry through a whole spectrum of appetites, full of resentment, he shuffled through the woods. He had been vaguely aware of the outskirts of a town not far from where the silver sphere had set him down. He would, he supposed, find what he wanted there, though wanting it was the only thing quite clear to him. How he was to get it was uncertain; but get it he must.

He was aware of the presence within him of the Medusa, observing, computing, but – not directing, cognizant as it was of the fact that the fine details of such an operation must be left to the species itself. Had it had its spheres and other machines available, there might have been a great deal it could do to assist Gurlick. But now – he was on his own.

He was in virgin forest, the interlocked foliage overhead dimming the mid-morning sunshine to an underwater green, and the footing was good, there being little underbrush and a gentle downslope. Gurlick gravitated downhill, knowing he would encounter a path or a road sooner or later, and monotonously cursed his empty stomach, his aching feet and his enemies.

He heard voices.

He stopped, shrank back against a tree-trunk, and peered. For a moment, he could detect nothing, and then, off to the right, he heard a sudden musical laugh. He looked towards the sound and saw a brief motion of something blue. He came out of hiding and scuttling clumsily from tree to tree, went to investigate.

There were three of them, girls in their mid-teens, dressed in halters and shorts, giggling over the chore of building a fire in a small clearing. They had a string of fish, pike and lake trout, and a frying pan, and seemed completely and hilariously preoccupied.

Gurlick, from a vantage point above them, chewed on his lower lip and wondered what to do. He had no delusions about approaching openly and sweet-talking his way into their circle. It would be far wiser, he knew, to slip away and go looking elsewhere, for something surer, safer. On the other hand . . .

He heard the crackle of bacon fat as one of the girls dropped the tender slivers into the frying pan. He looked at the three lithe young bodies, and at the waiting string of fish, half of which were scaled and beheaded, and quietly moaned. There was too much of what was wanted down there for him to turn his back.

Then a curl of fragrance from the bacon reached him and toppled his reason. He rose from his crouch and in three bounds was down the slope and in their midst, moaning and slavering. One of the youngsters bounded away to the right, one to the left. The third fell under his hands, shrieking.

'Now you jus' be still,' he panted, trying to hold his victim, trying to protect himself against her hysterical slappings, writhings, clawings. 'I ain't goin' to hurt you if you jus' – *uh!*'

He was bowled right off his feet by one of the escapees, who had returned at a dead run and crashed him with a hard shoulder. He rolled over and found himself staring up at the second girl who had run away, as she stood over him with a stone the size of a grapefruit raised in both hands. She brought it down; it hit Gurlick on the left cheekbone and the bridge of his nose, and filled the world with stars and brilliant tatters of pain.

He fell back, wagging his head, pawing at his face, trying to get some vision back and kick away the sick dizziness, and when at last he could see again, he was alone with the campfire, the frying pan, the string of fish.

'Li'l bastits,' he growled, holding his face. He looked at his hands, on which were flecks of his own blood, swore, turned in a circle as if to find and pursue them, and then squatted before the fire, reached for two cleaned fish and dropped them hissing into the pan.

Well, he'd got that much out of it, anyway.

He had eaten four of the fish and had two more cooking when he heard voices again, a man's deep 'Which way now? Over here?' and a girl's answer, 'Yes, where the smoke's coming from.'

Jailbait ... of course, of *course* they'd have gone for help! Gurlick cursed them all and lumbered downslope, away from the sound of voices. Boy, he'd messed up, but good. The whole hillside would be crawling with people hunting him. He had to get out of here.

He moved as cautiously as he could, quite sure he was being watched by hundreds of eyes, yet seeing no one until he glimpsed two men off to his left and below him. One had binoculars on a strap around his neck, the other a shotgun.

Gurlick, faint with terror, slumped down between a tree-trunk and a rock, and cowered there until he could hear their voices, and while he heard them, and after he heard them, with their curt certain syllables and their cold lack of mercy.

When all was quite quiet again, he rose, and at that moment became aware of an aircraft sound. It approached rapidly, and he dropped back into his hiding place, trembling, and peeped up at the glittering patches of blue in the leafy roof. The machine flew directly overhead, low, too slowly – a helicopter. He heard it thrashing the air off to the north, downhill from him, and for a while he could not judge if it was going or coming or simply circling down there.

In his pride, he was convinced that its business was Gurlick and only Gurlick, and in his ignorance he was certain it had seen him through the thick cover.

It went away at last and the forest returned to its murmuring silence. He heard a faint shout behind and above him, and scuttled from cover and away from the sound. Pausing for breath, he caught another glimpse of the man with the shotgun off to his left, and escaped to the right and down.

And thus pursued and herded, he came to the water's edge.

There was a dirt path there and no one in sight; and it was warm and sunny and peaceful. Slowly, Gurlick's panic subsided and, as he walked along the path, there was a deep throb of anticipation within him. He'd gotten away clear; and had outdistanced his enemies and now, enemies, beware!

The path curved closer to the bank of the lake. Alders stood thick here, and there was the smell of moss. The path turned and the shade was briefly darker here, at the verge of the floods of gold over the water. And there by the path it lay, the little pile of fabric, bright red, shiny black, filmy white with edges iced with lace. . . .

Gurlick stopped walking, stopped breathing until his chest

hurt. Then he moved slowly past this incredible, impossible consolidation of his dream, and went to the bushes at the water's edge.

She was out there – *she*.

He made a sharp wordless sound and stood forward, away from the bushes. She turned in the water and stared at him, her eyes round.

Emancipated now, free to be what she had always wished to be, and to do what she needed to do without fear or hesitation; swimming naked in the sun, sure and fearless, shameless; utterly oriented within herself and herself within the matrix of humanity and all its known data, Salome Carmichael stood up in the water, under the sun, and said, 'Hello, Handsome.'

So ended humanity within its planetary limits; so ended the self-contained, self-aware species-hive which had for such a brief time been able to feel to the ends of its world, its multifarious self. The end came some hours after the helicopter – the same one which had set her down by the pond – had come for Salome Carmichael, which it had the instant Gurlick quit the scene. Gurlick had seen it, from where he crouched guiltily in the bushes. After it had gone away, he slowly climbed to his feet and made his way back to the pond. He hunkered down with his back to a tree and regarded the scene unwinkingly.

It had been right there, on the moss.

Over there had lain the pretty little heap of clothes, so clean, so soft, so very red, shiny black, the white so pretty. The strangest thing that had ever happened to him in his whole life had happened here, stranger than the coming of the Medusa, stranger than the unpeopled factory back there in the mountains, stranger even than the overwhelming fact of this place, of her being here, of the unbelievable coincidence of it all with his dream. And that strangest thing of all was that once, when she was here, she had cried out, and he had then been gentle.

He had been gentle with all his heart and mind and body, for a brief while flooded, melted, swept away by gentleness.

No wrinkled raisin from out of space, no concept like the existence of a single living thing so large it permeated two galaxies and part of a third, could be so shockingly alien to him, everything he was and had ever been, as this rush of gentleness.

Its microscopic seed must have lain encysted within him all his life, never encountering a single thing, large or small, which could warm it to germination. Now it had burst open, burst him open, and he was shocked, shaken, macerated as never before in his bruised existence.

He crouched against the tree and regarded the moss, and the lake, and the place where the red and the black and the lace had lain, and wondered why he had run away. He wondered how he could have let her go. The gentleness was consuming him even now ... he had to find somewhere to put it down, but there wouldn't be anyone else, anyone or anything, for him to be gentle to, anywhere in the world.

He began to cry. Gurlick had always wept easily, his facile tears his only outlet for fear, and anger, and humiliation, and spite. This, however, was different. This was very difficult to do, painful in the extreme, and impossible to stop until he was racked, wrung out, exhausted. It tumbled him over and left him grovelling on the moss. Then he slept, abruptly, his whipped consciousness fleeing away to the dark.

What can travel faster than light?

Stand here by me, friend, on this hillside, under the black and freckled sky. Which stars do you know – Polaris? Good. And the bright one yonder, that's Sirius. Look at them now: at Polaris, at Sirius. Quickly now: Polaris, Sirius. And again Sirius, Polaris.

How far apart are they? It says in the book, thousands of light-years. How many? Too many: never mind. But how long does it take you to flick your gaze from one to the other and back? A second? A half-second next time, then a tenth? You can't say that nothing, absolutely nothing, has travelled between the two. Your vision has: your attention has.

You now understand, you have the rudiments of understanding what it is to flick a part of yourself from star to star, just as (given the skill) you may shift from soul to soul.

With such a shift, down such a path, came the Medusa at the instant of its marriage to humanity. In all the history of humanity, the one instant (save death) of most significance is the instant of syngamy, the moment of penetration by the sperm of the ovum. Yet almost never is there a heralding of this instant, nor a sign: it comes to pass in silence and darkness, and no one ever knows but the mindless flecks of complex jelly directly involved.

Not so now; and never before, and never again would marriage occur with such explosion. A microsecond after that melding, Gurlick's altered seed to the welcoming ovum of a human, the Medusa of space shot down its contacting thread, an unerring harpoon carrying a line to itself, and all of its Self following in the line, ready to reach and fill humanity, make of it a pseudopod, the newest member of its sprawling corpus.

But if the Medusa's bolt can be likened to a harpoon, then it can be said that the uprushing flood it met was like a volcano. The Medusa had not a micro-microsecond in which to realize what had happened to it. It did not die; it was not killed any more than humanity would have been killed had the Medusa's plan been realized. Humanity would have become a 'person' of the illimitable creature.

But now . . .

No, instead, humanity became the creature; flooded it, filled it to its furthermost crannies, drenched its most remote cells with the Self of humankind. Die? Never that; the Medusa was alive as never before, with a new and different kind of life, in which its slaves were freed but its motivations unified; where the individual was courted and honoured and brought special nutrients, body and mind, and where, freely, 'want to' forever replaced 'must'.

And all for want of a datum: that intelligence might exist in individuals, and that dissociated individuals might cooperate and yet not be a hive. For there is no structure on Earth which could not have been built by rats, were the rats centrally directed and properly motivated.

How could the Medusa have known? Thousands upon thousands of species and cultures throughout the galaxies have technological progress as advanced as that of Earth, and are yet composed of individuals no more highly evolved than termites, lemurs or shrews. What slightest hint was there for the Medusa that a hive-humanity would be a different thing than a super-rat?

Humanity had passed the barriers of language and of individual isolation on its planet. It passed the barriers of species now, and of isolation in its cosmos. As available to Guido as the faith of Mbala now became the crystal symphonies of the black planets past Ophiuchus. Charlotte Dunsay, reaching across the world to her husband in Hobart, Tasmania, might share with him a triple sunrise in the hub of Orion's great Nebula.

As one man could share the *being* of another here on Earth, so both, and perhaps a small child with them, could fuse their inner shelves with some ancient contemplative mind leeched to the rocks in some roaring methane cataract, or soar with some insubstantial life-forms adrift where they were born in the high layers of some dense planet's atmosphere.

So ended mankind, to be born again as hive-humanity; so ended the hive of Earth to become starman, the immeasurable, the limitless, the growing; maker of music beyond music, poetry beyond words, and full of wonder, full of worship.

So too ended Gurlick, the isolated, alone among humankind denied membership in the fusion of humans, full of a steaming fog, aglow with his flickerings of hate and the soft shine of corruption, member of something other than humankind. For, while humanity had been able to read him (and his dream) and herd him through the forest to its fulfilment, it had never been able to reach his consciousness, blocked as it was by the thought-lines of the Medusa.

These lines, however, were open still, and when humanity became Medusa, it flooded down to Gurlick and made him welcome. *Come!* it called, and whirled him up and outwards, showing and sharing its joy and strength and pride, showering him with wonders of a thousand elsewheres and a hundred heres; it showed him how to laugh at the most rarefied technician's joke and how to feel the structure of sestinae and sonnets, of bridges and Bach. It spoke to him saying *We* are granting him the right to regard it all and say *I*.

And more: he had been promised a kingship, and now he had it, for all this sentient immensity acknowledged to him its debt, and let him but make the phantom of a wish of a thought, and his desires would be fulfilled.

And it was at this that humanity swirled and steadied, perplexed. For Gurlick, numb and passive as he tossed like a chip on their ocean of wonders, had a wish, and had it, and had it.

True, none of this could have come about without him. This result could not have been with anyone else in his place, so – true enough – he was owed a debt. Pay it then.

Pay the debt; you do not reward a catalyst by changing it, the unchanging, into something else. So – take away hunger and poverty (of body and soul), deprivation and discomfort and humiliation, and you take away the very core of his being – his sole claim to superiority.

Don't ask him to look out among the stars and join in the revelries of giants. Don't thank him, don't treat him, and above all, do not take away from him his reasons to hate: they have become his life.

So they paid him, meticulously to the specifications he himself (though all unknowing) set up.

And as long as he lived, there would be a city corner holding drab streets and fumes, sullen pedestrians and careless, dangerous aimers of trucks and cabs; obligingly moist unbearable heat and bitter cold; and bars where Gurlick could go and put in his head, whining for a drink, and bartenders would obediently send him out into the wet with his hatred, back to a wrecked truck in a junkyard where he might lie in the dark and dream that dream of his.

'Bastits,' Gurlick would mutter in the dark, hating . . . happy. 'Lousy bastits.'

The Comedian's Children

The quiet third of the Twenty-First Century came to an end at ten o'clock on the morning of May 17, 2034, with the return to earth of a modified Fafnir space cruiser under the command of Capt. Avery Swope. Perhaps in an earlier or a later day, the visitation which began on the above date might have had less effect. But the earth was lulled and content with itself, and for good reason – international rivalries having reverted to the football fields and tennis courts, an intelligent balance of trade and redistribution of agriculture and industry having been achieved.

Captain Swope's mission was to accomplish the twelfth off-earth touchdown, and the body on which he touched was Iapetus (sometimes Japetus), the remarkable eighth satellite of Saturn. All Saturn's satellites are remarkable, each for a different reason. Iapetus' claim to fame is his fluctuating brilliance; he always swings brightly around the eastern limb of the ringed planet, and dwindles dimly behind the western edge. Obviously the little moon is half bright and half dark, and keeps one face turned always to its parent; but why should a moon be half bright and half dark?

It was an intriguing mystery, and it had become the fashion to affect all sorts of decorations which mimicked the fluctuations of the inconstant moonlet: cufflinks and tunic clasps which dimmed and brightened, bread-wrappers and book-jackets in dichotomous motley. Copies were reproduced of the mid-century master Pederson's magnificent oil painting of a space ship aground on one of Saturn's moons, with four suited figures alighting, and it became a sort of colophon for news stories about Swope's achievement and window displays of bi-coloured gimcrackery – with everyone marvelling at the Twentieth

Century artist's unerring prediction of a Fafnir's contours, and no one noticing that the painting could not possibly have been of Iapetus, which has no blue sky nor weathered rocks, but must certainly have been the meticulous Pederson's visualization of Titan. Still, everyone thought it was Iapetus, and since it gave no evidence as to why Iapetus changed its brightness, the public embraced the painting as the portrait of a mystery. They told each other that Swope would find out.

Captain Swope found out, but Captain Swope did not tell. Something happened to his Fafnir on Iapetus. His signals were faintly heard through the roar of an electrical disturbance on the parent world, and they were unreadable, and they were the last. Then, voiceless, he returned, took up his braking orbit, and at last came screaming down out of the black into and through the springtime blue. His acquisition of the tail-down attitude so very high – over fifty miles – proved that something was badly wrong. The extreme deliberation with which he came in over White Sands, and the constant yawing, like that of a baseball bat balanced on a fingertip, gave final proof that he was attempting a landing under manual control, something never before attempted with anything the size of a Fafnir. It was superbly done, and may never be equalled, that roaring drift down and down through the miles, over forty-six of them, and never a yaw that the sensitive hands could not compensate, until that last one.

What happened? Did some devil-imp of wind, scampering runt of a hurricane, shoulder against the Fafnir? Or was the tension and strain at last too much for weary muscles which could not, even for a split second, relax and pass the controls to another pair of hands? Whatever it was, it happened at three and six-tenths miles, and she lay over bellowing as her pilot made a last desperate attempt to gain some altitude and perhaps another try.

She gained nothing, she lost a bit, hurtling like a dirigible gone mad, faster and faster, hoping to kick the curve of the earth down and away from her, until over Arkansas, the forward section of the rocket liner – the one which is mostly inside the ship – disintegrated and she blew off her tail. She turned twice end over end and thundered into a buck-wheat field.

Two days afterwards a photographer got a miraculous picture. It was darkly whispered later that he had unforgivably carried the child – the three-year-old Tresak girl from the farm two miles away – into the crash area and had inexcusably posed her there; but this could never be proved, and anyway, how could he have known? Nevertheless, the multiple miracles of a momentary absence of anything at all in the wide clear background, of the shadows which mantled her and of the glitter of the many-sharded metal scrap which reared up behind her to give her a crown – but most of all the miracle of the child herself, black-eyed, golden-haired, trusting, fearless, one tender hand resting on some jagged steel which would surely shred her flesh if she were less beautiful – these made one of the decade's most memorable pictures. In a day she was known to the nation, and warmly loved as a sort of infant phoenix rising from the disaster of the roaring bird; the death of the magnificent Swope could not cut the nation quite as painfully because of her, as that cruel ruin could not cut her hand.

The news, then, that on the third day after her contact with the wreck of the ship from Iapetus, the Tresak child had fallen ill of a disfiguring malady never before seen on earth, struck the nation and the world a dreadful and terrifying blow. At first there was only a numbness, but at the appearance of the second, and immediately the third cases of the disease, humanity sprang into action. The first thing it did was to pass seven Acts, an Executive Order and three Conventions against any further off-earth touchdowns; so, until the end of the iapetitis epidemic, there was an end to all but orbital space flight.

'You're going to be all right,' she whispered, and bent to kiss the solemn, comic little face. (They said it wasn't contagious; at least, adults didn't get it.) She straightened up and smiled at him, and Billy smiled his half-smile – it was the left half – in response. He said something to her, but by now his words were so blurred that she failed to catch them. She couldn't bear to have him repeat whatever it was; he seemed always so puzzled when people did not understand him, as if he could hear himself quite plainly. So to spare herself the pathetic pucker which would worry the dark half of his face, she only smiled the more and said again, 'You're going to be all right,' and then she fled.

Outside in the corridor she leaned for a moment against the wall and got rid of the smile, the rigid difficult hypocrisy of that smile. There was something standing there on the other side of the scalding blur which replaced the smile; she said, because she had to say it to someone just then: 'How could I promise him that?'

'One does,' said the man, answering. She shook away the blur and saw that it was Dr Otis. 'I promised him the same thing myself. One just ... does,' he shrugged. 'Heri Gonza promises them, too.'

'I saw that,' she nodded. 'He seems to wonder "How could I?" too.'

'He does what he can,' said the doctor, indicating, with a motion of his head, the special hospital wing in which they stood, the row of doors behind and beyond, doors to laboratories, doors to research and computer rooms, store rooms, staff rooms, all donated by the comedian. 'In a way he has more right to make a promise like that than Billy's doctor.'

'Or Billy's sister,' she agreed tremulously. She turned to walk down the corridor, and the doctor walked with her. 'Any new cases?'

'Two.'

She shuddered. 'Any –'

'No,' he said quickly, 'no deaths.' And as if to change the subject, he said, 'I understand you're to be congratulated.'

'What? Oh,' she said wrenching her mind away from the image of Billy's face, half marble, half mobile mahogany. 'Oh, the award. Yes, they called me this afternoon. Thank you. Somehow it ... doesn't mean very much right now.'

They stood before his office at the head of the corridor. 'I think I understand how you feel,' he said. 'You'd trade it in a minute for –' he nodded down the corridor towards the boy's room.

'I'd even trade it for a reasonable hope,' she agreed. 'Good night, doctor. You'll call me?'

'I'll call you if anything happens. Including anything good. Don't forget that, will you? I'd hate to have you afraid of the sound of my voice.'

'Thank you, Doctor.'

'Stay away from the trideo this once. You need some sleep.'

'Oh Lord. Tonight's the big effort,' she remembered.

'Stay away from it,' he said with warm severity. 'You don't need to be reminded of iapetitis, or be persuaded to help.'

'You sound like Dr Horowitz.'

His smile clicked off. She had meant it as a mild pleasantry; if she had been less tired, less distraught, she would have had better sense. Better taste. Horowitz's name echoed in these of all halls like a blasphemy. Once honoured as among the greatest of medical researchers, he had inexplicably turned his back on Heri Gonza and his Foundation, had flatly refused research grants, and had publicly insulted the comedian and his great philanthropy. As a result he had lost his reappointment to the directorship of the Research Institute and a good deal of his professional standing. And like the sullen buffoon he was, he plunged into research – 'real research', he inexusably called it – on iapetitis, attempting single-handedly not only to duplicate the work of the Foundation, but to surpass it: 'the only way I know,' he had told a reporter, 'to pull the pasture out from under that clod and his trained sheep.' Heri Gonza's reply was typical: by deft sketches on his programmes, he turned Horowitz into an improper noun, defining a horowitz as a sort of sad sack or poor soul, pathetic, mildly despicable, incompetent and always funny – the kind of subhuman who not only asks for, but justly deserves a pie in the face. He backed this up with a widely publicized standing offer to Dr Horowitz of a no-strings-attached research grant of a half a million; which Dr Horowitz, after his first unprintable refusal (his instructions to the comedian as to what he could do with the money were preceded by the suggestion that he first change it into pennies), ignored.

Therefore the remark, even by a Nobel prizewinner, even by a reasonably handsome woman understandably weary and upset, even by one whose young brother lay helpless in the disfiguring grip of an incurable disease – such a remark could hardly be forgiven, especially when made to the head of the Iapetitis Wing of the Medical Centre and local chairman of the Foundation. 'I'm sorry, Dr Otis,' she said. 'I . . . probably need sleep more than I realized.'

'You probably do, Dr Barran,' he said evenly, and went into his office and closed the door.

'Damn,' said Iris Barran, and went home.

No one knew precisely how Heri Gonza had run across the idea of an endurance contest cum public solicitation of funds, or when he decided to include it in his bag of tricks. He did not invent the idea; it was a phenomenon of early broadcasting, which erupted briefly on the marriage of video with audio in a primitive device known as *television*. The performances, consisting of up to forty continuous hours of entertainment interspersed with pleas for aid in one charity or another, were headed by a single celebrity who acted as master of ceremonies and beggar-in-chief. The terminologically bastardized name for this production was *telethon*, from the Greek root *tele*, to carry, and the syllable *thon*, meaningless in itself but actually the last syllable of the word marathon. The telethon, sensational at first, had rapidly deteriorated, due to its use by numbers of greedy publicists who, for the price of a phone call, could get large helpings of publicity by pledging donations which, in many cases, they failed to make, and the large percentage of the citizenry whose impulse to give did not survive their telephoned promises. And besides, the novelty passed, the public no longer watched. So for nearly eighty years there were no telethons, and, if there had been, a disease to hang on would have been hard to find. Heart disease, cancer, multiple sclerosis, muscular dystrophy – these, and certain other infirmities on which public appeals had been based, had long since disappeared or were negligibly present.

Now, however, there was iapetitis.

A disorder of the midbrain and central nervous system, it attacked children between the ages of three and seven, affecting only one hemisphere, with no statistical preference for either side. Its mental effects were slight (which in its way was one of the most tragic aspects of the disease) being limited to aphasia and sometimes a partial alexia. It had more drastic effects on the motor systems, however, and on the entire cellular regeneration mechanisms of the affected side, which would gradually solidify and become inert, immobile. The most spectacular symptom was on the superficial pigmentation. The immobilized side turned white as bleached bone, the other increasingly dark, beginning with a reddening and slowly going through the red-browns to a chocolate in the latter stages. The division was exactly on the median line, and the bicolouration proceeded the same way in all cases, regardless of the original pigmentation.

There was no known cure.

There was no known treatment.

There was only the Foundation – Heri Gonza's Foundation – and all it could do was install expensive equipment and expensive people to operate it … and hope. There was nothing anyone else could do which would not merely duplicate Foundation's efforts, and besides, with one exception, the Foundation already had the top people in microbiology, neurology, virology, internal medicine, and virtually every other discipline which might have some bearing on the disease. There were, so far, only 376 known cases, every one of which was in a Foundation hospital.

Heri Gonza had been associated with the disease since the very beginning, when he visited a children's hospital and saw the appalling appearance of the first case, little Linda Tresak of Arkansas. When four more cases appeared in the Arkansas State Hospital after she was a patient there for some months, Heri Gonza moved with characteristic noise and velocity.

Within forty-eight hours of his first knowledge of the new cases, all five were ensconced in a specially vacated wing of the Medical Centre, and mobilization plans were distributed to centres all over the world, so that new clinics could be set up and duplicate facilities installed the instant the disease showed up. There were at present forty-two such clinics. Each child had been picked up within hours of the first appearance of symptoms, whisked to the hospital, pampered, petted, and ... observed. No treatment. No cure. The white got whiter, the dark got darker, the white side slowly immobilized, the dark side grew darker but was otherwise unaffected; the speech difficulty grew steadily (but extremely slowly) worse; the prognosis was always negative. Negative by extrapolation: any organism in the throes of such deterioration might survive for a long time, but must ultimately succumb.

In a peaceful world, with economy stabilized, population growing but not running wild any longer, iapetitis was big news. The biggest.

The telethon was, unlike its forebears, not aimed at the public pocket. It was to serve rather as a whip to an already aware world, information to the informed, aimed at earlier and earlier discovery and diagnosis. It was one of the few directions left to medical research. The disease was obviously contagious, but its transmission method was unknown. Some child, somewhere, might be found early enough to display some signs of the point of entry of the disease, something like a fleabite in spotted fever, the mosquito puncture in malaria – some sign which might heal or disappear soon after its occurrence. A faint hope, but it was a hope, and there was little enough of that around.

So, before a wide grey backdrop bearing a forty-foot insignia in the centre, the head and shoulders of a crying child vividly done in half silver, half mahogany, Heri Gonza opened his telethon.

Iris Barran got home well after it had started; she had rather overstayed her hospital visit. She came in wearily and slumped on the divan, thinking detachedly of Billy, thinking of Dr Otis. The thought of the doctor reminded her of her affront to him, and she felt a flash of annoyance, first at herself for having done it, and immediately another directed at him for being so touchy – and so unforgiving. At the same time she recalled his advice to get some sleep, not to watch the telethon; and in a sudden, almost childish burst of rebellion she slapped the arm of the divan and brought the trideo to life.

The opposite wall of the room, twelve feet high, thirty feet long, seemed to run to smoke, which cleared to reveal an apparent extension of the floor of the room, back and farther back, to Heri Gonza's great grey backdrop. All around were the sounds, the smells, the pressure of the presence of thousands of massed, rapt people. '. . . so I looked down and there the horse had caught its silly foot in my silly stirrup. "Horse," I says, "if you're gettin' on, I'm gettin' off!" '

The laugh was a great soft booming explosion, as usual out of all proportion to the quality of the witticism. Heri Gonza had that rarest of comic skills, the ability to pyramid his effects, so that the mildest of them seemed much funnier than it really was. It was mounted on a rapidly stacked structure of precious quips and jokes, each with its little store of merriment and all merriment suppressed by the audience for fear of missing not only the next joke, but the entire continuity. When the pyramid was capped, the release was explosive. And yet in that split instant between capper and explosion, he always managed to slip in a clear three or four syllables, 'On my way here – ' or 'When the president – ' or 'Like the horowitz who – ' which, repeated and completed after the big laugh, turned out to be the base brick for the next pyramid.

Watching his face during the big laughs – yocks, the knowledgeable columnists and critics called them – had become a national pastime. Though the contagion of laughter was in his voice and choice of phrase, he played everything deadpan. A small, wiry man with swift nervous movements, he had a face-by-the-million: anybody's face. Its notable characteristics were three: thin lips, masked eyes, impenetrable as onyx, and astonishing jug-handle ears. His voice was totally flexible, capable of almost any timbre, and, with the falsetto he frequently affected, his range was slightly over four octaves. He was an accomplished ventriloquist, though he never used the talent with the conventional dummy, but rather to interrupt himself with strange voices. But it was his ordinary, unremarkable, almost immobile face which was his audience's preoccupation. His face never laughed, though in dialogue his voice might. His voice could smile, too, even weep, and his face did not. But at the yock, if it was a big yock, a long one, his frozen waiting face would twitch; then thin lips would fill out a trifle: he's going to smile, he's going to *smile*! Sometimes, when the yock was especially fulsome, his mouth actually would widen a trifle; but then it was always time to go on, and, deadpan, he would. What could it matter to anyone whether or not one man in the world smiled? On the face of it, nothing: yet millions of people, most of whom were unaware of it, bent close to their trideo walls and peered raptly, waiting, waiting to see him smile.

As a result, everyone who heard him, heard every word.

Iris found herself grateful, somehow – able to get right out of herself; sweep in with that vast unseen crowd and leave herself, her worrying self, her angry, weary, logical, Nobel-prize-winning self asprawl on the divan while she hung on and smiled, hung on and tittered, hung on and exploded with the world.

He built, and he built, and the trideo cameras crept in on him until, before she knew it, he was standing as close to the invisible wall as belief would permit; and still he came closer, so that he seemed in the room with her; and this was a pyramid higher than most, more swiftly and more deftly built, so that the ultimate explosion could contain itself not much longer, not a beat, not a second. . . .

And he stopped in mid-sentence, mid-word, even, and, over at the left, fell to one knee and held out his arms to the right. 'Come on, honey,' he said in a gentle, tear-checked purr.

From the right came a little girl, skipping. She was a beautiful little girl, a picture-book little girl, with old-fashioned bouncing curls, shiny black patent-leather shoes with straps, little white socks, a pale-blue dress with a very wide, very short skirt.

But she wasn't skipping, she was limping. She almost fell, and Heri was there to catch her.

Holding her in his arms, while she looked trustingly up into his face, he walked to centre stage, turned, faced the audience. His eyes were on her face; when he raised them abruptly to the audience, they were, by some trick of the light (or of Heri Gonza) unnaturally bright.

And he stood, that's all he did, for a time, stood there with the child in his arms, while the pent-up laughter turned to frustrated annoyance, directed first at the comedian, and slowly, slowly, with a rustle of sighs, at the audience itself by the audience. Ah, to see such a thing and be full of laughter: how awful I am!

I'm sorry. I'm sorry.

One little arm was white, one pink. Between the too-tiny socks and the too-short skirt, the long thin legs were one white, one pink.

'This is little Koska,' he said after an age. The child smiled suddenly at the sound of her name. He shifted her in his elbow so he could stroke her hair. He said softly, 'She's a little Esthonian girl, from the far north. She doesn't speak very much English, so she won't mind if we talk about her.' A huskiness crept into his voice. 'She came to us only yesterday. Her mother is a good woman. She sent her to us the minute she noticed.'

Silence again, then he turned the child so their faces were side by side, looking straight into the audience. It was hard to see at first, and then it became all too plain – the excessive pallor of the right side of her face, the too-even flush on the left, and the sharp division between them down the centre.

'We'll make you better,' he whispered. He said it again in a foreign language, and the child brightened, smiled trustingly into his face, kept her smile as she faced the audience again: and wasn't the smile a tiny bit wider on the pink side than on the white? You couldn't tell. . . .

'Help me,' said Heri Gonza. 'Help her, and the others, help us. Find these children, wherever in the world they might be, and call us. Pick up any telephone in the world and say simply, I ... F. That's IF, the Iapetitis Foundation. We treat them like little kings and queens. We never cause them any distress. By trideo they are in constant touch with their loved ones.' Suddenly, his voice rang. 'The call you make may find the child who teaches us what we need to know. Your call – *yours!* – may find the cure for us.'

He knelt and set the child gently on her feet. He knelt holding her hands, looking into her face. He said, 'And whoever you are, wherever you might be, you doctors, researchers, students, teachers ... if anyone, anywhere, has an inkling, an idea, a way to help, any way at all – then call me. Call me now, call here – ' He pointed upwards and the block letters and figures of the local telephone floated over his head – 'and tell me. I'll answer you now, I'll personally speak to anyone who can help. Help, oh, help.'

The last word rang and rang in the air. The deep stage behind him slowly darkened, leaving the two figures, the kneeling man and the little golden girl, flooded with light. He released her hands and she turned away from him, smiling timidly, and crossed the wide stage. It seemed to take for ever, and as she walked, very slightly she dragged her left foot.

When she was gone, there was nothing left to look at but Heri Gonza. He had not moved, but the lights had changed, making of him a luminous silhouette against the endless black behind him ... one kneeling man, a light in the universal dark ... hope ... slowly fading, but there, still there ... no? Oh, there ...

A sound of singing, the palest of pale blue stains in deep centre. The singing up, a powerful voice from the past, an ancient, all but forgotten tape of one of the most moving renditions the world has ever known, especially for such a moment as this: Mahalia Jackson singing *The Lord's Prayer*, with the benefit of such audio as had not been dreamed of in her day ... with a cool fresh scent, with inaudible quasi-hypnotic emanations, with a whispering chorus a chorus of angels might learn from.

Heri Gonza had not said 'Let us pray'. He would never do such a thing, not on a global network. There was just the kneeling dimness, and the blue glow far away in the black. And if at the very end the glow looked to some like the sign of the cross, it might have been only a shrouded figure raising its arms; and if this was benediction, surely it was in the eye of the beholder. Whatever it was, no one who saw it completely escaped its spell, or ever forgot it. Iris Barran, for one, exhausted to begin with, heart and mind full to bursting with the tragedy of iapetitis; Iris Barran was wrung out by the spectacle. All she could think of was the last spoken word: *Help!*

She sprang to her phone and waved it active. With trembling fingers she dialled the number which floated in her mind as it had on the trideo wall, and to the composed young lady who appeared in her solido cave, saying, 'Trideo, C. A. O. Good evening,' she gasped, 'Heri Gonza – quickly.'

'One moment please,' said the vision, and disappeared, to be replaced instantly by another, even more composed, even lovelier, who said, 'I.F. Telethon.'

'Heri Gonza.'

'Yes, of course. Your name?'

'I-Iris Barran. Dr Iris Barran.'

The girl looked up sharply. 'Not the –'

'Yes, I won the Nobel prize. Please – let me speak to Heri Gonza.'

'One moment please.'

The next one was a young man with curly hair, a bell-like baritone, and an intensely interested face. He was Burcke of the network. He passed her to a jovial little fat man with shrewd eyes who was with Continuity Acceptance. Iris could have screamed out loud. But a worldwide appeal for calls would jam lines and channels for hours, and obviously a thorough screening process was essential. She was dimly aware that her name and face, only today in all the news, had already carried her to the top. Consciously, she thought of none of this; she held on and drove, wanting only to help ... *help* ... A snatch of the conversation she had had with Dr Otis drifted across her mind: *I guess you'd trade it for* ... and then a heart-rending picture of Billy's face, trying to smile with half a mouth. *I'd trade it all for a reasonable hope* ... and suddenly she was staring into the face of Heri Gonza. Reflexively she glanced over her shoulder at the trideo wall; Heri Gonza was there too, with a solidophone pillar in centre stage, its back to the audience so that only the comedian could see its cave. Light from it flickered on his face.

'I'd know that face anywhere!' he said raspingly.

'Oh,' she said faintly, 'Mr ... uh ...' and then remembered that one of his public affectations was never to permit anyone to call him Mister. She said, 'Heri Gonza, I ... I'm Iris B-Barran, and I – ' She realized that her voice could not be heard over the trideo. She was grateful for that.

He said, just as stridently, 'I know who you are. I know the story of your life too.' Switching to a comic quack, he said, 'So-o-o?'

'You know I just won the Nobel award. M – uh, Heri Gonza, I want to help, more than anything in the world, I want to help. My brother has it. W-would you like me to give the award money to you ... I mean, to the Foundation?'

She did not know what she expected in exchange for this stunning offer. She had not thought that far ahead. What she did not expect was ...

'You *what*?' he yelled, so loud she drew her head down, ungracefully, turtle-like. 'Listen, you, I got along without you before and I can get along without you now. You're getting from me, see, and I'm giving. What you got I don't want. I'm not up here to do *you* no good. I tell you what you got, you *got* a wrong number, and you *are*, s-s-s-s-so,' he hissed in a hilarious flatulent stutter, 's-s-so long.' And before she could utter another sound he waved her off and her phone cave went black.

Numb with shock, she slowly turned to the trideo wall, where Heri Gonza was striding downstage to the audience .His expressionless face, his gait, his posture, the inclination of his head, and his tone of voice all added to an amused indignation, with perhaps a shade more anger than mirth. He tossed a thumb at the phone and said, 'Wits we got calling, can you imagine? At a time like this. We got dimwits, half wits, and –' exactly the right pause; there was one bleat of laughter somewhere in the audience and then a thousand voices to chorus with him ' – horowitz!'

Iris sank back in the phone chair and covered her face, pressing so hard against her tired eyes that she saw red speckles. For a time she was shocked completely beyond thought, but at last she was able to move. She rose heavily and went to the divan, arrested her hand as she was about to click off the trideo. Heri Gonza was back at the stage phone, talking eagerly to someone, his voice honey and gentleness. 'Oh bless you, brother, and thank you. You may have an idea there, so I tell you what you do. You call the I.F. at Johannesburg and arrange a meeting with the doctors there. They'll listen ... No, brother, collect of course. What's-amatta, brother, you broke? I got news for you, for you-ee are-ee a-ee good-ee man-ee yes-ee indeedy-dee: you ain'ta broka no mo. A man like you? I got a boy on the way this very minute with a bag o' gold for the likes of you, brother ... oh now, don't say thanks, you make me mad. 'Bye.'

He waved off, and turned to the audience to intone, 'A man with an idea – little one, big one, who knows? But it's to help ... so bless him.'

Thunderous applause. Iris let her hand finish the gesture and switched off.

She went and washed her face, and that gave her strength enough to shower and change. After that she could think almost normally.

How *could* he?

She turned over impossible alternatives, explanations. His phone was a dummy; he couldn't see her, didn't know who was on the phone. Or it was his way of being funny, and she was too tired to understand. Or ... or ... it was no use: it had really happened, he had known what he was doing, he had a reason.

But *what* reason? Why? Why?

In her mind she again heard that roar from the audience: Horowitz. With difficulty, because it still stung, she pieced together the conversation and then, moving her forefinger towards her phone and the trideo, back and forth, puzzled out what had gone out over the air and what had not. Only then did she fully understand that Heri Gonza had done what he had done to make it seem that his first call was from Dr Horowitz. But if he needed that particular gag at that time, why didn't he fake it to a dead phone? Why actually converse with her, cut her down like that?

And he hadn't let her help. That was worse than any of the rudeness, the insult. He wouldn't let her help.

What to do? Making the gesture she had made had not been hard; having it refused was more than she could bear. She must help; she would help. Now of all times, with all this useless money coming to her; she didn't need it, and it might, it just might somehow help, and bring Billy back home.

Well then, expose Heri Gonza. Give him back some of his own humiliation. Call in the newsmen, make a statement. Tell them what she had offered, tell them just who was on the line. He'd *have* to take the money, and apologize to boot.

She stood up; she sat down again. No. He had known what he was doing. He had known who she was; he must have a telltale on his phone to get information on his callers from that screening committee. She knew a lot about Heri Gonza. He seemed so wild, so impulsive; he was not. He ran his many enterprises with a steel fist; he took care of his own money, his own bookings. He did not make mistakes or take chances. He had refused her and the Foundation would refuse her: the Foundation *was* Heri Gonza. He had his reasons, and if she had any defence at all against what he had done, he would not have done it.

She wasn't allowed to help.

Unless –

She suddenly ran to the phone. She dialled 5, and the cave lit up with the floating word DIRECTORY. She dialled H, O, R, and touched the *Slow* button until she had the Horowitzes. There were pathetically few of them. Almost everyone named Horowitz had filed unlisted numbers: many had gone so far as to change their names.

George Rehoboth Horowitz, she remembered.

He wasn't listed.

She dialled Information and asked. The girl gave her a pitying smile and told her the line was unlisted. And, of course, it would be. If Dr Horowitz wasn't the most hated man on earth, he was the next thing to it. A listed phone would be useless to him, never silent.

'Has he screening service?' Iris asked suddenly.

'He has,' said the girl, company-polite as always, but now utterly cold. Anyone who *knew* that creature to speak to ... 'Your name, please?'

Iris told her, and added, 'Please tell him it's very important.'

The cave went dark but for the slowly rotating symbol of the phone company, indicating that the operator was doing her job. Then a man's head appeared and looked her over for a moment, and then said, 'Dr Barran?'

'Dr Horowitz.'

She had not been aware of having formed any idea of the famous (infamous?) Horowitz; yet she must have. His face seemed too gentle to have issued those harsh rejoinders which the news attributed to him; yet perhaps it was gentle enough to be taken for the fumbler, the fool so many people thought he was. His eyes, in some inexplicable way, assured her that his could not be clumsy hands. He wore old-fashioned exterior spectacles; he was losing his hair; he was younger than she had thought, and he was ugly. Crags are ugly, tree-trunks, the hawk's pounce, the bear's foot, if beauty to you is all straight lines and silk. Iris Barran was not repulsed by this kind of ugliness.

She said, bluntly, 'Are you doing any good with the disease?' She did not specify: today, there was only one disease.

He said, in an odd way as if he had known her for a long time and could judge how much she would understand, 'I have it all from the top down to the middle, and from the bottom up to about a third. In between – nothing, and no way to get anything.'

'Can you go any farther?'

'I don't know,' he said candidly. 'I can go on trying to find ways to go farther, and if I find a way, I can try to move along on it.'

'Would some money help?'

'It depends on whose it is.'

'Mine.'

He did not speak, but tilted his head a little to one side and looked at her.

She said, 'I won ... I have some money coming in. A good deal of it.'

'I heard,' he said, and smiled. He seemed to have very strong teeth, not white, not even, just spotless and perfect. 'It's a good deal out of my field, your theoretical physics, and I don't understand it. I'm glad you got it. I really am. You earned it.'

She shook her head, denying it, and said, 'I was surprised.'

'You shouldn't have been. After ninety years of rather frightening confusion, you've restored the concept of parity to science – ' he chuckled – 'though hardly in the way anyone anticipated.'

She had not known that this was her accomplishment; she had never thought of it in those terms. Her demonstration of gravitic flux was a subtle matter to be communicated with wordless symbols, quite past speech. Even to herself she had never made a conversational analogue of it; this man had, though, not only easily, but quite accurately.

She thought, if this isn't his field, and he grasps it like that – just how good must he be in his own? She said, 'Can you use the money? Will it help?'

'God,' he said devoutly, 'can I use it. . . . As to whether it will help, Doctor, I can't answer that. It would help me go on. It may not make me arrive. Why did you think of me?'

Would it hurt him to know? she asked herself, and answered, it would hurt him if I were not honest. She said, 'I offered it – to the Foundation. They wouldn't touch it. I don't know why.'

'I do – ' he said, and instantly held up his hand. 'Not now,' he said, checking her question. He reached somewhere off-transmission and came up with a card, on which was lettered, AUDIO TAPPED.

'Who – '

'The world,' he overrode her, 'is full of clever amateurs. Tell me, why are you willing to make such a sacrifice?'

'Oh – the money. It isn't a sacrifice. I have enough: I don't need it. And – my baby brother. He has it.'

'I didn't know,' he said, with compassion. He made a motion with his hands. She did not understand. 'What?'

He shook his head, touched his lips, and repeated the motion, beckoning, at himself and the room behind him. Oh. *Come where I am.*

She nodded, but said only, 'It's been a great pleasure talking with you. Perhaps I'll see you soon.'

He turned over his card; obviously he had used it many times before. It was a map of a section of the city. She recognized it readily, followed his pointing finger, and nodded eagerly. He said, 'I hope it *is* soon.'

She nodded again and rose, to indicate that she was on her way. He smiled and waved off.

It was like a deserted city, or a decimated one; almost everyone was off the streets watching the telethon. The few people who were about all hurried, as if they were out against their wills and anxious to get back and miss as little as possible. It was known that he intended to go on for at least thirty-six hours, and still they didn't want to miss a minute of him. Wonderful, wonderful, she thought, amazed (not for the first time) at people – just people. Someone had once told her that she was in mathematics because she was so apart from, amazed at, people. It was possible. She was, she knew, very unskilled with people, and she preferred the company of mathematics, which tried so hard to be reasonable, and to say what was really meant. . . .

She easily found the sporting-goods store he had pointed out on his map, and stepped into the darkened entrance. She looked carefully around and saw no one, then tried the door. It was locked, and she experienced a flash of disappointment of an intensity that surprised her. But even as she felt it, she heard a faint click, tried the door again, and felt it open. She slid inside and closed it, and was gratified to hear it lock again behind her.

Straight ahead a dim, concealed light flickered, enough to show her that there was a clear aisle straight back through the store. When she was almost to the rear wall, the light flickered again, to show her a door at her right, deep in an ell. It clicked as she approached, and opened without trouble. She mounted two flights of stairs, and on the top landing stood Horowitz, his hands out. She took them gladly, and for a wordless moment they stood like that, laughing silently, until he released one of her hands and drew her into his place. He closed the door carefully and then turned and leaned against it.

'Well!' he said. 'I'm sorry about the cloak and dagger business.'

'It was very exciting.' She smiled. 'Quite like a mystery story.'

'Come in, sit down,' he said, leading the way. 'You'll have to excuse the place. I have to do my own housekeeping, and I just don't.' He took a test-tube rack and a cracked bunsen tube from an easy-chair and nodded her into it. He had to make two circuits of the room before he found somewhere to put them down. 'Price of fame,' he said sardonically, and sat down on a rope-tied stack of papers bearing the flapping label *Proceedings of the Pan-American Microbiological Society*. 'Where that clown makes a joke of Horowitz, other fashionable people make a game of Horowitz. A challenge. Track down Horowitz. Well, if they did, through tapping my phone or following me home, that would satisfy them. Then I would be another kind of challenge. Bother Horowitz. Break in and stir up his lab. with a stick. You know.'

She shuddered. 'People are . . . are so . . .'

'Don't say that, whatever it was,' said Horowitz. 'We're living in a quiet time, Doctor, and we haven't evolved too far away from our hunting and tracking appetites. It probably hasn't occurred to you that your kind of maths and my kind of biology are hunting and tracking too. Cut away our science bump and we'd probably hunt with the pack too. A big talent is only a means of hunting alone. A little skill is a means of hunting alone some of the time.'

'But . . . why must they hunt you?'

'Why must you hunt gravitic phenomena?'

'To understand it.'

'Which means to end it as a mystery. Cut it down to your size. Conquer it. You happen to be equipped with a rather rarefied type of reason, so you call your conquest understanding. The next guy happens to be equipped with fourteen inches of iron pipe and achieves his conquest with it instead.'

'You're amazing,' she said openly. 'You love your enemies, like – '

'Love thine enemies as thyself. Don't take any piece of that without taking it all. How much I love people is a function of how much I love Horowitz, and you haven't asked me about that. Matter of fact, *I* haven't asked me about that and I don't intend to. My God it's good to talk to somebody again. Do you want a drink?'

'No,' she said. 'How much do you love Heri Gonza?'

He rose and hit his palm with his fist and sat down again, all his gentleness folded away and put out of sight. 'There's the exception. You can understand anything humanity does if you try, but you can't understand the inhumanity of a Heri Gonza. The difference is that he knows what is evil and what isn't and doesn't care. I don't mean any numb by-rote moral knowledge learned at the mother's knee, the kind that afflicts your pipe-wielder a little between blows and a lot when he gets his breath afterwards. I mean a clear, analytical, extrapolative, brilliantly intelligent knowledge of each act and each consequence. Don't underestimate that devil.'

'He ... seems to ... I mean, he does love children,' she said fatuously.

'Oh, come on now. He doesn't spend a dime on his precious Foundation that he wouldn't have to give to the government in taxes. Don't you realize that? He doesn't do a thing he doesn't have to do, and he doesn't have to love those kids. He's using those kids. He's using the filthiest affliction mankind has known for a long time just to keep himself in front and centre.'

'But if the Foundation does find a cure, then he –'

'Now you've put your finger on the thing that nobody in the world but me seems to understand – why I won't work with the Foundation. Two good reasons. First, I'm 'way ahead of them. I don't need the Foundation and all those fancy facilities. I've got closer to the nature of iapetitis than any of 'em. Second, for all my love for and understanding of people, I don't want to find out what I'm afraid I would find out if I worked there and if a cure was found.'

'You mean he'd – he'd withhold it?'

'Maybe not permanently. Maybe he'd sit on it until he'd milked it dry. Years. Some would die by then. Some are pretty close as it is.'

She thought of Billy and bit her hand.

'I didn't say he would do that,' Horowitz said, more gently. 'I said I don't want to be in a position to find out. I don't want to know that any member of my species could do a thing like that. Now you see why I work by myself, whatever it costs. If I can cure iapetitis, I'll say so. I'll do it, I'll prove it. That's why I don't mind his kind of cheap persecution. If I succeed, all that harassment makes it impossible for him to take credit or profit in any way.'

'Who are you going to cure?'

'What?'

'He's got them all. He's on trideo right now, a telethon, the biggest show of the last ten years, hammering at people to send him every case the instant it's established.' Her eyes were round.

'The logician,' he whispered, as round-eyed as she. 'Oh my

God, I never thought of that.' He took a turn around the room and sat down again. His face was white. 'But we don't *know* that. Surely he'd give me a patient. Just one.'

'It might cost you the cure. You'd have to, you'd just *have* to give it to him, or you'd be the one withholding it!'

'I won't think about it now,' he said hoarsely. 'I can't think about it now. I'll get the cure. That first.'

'Maybe my brother Billy – '

'Don't even think about it!' he cried. 'He's already got it in for you. Don't get in his way any more. He won't let your Billy out of there and you know it. Try anything and he'll squash you like a beetle.'

'What's he got against *me*?'

'You don't know? You're a Nobel winner – one of the newsiest things there is. A girl, and not bad-looking at all. You're in the public eye, or you will be by noon tomorrow when the reporters get to you. Do you think for a minute he'd let you or anybody climb on his publicity? Listen, iapetitis is his sole property, his monopoly, and he's not going to share it. What'd you expect him to do, announce the gift on his lousy telethon?'

'I – I c-called him on his telethon.'

'You didn't!'

'He pretended the call was from you. But . . . but at the same time he told me . . . oh yes, he said, "What you got I don't want. I'm not up here to do you no good." '

Horowitz spread his hands. 'Q.E.D.'

'Oh,' she said, 'how awful.'

At that point somebody kicked the door open.

Horowitz sprang to his feet, livid. A big man in an open, flapping topcoat shouldered his way in. He had a long horse-face and blue jaw. His eyes were extremely sad. He said, 'Now just relax. Relax and you'll be all right.' His hands, as if they had a will of their own, busied themselves about pulling off a tight left-hand glove with wires attached to it and running into his side pocket.

'Flannel!' Horowitz barked. 'How did you get in?' He stepped forward, knees slightly bent, head lowering. 'You'll get out of here or so help me – '

'No!' Iris cried, clutching at Horowitz's forearm. The big man outreached and outweighed the biologist, and certainly would fight rougher and dirtier.

'Don't worry, lady,' said the man called Flannel sleepily. He raised a lazy right hand and made a slight motion with it, and a cone-nosed needler glittered in his palm. 'He'll be good – won't you, boy? Or I'll put you to bed for two weeks an' a month over.'

He sidled past and, never taking his gaze from Horowitz for more than a flickering instant, opened the three doors which led from the laboratory – a bathroom, a bedroom, a storage closet.

'Who is he? You know him?' Iris whispered.

'I know him,' growled Horowitz. 'He's Heri Gonza's bodyguard.'

'Nobody but the two of them,' said Flannel.

'Good,' said a new voice and a second man walked in, throwing off a slouch hat and opening the twin to the long, loose topcoat Flannel wore. 'Hi, chillun,' said Heri Gonza.

There was a long silence, and then Horowitz plumped down on his pile of *Proceedings*, put his chin in his hands, and said in profound disgust, 'Ah, for God's sake.'

'Dr Horowitz,' said Heri Gonza pleasantly, nodding, and 'Dr Barran.'

Iris said, shakily, 'I th-thought you were doing a sh-show.'

'Oh, I am, I am. All things are possible if you only know how. At the moment Chitsie Bombom is doing a monologue, and she's good for two encores. After that there's a solido of me sitting way up on the flats in the left rear, oh so whimsically announcing the Player's Pub Players. They have a long one-acter and a pantomime. I've even got a ballet company, in case this takes that long.'

'Phoney to the eyeballs, even when you work,' said Horowitz. 'Quickly and quietly and get the hell out of here, 'scuse me, Dr Barran.'

'Oh, that's all right,' she murmured.

'Please,' said the comedian softly, 'I didn't come here to quarrel with you. I want to end all that. Here and now, and for good.'

'We've got something he wants,' said Horowitz in a loud aside to Iris.

Heri Gonza closed his eyes and said, 'You're making this harder than it has to be. What can I do to make this a peaceful talk?'

'For one thing,' said Horowitz, 'your simian friend is breathing and it bothers me. Make him stop.'

'Flannel,' said Heri Gonza, 'get out.'

Glowering, the big man moved to the door, opened it, and stood on the sill. 'All the way,' said the comedian. Flannel's broad back was one silent mass of eloquent protest, but he went out and shut the door.

Deftly, with that surprising suddenness of nervous motion which was his stock in trade, Heri Gonza dropped to one knee to bring their faces on a level, and captured Iris's startled hands. 'First of all, Dr Barran, I came to apologize to you for the way I spoke on the telephone. I had to do it – there was no alternative, as you'll soon understand. I tried to call you back, but you'd already gone.'

'You followed me here! Oh, Dr Horowitz, I'm sorry!'

'I didn't need to follow you. I've had this place spotted since two days before you moved into it, Horowitz. But I'm sorry I had to strongarm my way in.'

'I yield to curiosity,' said Horowitz. 'Why didn't my locks alarm when you opened them? I saw Flannel's palm-print eliminator, but dammit, they should have alarmed.'

'The locks were here when you rented the place, right? Well, who do you think had them installed? I'll show you where the cut-off switch is before I leave. Anyhow – grant me this point. Was there any other way I could have got in to talk with you?'

'I concede,' said Horowitz sourly.

'Now, Dr Barran. You have my apology, and you'll have the explanation to go with it. Believe me, I'm sorry. The other thing I want to do is to accept, with thanks from the bottom of my heart, your very kind offer of the prize money. I want it, I need it, and it will help more than you can possibly realize.'

'No,' said Iris flatly. 'I've promised it to Dr Horowitz.'

Heri Gonza sighed, got to his feet, and leaned back against the lab. bench. He looked down at them sadly.

'Go on,' said Horowitz. 'Tell us how you need money.'

'The only two things I have never expected from you are ignorance and stupidity,' said Heri Gonza sharply, 'and you're putting up a fine display of both. Do you really think, along with all my millions of ardent fans, that when I land a two-million-dollar contract I somehow put two million dollars in the bank? Don't be childish. My operation is literally too big to hide anything in. I have city, county, state and federal tax vultures picking through my whole operational framework. I'm a corporation and subject to outside accounting. I don't even have a salary; I draw what I need, and I damn well account for it, too. Now, if I'm going to finish what I started with the disease, I'm going to need a lot more money than I can whittle out a chip at a time.'

'Then take it out of the Foundation money – that's what it's for.'

'I want to do the one thing I'm not allowed to do with it. Which happens to be the one thing that'll break this horrible thing – it has to!'

'The only thing there is like that is a trip to Iapetus.'

To this, Heri Gonza said nothing – absolutely nothing at all. He simply waited.

Iris Barran said, 'He means it. I think he really means it.'

'You're a big wheel,' said Horowitz at last, 'and there are a lot of corners you can cut, but not that one. There's one thing the government – all governments and all their armed forced – will rise up in wrath to prevent, and that's another landing and return from any place off earth – especially Iapetus. You've got close to four hundred dying kids on your hands right now, and the whole world is scared.'

'Set that aside for a moment.' The comedian was earnest,

warm-voiced. 'Just suppose it could be done. Horowitz, as I understand it, you have everything you need on the iapetitis virus but one little link. Is that right?'

'That's right. I can synthesize a surrogate virus from nucleic acids and exactly duplicate the disease. But it dies out of its own accord. There's a difference between my synthetic virus and the natural one, and I don't know what it is. Give me ten hours on Iapetus and half a break, and I'll have the original virus under an electron mike. Then I can synthesize a duplicate, a real self-sustaining virus that can cause the disease. Once I have that, the antigen becomes a factory process, with the techniques we have today. We'll have shots for those kids by the barrel lot inside of a week.'

Heri Gonza spread his hands. 'There's the problem, then. The law won't allow the flight until we have the cure. We won't have the cure unless we make the flight.'

Iris said, 'A Nobel prize is an awful lot of money, but it won't buy the shell of a space ship.'

'I've got the ship.'

For the first time Horowitz straightened up and spoke with something besides anger and hopelessness. 'What kind of a ship? Where is it?'

'A Fafnir. You've seen it, or pictures of it. I use it for globetrotting mostly, and VIP sightseeing. It's a deepspace craft, crew of twelve, and twelve passenger cabins. But it handles like a dream, and I've got the best pilot in the world, Kearsarge.'

'Kearsarge, God yes. But look, what you call deepspace is Mars and Venus. Not Saturn.'

'You don't know what's been done to that ship. She'll sleep four now. I have a lab. and a shop in her, and all the rest is nothing but power-plant, shielding and fuel. Hell, she'll make Pluto!'

'You mean you've been working on this already?'

'Man, I've been chipping away at my resources for a year and a half now. You don't know what kind of footsie I've been playing with my business managers and the banks and all. I can't squeak out another dime without lighting up the whole project. Dr Barran, *now* do you see why I had to treat you like that? You were *the* godsend, with your wonderful offer and your vested interest in Billy. Can you astrogate?'

'I – oh dear. I know the principles well enough. Yes, I could, with a little instruction.'

'You'll get it. Now look, I don't want to see that money. You two will go down and inspect the ship tomorrow morning, and then put in everything you'll need beyond what's already there. You've got food, fuel, water and air enough for two trips, let alone one.'

'God,' said Horowitz.

'I'll arrange for your astrogation, Dr Barran. You'll have to dream up a story, secret project or long solitary vacation or some such. Horowitz, you can drop out of sight without trouble.'

'Oh, sure, thanks to you.'

'Dammit, this time you're welcome,' said the comedian, and very nearly smiled. 'Now, you'll want one more crew member: I'll take care of that before flight time.'

'What about the ship? What will you say?'

'Flight test after overhaul. Breakdown in space, repair, return – some such. Leave that to Kearsarge.'

'I freely admit,' said Horowitz, 'that I don't get it. This is one frolic that isn't coming out of taxes, and it's costing you a packet. What's in it, mountebank?'

'You could ask that,' said the comedian, sadly. 'The kids that's all.'

'You'll get the credit?'

'I won't, I can't, I don't want it. I can't tie in to this jaunt – it would ruin me. Off-earth landings, risking the lives of all earth's kids – you know how they'd talk. No sir: this is your cooky, Horowitz. You disappear, you show up one day with the answer. I eat crow like a hell of a good sport. You get back your directorship if you want it. Happy ending. All the kids get well.' He jumped into the air and clicked his heels four times on the way down. 'The kids get well,' he breathed with sudden sobriety.

Horowitz said gently, 'Heri Gonza, what's with you and kids?'

'I like 'em.' He buttoned his coat. 'Good night, Dr Barran,
Please accept my apologies again, and don't think too badly
of me.'

'I don't,' she said smiling, and gave him her hand.

'But why do you like kids *that* much?' asked Horowitz.

Heri Gonza shrugged easily and laughed his deadpan laugh.
'Never had none,' he chuckled. He went to the door and stopped
facing it, suddenly immobile. His shoulders trembled. He whirled
suddenly, and the famous carven face was wet, twisted, the
mouth tortured and crooked. 'Never can,' he whispered, and
literally ran out of the room.

The weeks went by, the months. Iapetitis cases underwent
some strange undulations, and a hope arose that the off-world
virus was losing its strength. Some of the older cases actually
improved, and a blessing that was, too; for although overall
growth was arrested, there was a tendency for the mobile side
to grow faster than the other, and during the improvement
phase, the sides seemed to equalize. Then, tragically the improvement would slow; and stop.

Incidence of the disease seemed to be slackening as well. At
the last, there had been only three new cases in a year, though
they caused a bad flurry, occurring as they did simultaneously
in a Belgian village which had had no hint of the disease before.

Heri Gonza still did his weekly stint (less vacation) and still
amazed his gigantic audiences with his versatility, acting, singing, dancing, clowning. Sometimes he would make quiet
appearances, opening and closing the show and turning it over
to a theatre or ballet group. During the Old Timer's Celebration
he learned to fly a perfect duplicate of a century-old light aircraft with an internal combustion engine, and daringly took
his first solo during the show, with a trideo camera occupy-
ing the instructor's seat.

At other times he might take up the entire time-segment
alone, usually with orchestra and props, once – possibly his
most successful show – dressed in sloppy practice clothes on
a bare stage, without so much as a chair, and with no assistance

but lights and cameras and an occasional invisible touch from the hypnos and the scent generators. Single-handedly he was a parade, a primary schoolroom, a zoo in an earthquake, and an old lady telling three children, ages five, ten, and fifteen, about sex all at the same time.

And in between (and sometimes during) his shows, he faithfully maintained I. F. He visited his children regularly, every single one of the more than four hundred. He thrilled with their improvements, cheered them in their inevitable relapses. The only time he did not make one of his scheduled shows at all was the time the three cases appeared in Belgium, and then the slot was filled with news-items about the terrifying resurgence, and a world tour of I. F. clinics. He was a great man, a great comic, no question about it, right up to his very last show.

He didn't know it was his last show, which in its way was a pity, because with that knowledge he would have been more than good; he'd have been great. He was that kind of performer.

However, he was good, and was in and out of a vastly amusing variety show, using his old trick of standing offstage and singing with perfect mimicry while top vocalists stood centre stage and mouthed the words. He turned out to be one of the Japanese girls who built body-pyramids on their bicycles, and, powered by a spring device under the water, joined a succession of porpoises leaping to take fish out of a keeper's hand.

He played, as he preferred to do, in a large studio without an audience, but playing to the audience-response sound supplied to him. He made his cues well, filled in smoothly with *ad-libs* when a girl singer ran a chorus short of her arrangement, and did his easy stand-up comedy monologue to close. A pity he didn't smile on that show. When the on-the-airs went out and the worklights came on, he threw a sweat-shirt around his shoulder and ambled into the wings, where, as usual, the network man, Burcke, waited for him.

'How'd it look, Burckee ol' turkey?'

'Like never before,' said Burcke.

'Aw, you're cute yourself,' said the comedian. 'Let's have a look.' One of his greatest delights – and one reason for his fantastic polish – was the relaxed run-through afterwards, where he lounged in the projection-room and looked at the show he had just finished from beginning to end. He and Burcke and a few interested cast members, backstage people, and privileged strangers got arranged in the projection room. Beer was passed around and the small-talk used up. As usual they all deferred to Heri Gonza, and when he waved a negligent hand everybody shut up and the projectionist threw the switch.

Title and credits with moving cloud-blanket background. Credits fade, camera zooms towards clouds, which thin to show mountain range. Down through clouds, hover over huge misty lake. Water begins to heave, to be turbulent, suddenly shores rush together and water squirts high through the clouds in a thick column. Empty lake rises up out of clouds, is discovered to be Heri Gonza's open mouth. Pull back to show full face. Puzzled expression. Hand up, into mouth, extracts live goldfish.

GONZA: Welcome to the Heri Gonza show, this week 'As you lake it.' (*beat*) Which is all you can expect when you open with a punorama. What ho is (*beat*) What ho is yonder? A mountain. What ho is on the mountain? A mountain goat. What ho is the goat mountain? Why, another moun – Fellers, keep the lens on me, things are gettin' a little blue off camera. Now hear ye, Tom, now hear ye Dick, now hear ye hairy Harry, Heri's here. Hee hee, ho ho, here comes the show.

Soft focus and go to black. Long beat.

Heri took his beer away from his mouth and glared at the wall. 'God's sake, you send all that black?'

'Sure did,' said Burcke equably.

'Man, you don't do that for anything but the second coming. What you think they expect with all that black? It sucks 'em in, but boy, you got to pay off.'

'We paid off,' said Burcke. 'Here it comes.'

'The horse act, right?'

'Wrong,' said Burcke.

Dark stage. Desk, pool of light. Zoom in, Burcke, jaw clamped. In a face as sincere and interested as that, the clamped jaw is pretty grim.

BURCKE: Tonight the Heri Gonza show brings you a true story. Although the parts are played by professional actors, and certain scenes are shorted for reasons of time, you may be assured that these are real events and can be proved in every detail.

'What the hell is this?' roared Heri Gonza. 'Did you air this? Is this what went out when I was knocking myself out with that horse act?'

'Sit down,' said Burcke.

Heri Gonza sat down dazedly.

Burcke at desk. Lifts book and raps it.

BURCKE: This is a ship's rough log, the log of the Fafnir 203. How it comes to be on this desk, on your wall, is, I must warn you, a shocking story. The Fafnir is a twelve-cabin luxury cruiser with a crew of twelve, including stewards and the galley crew. So was the 203, before it was rebuilt. It was redesigned to sleep four with no room over, with two cabins rebuilt as a small-materials shop and biological laboratory, and all the rest taken up with powerplant, fuel and stores. The ship's complement was Dr Iris Barran, mathematician –
Fade in foredeck of Fafnir, girl standing by computer.

Dr George Rehoboth Horowitz, microbiologist –
Bespectacled man enters, crosses to girl, who smiles.

Yeager Kearsarge, pilot first class –
Kearsarge is a midget with a long, bony, hardbitten face. He enters from black foreground and goes to control console.

Sam Flannel, supercargo.
Widen lighting to pass cabin bulkhead, discovering large man strapped in acceleration couch, asleep or unconscious.

'I got it,' said Heri Gonza in the projection room. 'A rib. It's a rib. Pretty good, fellers.'

'It isn't a rib, Heri Gonza,' said Burcke. 'Sit down, now.'

'It's got to be a rib,' said Heri Gonza in a low voice. 'Slip me a beer. I should relax and enjoy the altogether funny joke.'
'Here. Now shush.'

BURCKE: ... mission totally contrary to law and regulation. Destination: Iapetus. Purpose: collection of the virus, or spores, of the dreaded children's affliction iapetitis, on the theory that examination of these in their natural habitat will reveal their exact internal structure and lead to a cure, or at the very least an immunization. Shipowner and director of mission: (*long beat*) Heri Gonza.
Fourteen hours out ...

Fade Burcke and desk and take out. Dolly in to foredeck. Horowitz crosses to side cabin, looks in on Flannel. Touches Flannel's face. Returns to computer and Iris.

HOROWITZ: He's still out cold. The tough boy is no spaceman.

IRIS: I can't get over his being here at all. Why ever did Heri want him along?

HOROWITZ: Maybe he'll tell us.

Small explosion. High whine.

KEARSARGE: A rock! a rock!

IRIS (*frightened*): What's a rock?

Kearsarge waddles rapidly to friction hooks on bulkhead, snatches off helmets, throws two to Horowitz and Iris, sprints with two more into cabin. Gets one on Flannel's lolling head, adjusts oxygen valve. Puts on his own. Returns to assist Iris, then Horowitz.

IRIS: What *is* it?

KEARSARGE: Nothing to worry you, lady. Meteorite. Just a little one. I'll get it patched.

From control console, sudden sharp hiss and cloud of vapour.

IRIS: Oh! what's *that*?

KEARSARGE: Now you got me.

Kearsarge goes to console, kneels, peers underneath. Grunts, fumbles.

HOROWITZ: What is it?

KEARSARGE: Ain't regulation, 'sall I know.

Horowitz kneels beside him and peers.

HOROWITZ: What's this?

KEARSARGE: Bottom of main firing lever. Wire tied to it, pulled that pin when we blasted off.

HOROWITZ: Started this timing mechanism. . . . What time did it pop?

KEARSARGE: Just about 14:30 after blastoff.

HOROWITZ: Think you can get it off there? I'd like to test for what was in it.

Kearsarge gets the device off, gives it to Horowitz, who takes it into the lab.

Cut to cabin, close-up to Flannel's helmeted face. He opens his eyes, stares blankly. He is very sick, pale, insane with dormant fear. Suddenly fear no longer dormant. With great difficulty raises head, raises strapped-down wrist enough to see watch. Suddenly begins to scream and thrash around. The releases are right by his hands but he can't find them. Iris and Kearsage run in. Kearsage stops to take in the situation, then reaches out and pulls releases. Straps fall away; Flannel, howling, leaps for the door, knocking the midget flat and slamming Iris up against edge of door. She screams. Kearsarge scrambles to his feet, takes off after Flannel like a Boston terrier after a bull. Flannel skids to a stop by the lifeboat blister, starts tugging at it.

KEARSARGE: What the hell are you doing?

FLANNEL (*blubbering*): 14:30 . . . 14:30 . . . I gotta get out, gotta get out . . . (*screams*).

KEARSARGE: Don't pull on that, y'damn fool! That's not the hatch, it's the release! We got spin on for gravity – y'll pitch the boat a hundred miles off!

FLANNEL: Oh, lemme out, it's too late!

Kearsarge punches upwards with both hands so unexpectedly that Flannel's grip is broken and he pitches over backwards. Kearsarge leaps on him, twists his oxygen valve, and scuttles back out of the way, Flannel staggers over to the boat blister, gets his hands on the wrong lever again,

but his knees buckle. Inside the helmet, his face is purpling.
Horowitz comes running out of the lab. Kearsarge puts out
an arm and holds him back, and together they watch Flan-
nel sag down, fall, roll, writhe. He puts both hands on
helmet, tugs at it weakly.

HOROWITZ: Don't for God's sake let him take off that helmet!

KEARSARGE: Don't worry. He can't.

Flannel slumps and lies still. Kearsarge goes to him and
opens valve a little. He beckons Horowitz and together
they drag him back to the cabin and with some difficulty
get him on the couch and strapped down.

HOROWITZ: What happened? I had my hands full of reagents
in there.

KEARSARGE: Space nutty. They get like that sometimes after
blackout. He wanted out. Tried to take the boat.

HOROWITZ: He say anything?

KEARSARGE: Buncha junk. Said, 14:30, 14:30. Said it was too
late, had to get out.

HOROWITZ: That snivvy under the console popped at 14:30.
He knew about it.

KEARSARGE: Did he now. What was it?

HOROWITZ: Cyanide gas. If we hadn't been holed and forced
to put the helmets on, we'd've had it.

KEARSARGE: Except him. He figured to be up' around lookin'
at his watch, and when she popped, he'd be in the boat headed
home and we'd keep blasting till the pile run dry, som'res out
t'ords Algol.

HOROWITZ: Can you fix those releases so he can't reach them?

KEARSARGE: Oh sure.

Fade. Lights pick up Burcke at the side.

BURCKE (*as narrator*): They got an explanation out of Flannel,
and it satisfied none of them. He said he knew nothing of any
cyanide. He said that Heri, knowing he was a bad spaceman,
had told him that if it got so bad he couldn't stand it, he
could always come back in the lifeboat. But if he did that,
he'd have to do it before 14:30 after blastoff or there
wouldn't be enough to decelerate, start back and manoeuvre

a landing. He insisted that that was all there was to it. He would not say what he was doing aboard, except to state that Heri Gonza wanted him to look out for Heri's interests.

No amount of discussion made anything clearer. Heri certainly could not have wanted the expedition to fail, or his ship hurled away from the solar system. They reluctantly concluded that some enemy of Heri Gonza's must have sabotaged them – someone they simply didn't know.

The weeks went by – not easy ones, by any means, in those quarters, without any event except Iris Barran's puzzling discovery that the ship required no astrogator after all: what the veteran Kearsarge couldn't handle in his head was easily treated in the computer. Why, then, had Heri Gonza insisted on her cramming on astrogation?

Zoom in to Saturn until it fills a quadrant. String out the moons.

Heri Gonza watched the bridge sequence, as Saturn swept colse and the moons rolled by like broken beads, and little Iapetus swam close. Iapetus is not a moon like most, round or oblate, but a rock, a drifting mountain some 500 miles in diameter. And before them was the solution to the mystery of the changing moonlight. Some unknown cataclysm has cloven Iapetus, so that it has one sheer face, nearly four hundred square miles of flat plain (or cliff, depending on how you look at it) made of pale grey basaltic material. Since Iapetus always maintains one face to Saturn, it always appears brighter as it rounds the eastern limb, and dimmer as it goes west, the albedo of the flat face being much higher than the craggy ruin of the rest of its surface.

'Burckee, Burckee, Burckee, ol' turkey,' murmured the comedian in accents of wonder, 'who the hell writes your stuff? Who writes your lousy, lousy stuff?'

Stock shot, Fafnir putting down tail-first on rocky plain, horizon washed out and black space brought down close. Rocks sharp-cornered, uneroded. Long shot, stabilizing jacks extend-

*ing widest. Ladder out. Two suited figures ride it down, the
other two climb down.*

   Close-up, all four at tail-base.

HOROWITZ (*filter mike*): Check your radios. Read me?

ALL: Check. Read you fine.

HOROWITZ: Each take a line. Walk straight out with the fin
   as a guide, and when you've passed our scorch area, get a
   rock scraping every five feet or so until you're far enough
   away that the horizon's a third of the way up the hull. Got
   that? No farther. (*Beat*) And I can almost tell you now, we
   aren't going to find one blessed thing. No virus, no spore, no
   nothing. My God, it's no more than twelve, thirteen degrees
   K in the shadows here. Anyway . . . let's go.

BURCKE (*Off*): Scratch and hop, scratch and hop. In this gravity,
   you don't move fast or push hard, or you'll soar away and
   take minutes to come down again. Shuffle and scratch,
   scratch and sweep, scratch and hop. It took them hours.

   Close-up Kearsarge, looking down.

KEARSARGE: Here's something.

   *Close-ups, each of the other three, turning head at the
   sound of Kearsarge's voice.*

HOROWITZ: What is it?

KEARSARGE: Scorch. A regular mess of it. Hell, you know
   what? Swope toppled his ship. I can see where he came down,
   where he took off, scraping along to the big edge there.

FLANNEL: Wonder he didn't wreck her.

KEARSARGE: He did. He couldn't hurt the hull any in this
   gravity, but he sure as hell wiped off his antennae, because
   there they are: landing, range, transmission – every one, by
   God. No wonder he come barrelling in the way he did. You
   can't land a Fafnir on manual, but you can try, and he tried.
   Poor ol' Swopie.

HOROWITZ: Everybody over there by Kearsarge. Maybe Swope
   picked up something where he scraped.

   *Long shot of the four working around long scorch and
   scrape marks.*

BURCKE (*off, narrating*): They filled their specimen sacks and brought them aboard, and then for seventy-two hours they went through their dust and stones with every test Horowitz could devise. . . . He had been quite right in his first guess. The moonlet Iapetus is as devoid of life as the inside of an autoclave.

Cut to foredeck set, but upended, the controls at highest point, the floor what was the after-bulkhead. Iris moving around with slow shuffle, setting out magnetized plates on a steel table, each one hitting loudly. In background, Flannel fusses with small electron mike, watching screen and moving objective screws. Lifeboat blister open, Kearsarge inside, working.

Airlock cycles, opens and Horowitz comes in, suited, with sack. He is weary. Iris helps with helmet.

HOROWITZ: I've had it. Let's get home. We can get just so duty-bound.

IRIS: What's this 'home'? I don't remember.

HOROWITZ: You for home, Kearsarge?

KEARSARGE: Any time you're through hoein' this rock.

HOROWITZ: What are you doing in there?

KEARSARGE: Just routine. Figured you might want to buzz around the other side with the boat.

HOROWITZ: No sir. I came close enough on foot. I say we're done here. A man could sit home with a pencil and paper and figure out the density of sub-microscopic growth this place would have to have to bring any back on the hull. We'd be hip deep in it. The iapetitis virus didn't come from Iapetus, and that, friends, is for sure and official.

KEARSARGE (*off*): Oh my holy mother. (*He pops out, putty-coloured.*) George, get over here.

IRIS (*curiously*): What is it?

She goes over and disappears for a moment inside the boat, with Kearsarge and Horowitz. Off, she gasps. Then, one by one they climb out and stand looking at Flannel. Sensing the silence, he looks up and meets their eyes.

FLANNEL: What I got, blue horns or something?

HOROWITZ: Show him, Kearsarge.

Kearsarge beckons. There is a strange pucker of grim amusement on his craggy face.

KEARSARGE: Come look, little feller. Then you can join our club.

Reluctantly, the big man goes over to the blister and follows Kearsarge into the lifeboat. Dolly after them, swing in to the instrument panel, under it and look up.

Lashed to the projecting lower end of the main thrust control is a silver can with a small cylinder at the near end.

FLANNEL (*pointing stupidly*): Is that ... that the same thing that –

KEARSARGE: A little smaller, but then you don't need as much cyanide for a boat.

FLANNEL (*angry*): Who the hell put it there? You?

KEARSARGE: Not me, feller. I just found it.

HOROWITZ: It's been there all along, Flannel. Kearsarge is right: you belong to the club too. You sure it was Heri Gonza told you to take the boat?

FLANNEL: Sure it was. He couldn't have nothing to do with this. (*Suddenly it hits him*) Jesus! I mighta –

HOROWITZ: We'll have plenty of time to talk this over. Let's pack up the testing stuff and haul out of here.

FLANNEL (*to no one*): Jesus.

Heri Gonza lay back in the projection room and sipped his beer and watched the stock shot at a Fafnir taking off from a rock plain. 'You really get all that glop out of that book, Burcke m' boy?'

'Every bit of it,' said Burcke, watching the screen.

'You know how it is in space, a fellow's got to do something with his time. Sometimes he writes, and sometimes it's fairy tales, and sometimes you can get a pretty good show out of a fairy tale. But when you do that, you call it a fairy tale. Follow me?'

'Yup.'

'This was really what went out on the air tonight?'

'Sure is.'

Very, very softly, Heri Gonza said, 'Poor Burcke. Poor, poor ol' Burcke.'

Close-up, hands turning pages in rough logbook. Pull back to show Burcke with book. He looks up, and when he speaks his voice is solemn.

BURCKE: Time to think, time to talk it over. Time to put all the pieces in the same place at the same time, and push them against each other to see what fits.

Fade to black; but it is not black after all: instead, starry space. Pan across to pick up ship, a silver fish with a scarlet tail. Zoom in fast, dissolve through hull, discovering foredeck. The four lounge around, really relaxed, willing to think before speaking, and to speak carefully. Horowitz and Kearsarge sit at the table ignoring a chessboard. Iris is stretched on the deck with a rolled-up specimen sack under her head. Flannel kneels before a spread of Canfield solitaire. Horowitz is watching him.

HOROWITZ: I like to think about Flannel.

FLANNEL: Think what?

HOROWITZ: Oh . . . the alternatives. The 'ifs'. What would Flannel do if this had been different, or that.

FLANNEL: There's no sense in that kind of thinkin' – if this, if that. This happened, or that happened, and that's all there is to it. You got anything special in mind?

HOROWITZ: I have, as a matter of fact. Given that you had a job to do, namely to cut out and leave us with our cyanide bomb at the start of the trip –

FLANNEL (*aroused*): I tol' you and *tol'* you that wasn't a job. I didn't know about the damn cyanide.

HOROWITZ: Suppose you had known about it. Would you have come? If you had come, would you have tipped us off about it? And here's the question I thought of: if the first bomb had failed – which it did – and there had been no second bomb to tell you that you were a member of the Exit Club, would you have tried to do the job on the way home?

FLANNEL: I was thinkin' about it, about what to do.

HOROWITZ: And what did you decide?

FLANNEL: Nothin'. You found the bomb in the boat so I just stopped thinkin'.

IRIS (*suddenly*): Why? Did that really make a difference?

FLANNEL: All the diff'nce in the world. Heri Gonza tol' me to get in the lifeboat before fourteen an' a half hours and come back and tell him how things went. Now if there was just *your* bomb, could be that Heri Gonza wanted you knocked off. There was an accident and it din't knock you off, and here I am working for him and wonderin' if I shoon't take up where the bomb left off.

IRIS: Then we found the second bomb, and you changed your mind. Why?

FLANNEL (*exasperated*): Whata ya all, simple or somepin? Heri Gonda, *he tol' me to come back and tell him how it went.* If he tells me that an' then plants a bomb on me, how could I get back to tell him? A man's a fool to tell a guy to do somethin' an' then fix it so he can't. He's no fool, Heri Gonza I mean, an' you know it. Well then: If he din't plant my bomb, he din't plant your bomb, because anyone can see they was planted by the same guy. An' if he din't plant your bomb, he don't want you knocked off, so I stopped thinkin' about it. Is that simple enough for ya?

IRIS: I don't know that it's simple, but it sure is beautiful.

HOROWITZ: Well, one of us is satisfied of Heri Gonza's good intentions. Though I still don't see what sense it made to go to all the trouble of putting you aboard just to have you get off and go back right at the start.

FLANNEL: Me neither. But do I have to understand everything he tells me to do? I done lots of things for him I didn't know what they was about. You too, Kearsarge.

KEARSARGE: That's right. I drive this can from here to there, and from there to yonder, and I don't notice anything else, but if I notice it I forget it, but if I don't forget it I don't talk about it. That's the way he likes it and we get along fine.

IRIS (*forcefully*): I think Heri Gonza wanted us all killed.

HOROWITZ: What's that – intuition? And … shouldn't that read 'wants'?

IRIS: 'Wants,' yes. He wants us all killed. No, it's not intuition. It formulates. Almost. There's a piece missing.

FLANNEL: Ah, y'r out of y'r mind.

KEARSARGE: Doubled.

HOROWITZ (*good-naturedly*): Shut up, both of you. Go on with that, Iris. Maybe by you it formulates, but by me it intuits. Go on.

IRIS: Well, let's use as a working hypothesis that Heri Gonza wants us dead – us four. He wants more than that: he wants us to disappear from the cosmos – no bodies, no graves, no nothing.

KEARSARGE: But *why*?

HOROWITZ: Just you listen. We start with the murders and finish with the why. You'll see.

IRIS: Well then, the ship will do the removal. The cyanide – both cyanides – do the actual killing, and it hits so fast that the ship keeps blasting, out and out until the fuel is gone, and forever after that. We three are on it; Flannel crashes in a small craft and if anybody wonders about it they don't wonder much. Is there any insignia on that boat, by the way, Kearsarge?

KEARSARGE: Always.

IRIS: Go look, will you? Thanks. Now, what about the traces we leave behind us? Well, we took off illegally so notified no one and filed no clearances. You, George, were already in hiding from Heri Gonza's persecutions. Kearsarge here is so frequently away on indeterminate trips of varying lengths that he would soon be forgotten; Flannel here – no offence, Flannel – I don't think anyone would notice that you're gone for good. As for me, Heri Gonza himself had me plant a story about going off secretly for some solitary research for a year or so. What's the matter, Kearsarge?

KEARSARGE: I wouldn'ta believed it. No insignia. Filed off and sanded smooth and painted. Numbers off the thrust block. Trade-name off the dash, even. I … I wouldn'ta believed it.

HOROWITZ: Now you'd better listen to the lady.

IRIS: No insignia. So even poor Flannel's little smash-up is thoroughly covered. Speaking of Flannel, I say again that it was stretching credibility to put him aboard that way – unless you assume that he was put aboard like the rest of us, to be done away with. I certainly came under false pretences: Heri Gonza not only told me he needed an astrogater for the trip, which he didn't, but had me bone up on the subject.

Now we can take a quick look at motive. George Horowitz here is the most obvious. He has for a long time been a thorn in the flesh of that comedian. Not only has he concluded that Heri Gonza doesn't really want to find a cure for iapetis – he says so very loudly and as often as he can. In addition, George is always on the very verge of whipping the disease, something that frightens Heri Gonza so much that he's actually hoarding patients so George can't get to them. Also, he doesn't like George.

Why kill Flannel? Is he tired of you, Flannel? Did you boggle something he asked you to do?

FLANNEL: He don't have to kill me, Miss Iris. He could fire me any time. I'd feel real bad, but I wouldn't bother him none. He knows that.

IRIS: Then you must know too much. You must know something about him so dangerous he won't feel safe until you're dead.

FLANNEL: So help me lady, there ain't a single thing like that I know about him. Not one. Not that I know of.

HOROWITZ: There's the key, Iris. He doesn't know he knows it.

KEARSARGE: Then that's me too, because if there's a single thing I know that he'd have to kill me for then I don't know what it is.

IRIS: You said 'key.' Lock and key. A combination of things. Like if you put what Flannel knows with what Kearsarge knows, they will be dangerous to Heri Gonza.

Flannel and Kearsarge gape at each other blankly and simultaneously shrug.

HOROWITZ: I can give you one example of a piece of knowledge we all have that would be dangerous to him. We now
know that the disease virus does not originate on Iapetus.
Which means that poor Swope was not responsible for bring-
ing it to earth, and, further, the conclusion that the little
Tresak girl – the first case – caught it from the wreckage of
the space ship was unwarranted.

FLANNEL: I brung that picture of that little girl standing in
the wreck, I brung it to Heri Gonza. He liked it.

IRIS: What made you do that?

FLANNEL: I done it all the time. He told me to.

HOROWITZ: Bring him pictures of little girls?

FLANNEL: Girls, boys ... but pretty ones. I got to know just
the ones he would like. He liked to use 'em on his show.
    *Iris and Horowitz lock glances for one horrified second,
    and then pounce all but bodily on Flannel.*

IRIS: Did you ever show him a picture of any child who later
contracted the disease?

FLANNEL (*startled*): Wh ... I dunno.

IRIS (*shouting*): Think! Think!

HOROWITZ (*also shouting*): You did! You did! The Tresak girl
– that photograph of her was taken before she had the
disease!

FLANNEL: Well yeah, her. And that little blonde one he had
on the telethon that din't speak no English from Est'onia, but
you're not lettin' me think.

HOROWITZ: What?

KEARSARGE: I remember that little blonde girl. I flew her from
Esthonia.

IRIS: Before or after she had the disease?

KEARSARGE (*shrugging*): The kind of thing I never noticed.
She ... she looked all right to me. Real pretty little kid.

IRIS: How long before the telethon was that?

KEARSARGE: Week or so. Wait, I can tell you to the day.
(*He rises from the chess table and goes to a locker, from
which he brings a notebook. He leafs.*) Here it is. Nine
days.

IRIS (*faintly*): He said, on the telethon, three days ... first symptoms.

HOROWITZ (*excitedly*): May I see that? (*Takes book, riffles it, throws it on the table, runs to lab., comes back with cardboard file, fans through it, comes up with folder.*) Iris, take Kearsarge's book. Right. Now did he fly to Belem on the ninth of May?

IRIS: The sixth.

HOROWITZ: Rome, around March twelfth.

IRIS: March twelfth, March – here it is. The eleventh.

HOROWITZ: One more, Indianapolis, middle of June.

IRIS: Exactly. The fifteenth. What is that you have there?

He throws it down in front of her.

HOROWITZ: Case files. Arranged chronologically by known or estimated date of first symptom, in an effort to find some pattern of incidence. No wonder there was never any pattern. God in Heaven, if he wanted a clinic in Australia, cases would occur in Australia.

FLANNEL (*bewildered*): I don't know what you are talkin' about.

KEARSARGE (*grimly*): I think I do.

IRIS: *Now* do you think you're worth murdering – you who can actually place him on the map, at the time some child was stricken, every single time?

KEARSARGE (*huskily*): I'm worth murdering. I . . . didn't know.

FLANNEL (*poring over the case file*): Here's that one I seen in Bellefontaine that time, she had on a red dress. And this little guy here, he got his picture in a magazine I found on the street in Little Rock and I had to go clear to St Louis to find him.

Kearsarge hops up on a chair and kicks Flannel in the head.

FLANNEL (*howling*): Hooo – wow! What you wanna hafta do that for? Ya little –

HOROWITZ: Cut it out, you two. *Cut it out!* That's better. We don't have room for that in here. Leave him alone, Kearsarge. His time will come. Heaven help me, Iris, it's been in front of my nose right from the start, and I didn't see it. I even told you once that I was so close because I could synthesize a virus which would actually cause the disease – but it wouldn't maintain it? I had this *idée fixe* that it was an extra-terrestrial disease. Why? Because it acted like a synthetic *and no natural terran virus does.* Serum from those kids always acted that way – it would cause a form of iapetitis which would fade out in three months or less. *All you have to do to cure the damn thing is to stop injecting it!*

IRIS: Oh, the man, the lovely clever man and his family all over the world, the little darlings, the prettiest ones he could find, whom he never, never failed to visit regularly ... (*Suddenly, she is crying*) I was so s-sorry for him! Remember the night he ... tore himself open to tell us he c'couldn't have k-kids of his own?

KEARSARGE: Who you talking about – Heri Gonza? For Pete's sake, he got an ex-wife and three kids he pays money to keep 'em in Spain, and another ex-wife in Paris France with five kids, three his, and that one in Pittsburgh – man, that comedian's always in trouble. He *hates* kids – I mean really hates 'em.

(*Iris begins to laugh. Probably hysteria.*)

Dissolve to black, then to starry space. To black again, bring up pool of light, resolve it into:
Burcke, sitting at desk. He closes log book.
BURCKE: This is, I regret to say, a true story. The Fafnir 203 came in at night six days ago at a small field some distance from here, and Dr Horowitz phoned me. After considerable discussion it was decided to present this unhappy story to you in the form written up by four people who actually experienced it. They are here with me now. And here is a much maligned man, surely one of the greatest medical researchers alive – Dr Horowitz.

HOROWITZ: Thank you. First, I wish to assure everyone within reach of my voice that what has been said here about iapetitis is true: it is a synthetic disorder which is, by its very nature, harmless, and which, if contracted, will pass away spontaneously in from two to twelve weeks. Not a single child has died of it, and those who have been its victims the longest – some up to two years – have unquestionably been lavishly treated. A multiple murder was attempted upon my three companions and myself, of course, but it was our greatest desire to see to it that that charge is not pressed.

BURCKE: I wish to express the most heartfelt apologies from myself and all my colleagues for whatever measure of distress this network and its affiliates may have unwittingly brought you, the public. It is as an earnest of this that we suffer, along with you, through the following film clip, taken just two days ago in the I. F. clinic in Montreal. What you see in my hand here is a thin rubber glove, almost invisible on the hand. Fixed to its fingertips is a microscopic forest of tiny sharp steel points, only a few thousandths of an inch long. And this metal box, just large enough to fit unobtrusively in a side pocket, contains a jellied preparation of the synthetic virus.

   Fade to:

   Wild hilarity in hospital ward. Children in various stages of iapetitis, laughing hilariously at the capering, growling, gurling, belching funny man as he moves from bed to bed, Peep! at you, peep-peep at you, and one by one ruffling the little heads at the nape, dipping the fingertips in the side jacket pocket between each bed.

   Dissolve, and bring up Burcke.

BURCKE: Good night, ladies, gentlemen, boys and girls . . . *I'm sorry.*

The lights came up in the projection room. There was nobody there with Heri Gonza but Burcke: all the others had quietly moved and watched the last few scenes from the doorway, and slipped away.

'You did air it?' asked the comedian, making absolutely sure.

'Yes.'

Heri Gonza looked at him without expression and walked

towards the stage door. It opened as he approached, and four people came in. Flannel, Kearsarge, Horowitz, Iris Barran.

Without a word Flannel stepped up to the comedian and hit him in the stomach. Heri Gonza sank slowly to the floor, gasping.

Horowitz said, 'We've spent a lot of time deciding what to do about you, Heri Gonza. Flannel wanted just one poke at you and wouldn't settle for anything else. The rest of us felt that killing was too good for you, but we wanted you dead. So we wrote you that script. Now you're dead.'

Heri Gonza rose after a moment and walked through the stage door and out to the middle of acres and acres of stage. He stood there alone all night, and in the morning was gone.

The [Widget], the [Wadget], and Boff

Throughout the continuum as we know it (and a good deal more, as we don't know it) there are cultures that fly and cultures that swim; there are boron folk and fluorine fellowships, cupro-coprophages and (roughly speaking) immaterial lifeforms which swim and swirl around each other in space like so many pelagic shards of metaphysics. And some organize into super-entities like a beehive or a slime-mould so that they live plurally to become singular, and some have even more singular ideas of plurality.

Now, no matter how an organized culture of intelligent beings is put together or where, regardless of what it's made of or how it lives, there is one thing all cultures have in common, and it is the most obvious of traits. There are as many names for it as there are cultures, of course, but in all it works the same way – the same way the inner ear functions (with its contributory synapses) in a human being when he steps on Junior's roller skate. He doesn't think about how far away the wall is, some wires or your wife, or in which direction: he *grabs*, and, more often than not he *gets* – accurately and without analysis. Just so does an individual reflexively adjust when imbalanced in his sociocultural matrix: he experiences the reflexes, a thing as large as the legendary view afforded a drowning man of his entire past, in a single illuminated instant wherein the mind moves, as it were, at right angles to time and travels high and far for its survey.

And this is true of every culture everywhere, the cosmos over. So obvious and necessary a thing is seldom examined: but it was once, by a culture which called this super-reflex 'Synapse Beta sub Sixteen'.

What came out of the calculator surprised them. They were, after all, expecting an answer.

Human eyes would never have recognized the device for what it was. Its memory bank was an atomic cloud, each particle of which was sealed away from the others by a self-sustaining envelope of force. Subtle differences in nuclei, in probability shells, and in internal tensions were the coding, and fields of almost infinite variability were used to call up the particles in the desired combinations. These were channelled in a way beyond description in earthly mathematics, detected by a principle as yet unknown to us, and translated into language (or, more accurately, an analogue of what we understand as language). Since this happened so far away, temporally, spatially, and culturally, proper nouns are hardly proper; it suffices to say that it yielded results, in this particular setting, which were surprising. These were correlated into a report, the gist of which was this:

Prognosis positive, or prognosis negative, depending upon presence or absence of Synapse Beta sub Sixteen.

The pertinent catalogue listed the synapse in question as 'indetectible except by field survey'. Therefore an expedition was sent.

All of which may seem fairly remote until one realizes that the prognosis was being drawn for that youthful and dangerous aggregate of bubbling yeasts called 'human culture', and that when the term 'prognosis negative' was used it meant *finis*, the end, zero, *ne plus ultra* altogether.

It must be understood that the possessors of the calculator, the personnel of the expedition to Earth, were not Watchers in the Sky and Arbiters of Our Fate. Living in our midst, here and now, is a man who occupies himself with the weight-gain of amoebae from their natal instant to the moment they fission. There is a man who, having produced neurosis in cats, turns them into alcoholics for study. Someone has at long last settled the matter of the camel's capacity for, and retention of, water. People like these are innocent of designs on the destinies of amoebae, cats, camels and cultures; there are simply certain things they want to know. This is the case no matter how unusual, elaborate, or ingenious their methods might be. So – an expedition came here for information.

EXCERPT FROM FIELD EXPEDITION [NOTEBOOK][1]. [VOLUME]ONE:CONCLUSION... to restate the obvious, [we] have been on Earth long enough and more than long enough to have discovered anything and everything [we] [wished] about any [sensible-predictable-readable] culture anywhere. This one, however, is quite beyond [understanding-accounting-for]. At first sight [one] was tempted to conclude immediately that it possesses the Synapse, because no previously known culture had advanced to this degree without it, ergo ... And then [we] checked it with [our] [instruments] [! ! !] [Our] [gimmick] and our [kickshaw] gave [us] absolutely negative readings, so [we] activated a high-sensivity [snivvy] and got results which approximate nonsense: the Synapse is scattered through the population randomly, here non-existent or dormant, there in brief full activity at [unheard-of] high levels. [I] thought [Smith] would go [out of [his] mind] and as for [myself], [I] had a crippling attack of the [   ]s at the very concept. More for [our] own protection than for the furtherance of the Expedition, [we] submitted all our data to [our] [ship]'s [computer] and got what appeared to be even further nonsense: the conclusion that this species possesses the Synapse but to all intents and purpose does not use it.

How can a species possess Synapse Beta sub Sixteen and not use it? Nonsense, nonsense, nonsense!

So complex and contradictory are [our] data that [we] can only fall back on a microcosmic analysis and proceed by its guidance. [We] shall therefore isolate a group of specimens under [laboratory] control, even though it means using a [miserable] [primitive] [battery]-powered [wadget]. [We]'ll put our new-model [widget] on the job, too. [We]'ve had enough of this [uncanny, uncomfortable] feeling of standing in the presence of [apology-for-obscenity] paradox.

---

[1] TRANSLATOR'S NOTE: Despite the acknowledged fact that the translator is an expert on extra-terrestrial language, culture, philosophy, and the theory and design of xenological devices, the reader's indulgence is requested in this instance. To go into detail about these machines and the nature and modes of communication of the beings that operate them would be like writing the story of a young lover on the way to his reward, springing up his beloved's front

I

The town was old enough to have slums, large enough to have
no specific 'tracks' with a right and wrong side. It's nature was
such that a boarding house could, without being unusual, contain such varied rungs on the social ladder as a young, widowed
night-club hostess and her three-year-old son; a very good
vocational guidance expert; a young law clerk; the librarian
from the high school; and a stage-struck maiden from a very
small small town. They said Sam Bittelman, who nominally
owned and operated the boarding house, could have been an
engineer, and if he had been, a marine architect as well, but
instead he had never risen higher than shop foreman. Whether
this constituted failure or success is speculative; apply to a
chief petty officer or top sergeant who won't accept a com-
mission, and to the president of your local bank, and take your
pick of their arguments. It probably never occurred to Sam
to examine the matter. He had other things to amuse him.
Tolerant, curious, intensely alive, old Sam had apparently never
retired from anything but his job at the shipyards back east.

He in turn was owned and operated by his wife, whom everyone called 'Bitty' and who possessed the harshest countenance
and the most acid idiom ever found in a charter member of
the Suckers for Sick Kittens and Sob Stories Society. Between
them they took care of their roomers in that special way possible only in boarding houses which feature a big dining table
and a place set for everyone. Such places are less than a family,
or more if you value your freedom. They are more than a hotel,
or less if you like formality. To Mary Haunt, who claimed to
be twenty-two and lied, the place was the most forgettable and

steps, ringing the bell – and then stopping to present explicit detail
about the circuitous wiring and dry, dry, cells. It is deemed more
direct and more economical to use loose convenient translations
and to indicate them by brackets, in order to confine the narrative
to the subject at hand. Besides, it pleases the translator's modesty
to be so sparing with his [omniscience].

soon-to-be-forgotten of stepping stones; to Robin it was home and more: it was the world and the universe, an environment as ubiquitous, unnoticed and unquestioned as the water around a fish; but Robin would, of course, feel differently later. He was only three. The only other one of the Bittelmans' boarders who breathed what was uniquely the Bittelman quality as if it were air was Phil Halvorsen, a thoughtful young man in the vocational guidance field, whose mind was on food and housing only when they annoyed him, and since the Bittelmans made him quite comfortable, in effect they were invisible. Reta Schmidt appreciated the Bittelmans for a number of things, prime among which was the lengths to which her dollar went with them, for Miss Schmidt's employers were a Board of Education. Mr Anthony O'Banion permitted himself a genuine admiration of almost nothing in these parts. So it remained for Sue Martin to be the only one in the place who respected and admired them, right from the start, with something approaching their due. Sue was Robin's widowed mother and worked in a night club as hostess and sometimes entertainer. She had done, in the past, both better and worse. She still might do better for herself, but only that which would be worse for Robin. The Bittelmans were her godsend. Robin adored them, and the only thing they would not do for him was to spoil him. The Bittelmans were there to give him breakfast in the mornings, to dress him when he went out to play, to watch over him and keep him amused and content until Sue rose at eleven. The rest of the day was for Sue and Robin together, right up to his bedtime, when she tucked him in and storied him to sleep. And when she left for work at 9 p.m., the Bittelmans were there, safe and certain, ready and willing to cope with anything from a bladder to a blaze. They were like insurance and fire extinguishers, hardly ever used but comforting by their presence. So she valued them . . . but then, Sue Martin was different from most people. So was Robin; however, this is a truism when speaking of three-year-olds.

Such was the population of Bittelmans' boarding house, and if they seem too many and too varied to sort out all at once,

have patience and remember that each of them felt the same
way on meeting all the others.

2

A pawnshop is a dismal place.

A pawnshop in the rain. A closed pawnshop in the rain, on
a Sunday.

Philip Halvorsen did not object. He had a liking for harmony,
and the atmosphere suited him well just now, his thoughts, his
feelings. A sunbeam would have been a intrusion. A flower shop
could not have contributed so much. People, just now, would
have been intolerable.

He leaned his forehead against the wet black steel of the
burglar-proof gate and idly inventoried the contents of the
window and his thoughts about them. Like the window and its
contents, and the dark recesses inside, his thoughts were mis-
cellaneous, cluttered, captured in that purgatory of uselessness
wherein things are not dead, only finished with what they have
been and uncaring of what will happen to them and when. His
thoughts were binoculars without eyes, cameras without film,
silent guitars and unwound watches.

He found himself approving more of the guitars than the two
dirty violins hanging in the window. He almost wondered why
this should be, almost let the question disappear into lethargy,
and at last sighed and ran the matter down because he knew it
would bother him otherwise and he was in no mood to be
bothered. He looked at the instruments lazily, one, the other,
analysing and comparing. They had a great deal in common,
and some significant differences. Having a somewhat sticky
mind, to which windblown oddments of fact had been adhering
for nearly thirty years now, he knew of the trial-and-error
evolution of those resonance-chambers and of the high degree
of perfection they had come to. Given that design followed
function in both the violin and the guitar, and aside from any
preference in the sounds they made (actually Halvorsen was
completely indifferent to music anyway), then why should he

intuitively prefer the guitars he saw to the violins? Size, proportion, numbers of strings, design of bridge, frets or lack of them, finish, peg and tailpiece mechanics – all these had their differences and all were perfect for the work they did.

Suddenly, then, he saw it, and his mind swiftly thumbed through the mental pictures of all the violins he had ever seen. They all checked out. One flickering glance at the guitars in the window settled the matter.

All violins have a scroll carved at the end of the neck – *all* of them. There is scrollwork on some guitars, none on others; it's obviously optional. The back-bending spiral at the end of a violin's neck is not optional, but traditional, and it has no function. Halvorsen nodded slightly and permitted his mind to wander away from the matter. It wasn't important – not in itself; only settling it was important. His original, intuitive approval of guitars over violins was not a matter of moment either; his preference for the functional over the purely traditional was just that – a preference.

None of this required much of Halvorsen's conscious effort or attention. The survey, the sequence, was virtually reflexive, and his thoughts moved as fish in some deep clear pool might move, hanging and hanging, fanning, then suddenly darting about with a swirl and a splash, to hang again fanning, alive and waiting.

He stood motionless, the fine rain soaking into the back of his collar and his eyes unseeking but receptive. Binoculars with mother-of-pearl; binoculars without. A watch with glass rubies in the face. Display cards, cheap combs, cheap wallets, cheap pens. An electric steam iron with a frayed cord. A rack of second-hand clothing.

Guns.

He felt again that vague dissatisfaction, set up a certain amount of lethargic resistance to it, and when it came through anyway he patiently gave it its head. He looked at the guns. What bothered him about the guns?

One had a pearl handle and rococo etching along the barrel, but that wasn't it. He glanced down the row and settled on a

.38 automatic, about as functional an artifact as could be imagined – small, square, here knurled and there polished, with
the palm-safety and lock-safety just where they should be. And
still he felt that faint disapproval, that dissatisfaction that
spelt criticism. He widened his scan to all the guns, and felt it
just as much. Just as little.

It was categorical then. It had to do with all these guns, or
with all guns. He looked again, and again, and within this scope
found no crevice for the prying of his reason, so he turned the
problem on its back and looked again: what would a gun be
like if it satisfied this fastidious intuition of his?

It came in a flash, and he hardly believed it: a flimsy structure of rolled sheet metal with a simple firing pin on a piece
hinged and sprung like the business part of a mousetrap. There
was no butt, there were no sights. No trigger either; just a
simple catch and – what was that? – and a piece of string. He
visualized it sitting on a polished surface on a wire stand, its
thin barrel angled upwards about 45°, like a toy cannon. Its
calibre was about .38. The feature which struck him most was
the feeling of fragility, lightness, in the whole design. Design!
What would an object like that be designed for?

He looked again at the pawned guns. Among the things they
had in common was massiveness. Breeches were cast steel,
muzzles thick-walled, probably all rifled; parts were tempered,
hardened, milled, designed and built to contain and direct
repeated explosions, repeated internal assaults by hot hurtling
metal.

It was as if a little red signal-light flickered on the concept
repeated. Was that it, that all these guns were designed for
repeated use? Was he dissatisfied with that? Why?

He conjured up the image of a single-shot duelling pistol he
had once handled: long-barrelled, muzzle-loading, with a
powder-pan for priming and a chip of flint fixed to the hammer.
To his surprise he found the little mental red light still aflicker;
this was a design that displeased him too, somewhere in the
area labelled *repeated*.

Even a single-shot pistol was designed to be used over again;

that must be it. Then to him, a gun satisfied its true function only if it was designed to be used only once. *Enough* is the criterion of optimum design, and in this case once was enough.

Halvorsen snorted angrily. He disliked being led by rational means to a patently irrational conclusion. He cast back over his reasoning, looking for the particular crossroads where he must have taken a wrong turning.

There was none.

At this point his leisurely, almost self-powered curiosity was replaced by an incandescent ferocity of examination. Logic burned in Halvorsen as fury did in other men, and he had no tolerance for the irrational. He attacked it as a personal indignity, and would not let up until he had wrapped it up, tied it down, in the fabric of his understanding.

He let himself visualize the 'gun' of his satisfied imagination, with its mousetrap firing mechanism, its piece of string, its almost useless flimsiness, and for a moment pictured police, cattlemen, Army officers handling such a ridiculous object. But the vision dissolved and he shook his head; the guns ordinarily used by such people satisfied his sense of function perfectly. He slipped (hypothetically) into the consciousness of such a man and regarded his gun – *a* gun – any gun with satisfaction. No, this seemed a personal matter, unlike the dissatisfaction everyone should feel (if they cared) about the extraordinary fact that automobiles are streamlined only where they show, and are powered by a heat-engine which is inoperable without a cooling system.

What's so special about my mousetrap gun? he demanded of himself, and turned his eye inwards to look at it again. There it sat, on a polished surface – table-top, was it? – with its silly piece of string leading forward towards him and its muzzle tilted upwards, unabashedly showing off its sleazy construction.

Why could he see how thin the metal of that muzzle was?

Because it was aimed right at the bridge of his nose.

Make a statement, Halvorsen, and test it. Statement: Other guns satisfy other men because they can be used over and over again. This gun satisfies me because it goes off once, and once is enough.

Test: A duelling pistol goes off only once; yet it can be reloaded and used again. Why not this? Answer: Because whoever uses a duelling pistol expects to be able to use it again. Whoever sees it used expects it will be used again, because the world goes on.

After Halvorsen's mousetrap gun went off, the world wouldn't go on. Not for Halvorsen – which of course is the same thing. 'I am the core and centre of the universe' is a fair statement for anyone.

So restate, and conclude: The optimum gun design is that which, having shot Halvorsen between the eyes, need no longer exist. Since *optimum* carried with it the flavour of *preferred performance*, it is fair to state that within himself Halvorsen found a preference for being shot to death. More specifically, for dying. Correction: for being dead – gladly.

Momentarily, Halvorsen felt such pleasure at having solved his problem that he neglected to look at the solution, and when he did, it chilled him far more than the fine rain could.

Why should he want to be dead?

He glanced at the racked guns in the pawnshop and saw them as if for the first time, each one very real and genuinely menacing. He shuddered, clung for a moment to the wet black steel of the gate, then abruptly turned away.

In all his thoughtful – thought-*filled* – life he had never consciously entertained such a concept. Perhaps this was because he was a receptive person rather than a transmissive one. What he collected he used on his external world – his job – rather than on himself. He had no need for the explanations and apologies, the interpretations and demands-to-be-heard of the out-going person, so he had no need to indulge in self-seeking and the complicated semantics of ego-translation. He was rather a clearing-house for the facts he found, taking knowledge and experience from *here* and storing them virtually untouched until they could be applied *there*.

He walked slowly homeward, in a state that would be numbness except for the whirling, wondering core which turned and poked and worried at this revelation. Why should he want to be dead?

Philip Halvorsen loved being alive. Correction: He enjoyed being alive. (Question: Why the correction? File for later.) He was a vocational guidance worker employed by a national social service organization. He was paid what he should be, according to his sense of values, and thanks to the Bittelmans he lived a little better on it than he might otherwise. He did not work for money, anyway; his work was a way of thinking, a way of life. He found it intriguing, engrossing, deeply satisfying. Each applicant was a challenge, each placement a victory over one or more of the enemies that plague mankind – insecurity, inferiority, blindness and ignorance. Each time he looked up from his desk and saw a new applicant entering his cubicle, he experienced a strange silent excitement. It was a pressure, a power, like flicking on the master switch of a computing machine; he sat there with all relays open and all circuits blank, waiting for the answers to those first two questions: 'What are you doing now?' and 'What do you want to do?' Just that; it was enough for that indefinable sense of satisfaction or dissatisfaction to make itself known to him. And just as he had analysed its source in the matter of guns, so he analysed his clients. That flickering light signalling wrongness, misapplication, malfunction, misevaluation – all the flaws in design, the false goals, the frustrations and hurts of those who wonder if they have chosen the right vocation – that light burned on while he worked on each case, and would not go out until he found an answer. Once or twice he had wished, whimsically, that his imagined signal light would illuminate a sign for the client which said *Steeplejack* and for that one which said *Frog Farmer*, but it refused to be so obliging. It only told him when he was wrong. Being right involved laborious and meticulous work, but he did it gladly. And when at last he was satisfied, he frequently found that his work had just begun: to tell an eighty-dollar-a-week bank clerk that his proper niche is in freight-handling with a two-year apprenticeship at fifty is initially a thankless task. But Halvorsen knew how to be quiet and wait, and had become a past master at the art of letting a client fight himself, defeat himself, reconstruct himself, and at last persuade himself that the vocational counsellor was right. And all of it, Halvorsen liked, from the challenge to the accomplishment. Why, why should there be a wish in him to have this cease, to end the world in which all these intriguing problems existed? And to be glad of its ending?

What would he advise a client, a stranger, if that stranger blurted out such a desire?

Well, he wouldn't. It would depend. He would simply throw that in with everything else about the client – age, education, temperament, marital status, I.Q., and all the rest of it, and let the death-wish throw its weight along with all the other factors. It would, however, predispose him to conclude that the man was intolerably misplaced in some area: in a marriage, a family situation, a social beartrap of some kind ... or his job. His job. Was he, Halvorsen, judge and arbiter of occupations – was he in the wrong job?

He slouched along in the rain, huddled down into himself to escape a far more penetrating chill than this drenching mist. So uncharacteristically wrapped in his inward thought was he that he had taken three steps on dry pavement before he became aware of it. He stopped and took his bearings.

He stood under the marquee of the smallest and cheapest of the town's four theatres. It was closed and dark, this being Sunday in a 'blue-law' district, but dead bulbs and locked doors did not modify the shrillness of its decorations. Over the main entrance were two groups of huge letters, one for each of the two features on the bill. SIN FOR SALE, one shrieked, and the other blared back SLAVES OF THE HELL-FLOWER. Under these was a third sign, offering as a special added attraction *Love Rites of a South Sea Eden*. From the sidewalk on the far left, up to the marquee, across and down the other side was an arch of cardboard cutouts of women, wilting and wet, unnaturally proportioned and inhumanly posed, with scraps of ribbon and drape, locks of hair and induced shadows performing a sort of indicative concealment on their unbelievable bodies. Over the box-office was the stern advice *Adults only!!!* and papering the supporting pillars just inside the mirrored cavern of a lobby were still photographs of highlights of the pictures: A bare-backed female with her hands trussed to a high tree-branch, being whipped; a man standing, gun in hand, over a delectable corpse whose head hung back and down over the edge of a bed so that her carefully arranged hair swept the floor, and some flyblown samples of the South Sea den with the portraits of its inhabitants smeared strategically with rubber-stamp ink in angry and careless obedience to some local by-law.

At the best of times this sort of display left Phil Halvorsen cold. At the worst of times (up to now) he would have felt a mild disgust leavened by enough amusement at the out-house crudity of it to make it supportable – and forgettable. But at the moment things were a little worse than the worst had ever been before. It was as if his earlier unpleasant revelation had in some obscure way softened him up, opened a seam in a totally unexpected place in his armour. The display smote him like a blast of heat. He blinked and stepped back a pace, half-raising his hands and screwing his eyes shut. Behind the lids the picture of his ridiculous one-shot cannon rose up roaring. He thought he could see a bullet emerging from its smoking muzzle like the tip of a hot black tongue. He shuddered away from the millisecond nightmare and opened his eyes, only to get a second and even more overwhelming reaction from the theatre-front.

My God, what's happening to me? he silently screamed to himself. He pounded his forehead with his fists twice, then put his head down and ran up the street, up the hill. His photographic eye had picked up the banner inside the lobby, and as he ran, part of him coldly read it:

SEE (in flaming scarlet) the big-city orgies
SEE the temptation of a teenager
SEE lust run riot
SEE the uncensored rites of an island cult

SEE ... SEE ... There was more. As he ran, he moaned.

And then he thought, at the Bittelmans there are people, it is light, it is warm, it is almost home.

He began to run to something instead of away.

3

The Bittelmans' kitchen was a vague 'backstairs' area to O'Banion and a functional adjunct of the boarding house to Halvorsen; to Miss Schmidt it was forbidden ground which excited no special interest for that – almost all the world was forbidden ground to Miss Schmidt. In it Sue Martin was as content as she was anywhere, and among the torments of Mary Haunt, the kitchen was a special hell. But in Robin's world it was central, more so than the bedroom he shared with his mother, more so than his crib. He ate in the kitchen, played there when it was raining or especially cold. When he went outdoors it was through the kitchen door, and it was a place to come back to with a bruised knee, with a hollow stomach, with a sudden flood of loneliness or of a three-year-old's wild manic passion. It was big and warm and full of friends.

The most resourceful of these friends was, of course, Bitty, who without ever losing her gruffness knew the right time to apply a cookie or a story (usually about a little boy with a beautiful mother) or a swat on the bottom. Sam was a friend, too, mostly as something safe to climb on. Of late, O'Banion had carved a rather special niche for himself, and Robin had always liked a limited amount of Miss Schmidt's self-conscious passiveness; she was a wonderful listener. He treated Halvorsen with cheerful respect, and Mary Haunt as if she did not exist. There were other people, too, every bit as much so as anyone who ate and had a job and occupied rooms elsewhere in the house. There was the electric mixer and the washing machine – in Robin's economical language 'Washeen' – the blender and the coffee-pot; in short, everything which had a motor in it. (The presence or absence of motors in percolators is arguable only by those with preconceptions.) To him they were all alive, responsive and articulate, and he held converse with them all. He showed them his toys and he told them the news, he bade them good-bye and good morning, hello, what's the matter, and happy birthday.

And besides all these people, there were Boff and Googie, who, though by no means limited to the kitchen, were often there.

They were not there on that dark Sunday while the sky grieved and Halvorsen fought his personal devils outdoors. 'Mitster, Boff an' Googie gone for ride,' Robin informed the electric mixer. Its name, Mits-ter, was identical in his vocabulary with 'Mister' and was a clear link between the machine and the males he heard spoken of, and just another proof of the living personalty he assigned to it. He got a kitchen chair and carried it effortlessly over to the work-table, where he put it down and climbed on it. He tilted the mixer up and back and turned its control-cowling, and it began to hum softly. Bitty kept the beaters in a high drawer well out of his reach and let him play with the therefore harmless machine to his heart's content. '*Ats* right, Mitster,' he crooned. 'Eat your yunch. Hey, Washeen!' he called to the washing machine, 'Mitster's eatin' his yunch all up, I go' give him a cookie, he's a *good* boy.' He revved the control up and down, the machine whining obediently. He spun the turntable, turned the motor off, listened to the ball-bearings clicking away in the turntable, stopped it and turned on the motor again. He turned suddenly at the nudge of some sixth sense and saw O'Banion in the doorway. 'Goo' morning, Tonio,' he called, beaming. 'Go picnic now?'

'Not today, it's raining,' said O'Banion, 'and it's "good afternoon" now.' He crossed to the table. 'What you up to, fellow?'

'Mitster eatin' his yunch.'

'Your mother asleep?'

'Yis.'

O'Banion stood watching the child's complete preoccupation with the machine. Little son of a gun, he thought, how did you do it?

The question was all he could express about the strangely

rewarding friendship which flowered between him and Robin. He had never liked (nor, for that matter, disliked) a child in his life. He had never been exposed to one before; his only sibling was an older sister and he had never associated with anyone but contemporaries since he was a child himself.

Robin had caught him alone one day and had demanded to know his name. 'Tony O'Banion,' he had growled reluctantly. 'Tonio?' 'Tony O'Banion,' he had corrected distinctly. 'Tonio,' Robin had said positively, and from then on that was inalterably that. And surprisingly, O'Banion had come to like it. And when, on the outskirts of town, someone had set up something called a Kiddie Karnival, a sort of miniature amusement park, and he had been assigned to handle land rentals there for his firm, he found himself thinking of Robin every time he saw the place, and of the Karnival every time he saw Robin, until one warm Sunday he startled himself and everyone else concerned by asking Sue Martin if he could take the boy there. She had looked at him gravely for a moment and said, 'Why?'

'I think he might like it.'

'Well, thanks,' she had said warmly, 'I think that's wonderful.' And so he and Robin had gone.

And they'd gone again, several times, mostly on Sunday when Sue Martin was taking her one luxurious afternoon nap of the week, but a couple of times during the week, too, when O'Banion had business out there and could conveniently pick the child up on the way out from the office and drop him again on the way back. And then, just for a change, a picnic, Robin's very first, by the bank of a brook where they had watched jewel-eyed baby frogs and darting minnows and a terrifying miniature monster that he later identified as a dragonfly nymph; and Robin had asked so many questions that he had gone to a bookstore the next day and bought a bird book and a wildflower guide.

Occasionally he asked himself *why*? What was he getting out of it? and found the answers either uncomfortable or elusive. Perhaps it was the relaxation: for the first time he could have communion with another human being without the cautious and watchful attention he usually paid to 'Where did you go to school?' and 'Who are your people?' Perhaps it was the warmth of friendship radiating from a face so disturbingly like the one which still intruded itself between his eyes and his work once in a while, and which was so masked and controlled when he encountered it in the flesh.

And there had been the Sunday when Sue Martin, after having given her permission for one of these outings, had suddenly said, 'I haven't much to do this afternoon. Are these excursions of yours strictly stag?' 'Yes,' he had said immediately, 'they are.' He'd told *her*. But – it didn't feel like a victory, and she had not seemed defeated when she shrugged and smiled and said, 'Let me know when you go coeducational.' After that she didn't put a stop to the picnics, either, which would have pleased him by permitting him to resent her. He found himself wishing she would ask again, but he knew she would not, not ever. And if he should ask her to come, and she should refuse . . . he could not bear the thought. Sometimes he thought the whole business of amusing the child was done to impress the mother; he had overheard Mary Haunt make a remark to Miss Schmidt once that intimated as much, and had furiously sworn off for all of six hours, which was when Robin asked him where they would go next. As long as it was simple, a matter between him and the child, it required no excuses or explanations. As soon as he placed the matter in any matrix, he became confused and uncertain. He therefore avoided analyses, and asked himself admiringly and academically, little son of a gun, how did you do it? while he watched Robin's animated conversation with the electric mixer.

He rumpled Robin's hair and went to the stove, where he picked up the coffeepot and swirled it. It was almost full, and he lit the gas under it.

'Wha' you do, Tonio? Make coffee?'

'Yea, bo.'

'Okay,' said Robin, as if granting permission. 'Boff doesn't drink coffee, Tonio,' he confided. 'Oh no.'

'He doesn't, hm?' O'Banion looked around and up. 'Is Boff here?'

'No,' said Robin. 'He not here.'

'Where'd he go? Out with the Bittelmans?'

'Yis.' The coffee-pot grumbled and Robin said, '*Hello*, Coffee-pot.'

Halvorsen came in and stood blindly in the doorway. O'Banion looked up and greeted him, then said under his breath, 'My God!' and crossed the room. 'You all right, Halvorsen?'

Halvorsen directed blind eyes at the sound of his voice, and O'Banion could watch seeing enter them slowly, like the fade-in on a movie screen. 'What?' His face was wet with the rain, fish-belly pale, and he stood slumping like a man with a weight on his back, raising his face to look up rather than lifting his head.

'You'd better sit down,' said O'Banion. He told himself that this unwonted concern for the tribulations of a fellow-human was purely a selfish matter of not wanting to shovel the stunned creature up off the floor. Yet as Halvorsen turned towards the ell with its wooden chairs. O'Banion caught at the open front of Halvorsen's coat. 'Let me take this, it's sopping.'

'No,' said Halvorsen. 'No.' But he let O'Banion take the coat; rather, he walked out of it, leaving O'Banion with it foolishly in his hands. O'Banion cast about him, then hung it up on the broom-hook and turned again to Halvorsen, who had just fallen heavily back into a chair.

Again Halvorsen went through that slow transition from blindness to sight, from isolation to awareness. He made some difficult, internal effort and then said, 'Supper ready?'

'We roll our own,' said O'Banion. 'Bitty and Sam are taking their once-a-month trip to the fleshpots.'

'Fleshpots,' said Robin, without turning his head.

Carefully controlling his face and his voice, O'Banion continued, 'They said to raid the refrigerator, only hands off the leg o' lamb, that's for tomorrow.' Motioning towards Robin with his head, he added, 'He doesn't miss a trick,' and at last released a broad grin.

Halvorsen said, 'I'm not hungry.'

'I've got some coffee going.'

'Good.'

O'Banion dropped a round asbestos mat on the table and went for the coffee-pot. On the way back he got a cup and saucer. He put them on the table and sat down. Sugar was already there; spoons were in a tumbler, handles down, country-style. He poured and added sugar and stirred. He looked across at Halvorsen, and saw something on that reserved face that he had read about but had never seen before; the man's lips were blue. Only then did it occur to him to get a cup for Halvorsen. He went for it, and remembered milk, too, just in case. He brought them back, hesitated, and then poured the second cup. He put a spoon in the saucer, and with sudden shyness pushed it and the milk towards the other man. 'Hey!'

'What?' Halvorsen said in the same dead, flat tone, and 'Oh. Oh! Thanks, O'Banion, thanks very I'm sorry.' Suddenly he laughed forcefully and without mirth. He covered his eyes and said plaintively, 'What's the *matter* with me?'

It was a question neither could answer, and they sat sipping coffee uncomfortably, a man who didn't know how to unburden himself and a man who had never taken up another's burden. Into this tableau walked Mary Haunt. She had on a startling yellow hostess gown and had a magazine tucked under her arm. She threw one swift gaze around the room and curled her lip.

'Grand Central Station,' she growled and walked out.

O'Banion's anger came as a great relief to him at just that moment; he was almost grateful to the girl. 'One of these days someone's going to grab that kid by the scruff of the neck and housebreak her,' he snorted.

Halvorsen found a voice, too, and probably was as grateful for the change in focus. 'It won't last,' he said.

'What do you mean?'

'I mean she can't go on that way much longer,' said Halvorsen thoughtfully. He paused and closed his eyes; O'Banion could see him pulling himself hand over hand out of his personal swamp, moving to dry ground, high ground, where he could look with familiarity at a real world again. When he opened his eyes he gave O'Banion a strange little smile and said, as if in parenthesis, 'Thanks for the coffee, O'Banion,' and went on 'She's waiting for the Big Break. She thinks she deserves it and that it will come to her if she only waits. She really believes that. You've heard of high-school kids who perch on drugstore stools hoping for a movie scout to come along and discover them. That's harmless as long as they do it an hour or two a day. But Mary Haunt does it every minute she's out of this house. None of us here could help her, so she treats us the way anyone treats useless things. But you ought to see her down at the station.'

'What station?'

'She types continuities at the radio station,' said Halvorsen. 'From what I hear, she's not very good, but on the other hand they don't pay her much money, so nobody kicks. But to her a radio station is the edge of the world she wants to crash – it starts there and goes to TV and to the movies. I'll bet you anything you like she has a scene all rehearsed in her mind, where a big producer or director stops here and drops in at the radio station to see someone, and *bang!* our Mary's a starlet being groomed for the top.'

'She'd better learn some manners,' grumbled O'Banion.

'Oh, she's got manners when she thinks they'll do her some good.'

'Why doesn't she use them on you, for example?'

'Me?'

'Yes. Don't you get people better jobs, that sort of thing?'

'I see a lot of people, a lot of different kinds of people,' said Halvorsen, 'but they have one thing in common: they aren't sure what they want to do, to be.' He pointed his spoon at the doorway. 'She is. She may be wrong, but she's certain.'

'Well, what about Sue Martin?' said O'Banion. He pursued the subject quickly, almost thoughtlessly, because of a vague feeling that, if he didn't, Halvorsen would slip back into that uncomfortable introspective silence. 'Surely there's a lot about show business Mary Haunt could learn from her.'

Halvorsen gave the nearest thing yet to a grin and reached for the coffee-pot. 'Mrs Martin's a night-club entertainer,' he said, 'and as far as Mary Haunt's concerned, night clubs are slums.'

O'Banion blushed violently and cursed himself for it. 'Why that little – no background, no – no – how could *she* look down on ... I mean, she's a little *nobody*!' Conscious that he was spluttering under the direct and passionless gaze of Halvorsen's dark eyes, he reached for the first thing he could think of that was not an absolute *non sequitur*: 'One night a couple of months ago Mrs Martin and I saw her throw a fit of hysterics over something ... oh, Miss Schmidt had a magazine she wanted ... anyway, after it was all over, Mrs Martin said something about Mary Haunt that could have been a compliment. I mean, to some people. I can't think of Mary Haunt ever doing as much for her.'

'What did she say?'

'Mrs Martin? Oh, she said anybody who gets between Mary Haunt and what she wants is going to have a Mary-sized hole through them.'

'It wasn't a compliment,' said Halvorsen immediately. 'Mrs Martin knows as well as you or I do what's between that girl and her Big Break.'

'What is?'

'Mary Haunt.'

O'Banion thought about that for a moment and then chuckled. 'A Mary-sized hole wouldn't leave much.' He looked up. 'You're quite a psychologist.'

'Me?' said Halvorsen in genuine surprise. At that moment Robin, who had all this while been murmuring confidences to the mixed, switched off the machine and looked up. 'Boff!' he cried joyously. 'Hello, *Boff*!' He watched something move towards him, turning slightly to follow it with his eyes until it settled on the spice shelf over his table. 'Wash you doin', Boff? Come for dinner?' Then he laughed, as if he had thought of something pleasant and very funny.

'I thought Boff was out with the Bittelmans, Robin,' O'Banion called.

'No, he hide,' said Robin, and laughed uproariously. 'Boff right here. He come back.'

Halvorsen watched this with a dazed smile. 'Who on earth is Boff?' he asked O'Banion.

'Imaginary playmate,' said O'Banion knowledgeably. 'I'm used to it now but I don't mind telling you it gave me the creeps at first. Lots of kids have them. My sister did, or so Mother says – Sister doesn't remember it now. A little girl named Ginny who used to live in the butler's pantry. You laugh off this "Boff" and the other one – her name's Googie – until you see Robin holding the door open to let them in, or refusing to go out to play until they get downstairs. And he isn't kidding. That's a nice little kid most of the time, Halvorsen, but some things will make him blow up like a bottle of nitro, and one of 'em is to deny that Boff and Googie are real. I know. I tried it once and it took half a day and six rides on a merry-go-round to calm him down.' He emphasized with a forefinger: 'Six rides for Boff and Googie too.'

Halvorsen watched the child. 'I'll be darned.' He shook his head slightly. 'Is that – uh – healthy?'

'I bought a book,' said O'Banion, and, unaccountably, found himself blushing again, 'and it says so, long as the child has good contact with reality, and believe me, he has. They grow out of it. Nothing to worry about.'

Just then Robin cocked his head up to the spice shelf, as if he had heard a sound. Then he said, 'Okay, Boff,' climbed down from his chair, carried the chair across the kitchen to its place against the wall, and said cheerfully, 'Tonio, Boff wan see cars. Okay. Shall we?'

O'Banion rose, laughing. 'My master's voice. I got the *Popular Electrics* special issue on this year's automobiles and Boff and Robin can't get enough of it.'

'Oh?' Halvorsen smiled. 'What do they like this year?'

'Red ones. Come on, Robin. See you, Halvorsen.'

'See you.'

Robin trotted after O'Banion, paused near the door. 'Come on, Boff!'

He waved violently at Halvorsen. 'See you, Have-sum-gum.'

Halvorsen waved back, and they were gone.

Halvorsen sat numbly for a while, his hand still raised. The presence of the other man and the child had been a diversion from his strange inner explosion and its shock-waves. Now they were gone, but he would not permit himself to sink into that welter of approaching bullet, rain-damped torsos, *why do I want to be dead?* So he hung motionless for a moment between disturbance and diversion. He thought of following O'Banion into the parlour. He thought of sinking back into his panic, facing it, fighting it. But he wasn't ready to fight, not yet, and he didn't want to run ... and he couldn't stay like this. It was like not breathing. Anyone can stop breathing, but not for long.

'Mr Halvorsen?'

Soft-footed, soft-voice, timidly peering about her to be sure she was not intruding, Miss Schmidt came in. Halvorsen could have hugged her. 'Come in, come in!' he cried warmly.

The half-alive smile brightened like fanned embers at his tone. 'Good afternoon, Mr Halvorsen. I was looking, that is, wondering, you know, if Mr Bittelman was back yet, and I thought perhaps that ...' She wet her lips and apparently thought it was worth another try. 'I wanted to see him about – I mean to say, ask him if he – about something.' She exhaled, took a breath, and would surely have come out with more of the same, but Halvorsen broke in.

'No, not yet. Sure picked a miserable day for a joy-ride.'

'It doesn't seem to matter to the Bittelmans. Every fourth week, like clockwork.' She suddenly uttered a soft little bleat of a laugh. 'I'm sure I don't mean clockwork, Mr Halvorsen, I mean, four weeks.'

He laughed politely, for her sake. 'I know what you mean.' He saw her drop her eyes to her kneading hands, divined that her next movement would be towards the door. He felt he couldn't bear that, not just now. 'How about – uh – a cup of tea or something. Sandwich. I was just going to – ' He rose.

She went pink and smiled again. 'Why, I –'

There was a short, sibilant sound in the doorway, a sniff, a small snort of anger. Mary Haunt stood there glowering. Miss Schmidt said, faintly, 'No, no thank you, I'd better, I mean, just go and ... I only wanted to see if Mr Bittelman was – ' She faded out altogether and tiptoed apologetically to the door. Mary Haunt swung her shoulders but did not move her feet. Miss Schmidt slid out and escaped past her.

Halvorsen found himself standing, half angry, half foolish. His own last words echoed in his mind: 'Sandwich. I was just going to – ' and he let them push him to the other end of the kitchen. He was furious, but why? Nothing had happened; a lot had happened. He would have liked to rear back on his hind legs and blast her for persecuting a little defenceless rabbit like Miss Schmidt; yet what had she actually done? Couldn't she say with absolute truth, 'Why, I never said a word to her!'? He felt ineffectual, unmanned; and the picture of the flimsy gun flickered inside his eyelids and shocked him. He trembled, pulled himself together, painfully aware of the bright angry eyes watching his back from the doorway. He fumbled into the bread-box and took out half a loaf of Bitty's magnificent home-baked bread. He took down the bread-board and got a knife from the drawer, and began to saw. Behind him he heard a sharp slap as Mary Haunt tossed her magazine on the table beside the coffee-pot, and then he was conscious of her at his elbow. If she had said one word, she would have faced a blaze of anger out of all proportion to anything that had happened. But she didn't, and didn't: she simply stood there and watched him. He finished cutting the first slice, started on the second. He almost swung to face her but checked the motion, whereupon the knife bit into the first joint of his thumb. He closed his eyes, finished cutting the bread, and turned away to the refrigerator. He opened it and then bent over the shelves, holding his cut thumb in his other hand.

'What do you think you're doing?' asked the girl.

'What's it look like?' he growled. His cut suddenly began to hurt.

'I couldn't say,' said Mary Haunt. She stepped to the bread-board, picked up the knife and with it whisked the bread he had cut into the sink.

'Hey!'

'You better push the cut up against the freezer coils for a second,' she said with composure. She put a hand on the loaf and with one sweep straightened its hacked end. 'Sit down,' she said as he filled his lungs to roar at her. 'If there's anything I hate it's to see someone clumsy paddling around in food.' One, two, three, four even slices fell to the board as she spoke. And again she interrupted him just as he was forming a wounded-bear bellow, 'You want a sandwich or not? Just sit down over there and stay out from under-foot.'

Slackjawed, he watched her. Was she doing him a kindness? Mary Haunt doing someone a *kindness*?

He found himself obeying her, pressing his cut against the freezer coils. It felt good. He withdrew his hand just as she came towards the refrigerator, and dodged out of her way. He backed to the table, sat down, and watched her.

She was something to watch. The pale, over-manicured hands flew. She set out mayonnaise, cream cheese, a platter of cold-cuts, parsley, radishes. With almost a single motion she put a small frying pan and a butter-melter on the stove and lit the fire under them. Into the frying pan went a couple of strips of bacon; into the other, two tablespoons of water and half the fluid from a jar of capers. She added spices, 'by ear' – a shake, a pinch: poultry seasoning, oregano, garlic salt. The tiny pan began to hiss, and suddenly the kitchen smelt like the delivery entrance to paradise. She snatched it off, scraped the contents into a bowl, added cream cheese and mayonnaise, and thrust it under the electric mixer. She turned the bacon, shoved two of the bread slices into the toaster, and busied her-self with a paring knife and the radishes.

Halvorsen shook his head unbelievingly and muttered an exclamation. The girl threw him a look of such intense scorn that he dropped his eyes. He found them resting on her magazine. It was called *Family Day* and was a home-making publication from a chain supermarket – in no way a movie magazine.

Out of the frying pan came the bacon, crackling. She drained it on a paper towel and crumbled it into the bowl where the mixer was working. As if some kitchen choreographer was directing the work, the toast popped up as she reached out her hand for it. She dropped in the other two slices and went back to her alchemy with the radishes. In a moment she turned off the mixer and spread the contents of the bowl on the toast. On this she laid cold-cuts, narrow strips of various kinds, deftly weaving them so they formed a beautiful basket pattern. As she finished the first two, the second pair popped out of the toaster; it was a continuous thing, the way she did all the different things she did; it was like music or a landscape flowing by a train window.

She did something swift with the knife, and set the results out on two plates: bite-sized sandwiches arranged like a star, and in the centre what looked like a tiny bouquet of rosebuds – the radishes, prepared with curled petals and nested in a neat bed of parsley, its stems all drawn together by one clever half-hitch in one of them. The whole amazing performance had taken perhaps six minutes. 'You can make your own coffee,' she snapped.

He came over and picked up one of the plates. 'Why, this is – is – well, *thanks*!' He looked at her and smiled. 'Come on, let's sit down.'

'With *you*? She stalked to the table, carrying the other plate, and scooped up the magazine as if it were a guilty secret. She went to the door. 'You can clean up,' she said, 'and if you ever tell anyone about this I'll snatch you bald-headed.'

Staring after her, stunned, he absently picked up one of the sandwiches and bit into it, and for a moment forgot even his amazement, it was so delicious. He sat down slowly, and for the first time since he had started comparing violins with guitars in the pawn-shop, he gave himself up completely to his senses and forgot his troubles. He ate the sandwiches slowly and appreciatively and let them own him.

EXCERPT FROM FIELD EXPEDITION [NOTEBOOK]:

So [weary-irritated] [I] can barely [write]. As if this kind of research wasn't arduous enough at the best of times, which this is not, with the best of equipment, which [we] lack, [I] am plagued by a [partner-teammate] with insuperable enthusiasm and a quality [I] can only describe as head-long stubbornness. [Smith] means well, of course, but the universe is full of well-meaning [individuals] [who] have succeeded only in making [   ]s of themselves.

All during the tedious and infuriating process of re[charging] the [wadget] [Smith] argued that purely objective observation would get [us] nowhere and would take [forever]; that [we] have sufficient data now to apply stimuli to these specimens and determine once and for all if a reliable, functional condition of Synapse Beta sub Sixteen is possible to them. [I] of course objected that it is against [our] highest [ethic] to apply [force] to alien species; [Smith] then argued that it would not really be [force], but only the [magnification-amplification-increased efficiency] of that which they already possessed. [I] then pointed out that even if [we] succeed, [we] can only test the final result by means which may readily kill some or all of the specimens. [Smith] is willing to worry about only when the time comes. [I] pointed our further that in order to supply the necessary stimuli [we] shall have to re[wire] not only the [widget], but that [   ]ed, inefficient, [stone] age excuse for a [mechanism], the [wadget]. [Smith] readily agreed, and while [I] went on arguing [he] began re[wiring], and [I] argued, and [he] [wired], and by the time [I]'d [made my point] [he] was practically finished and [I] found [myself] holding the [light] as well.

[I] forgot to ask [Smith] what [he] planned to do if one of the specimens finds out what [we]'re up to. Kill it? Kill them all? It wouldn't [surprise] [me]. In the name of [research] [Smith] would happily [watch] [his] [elderly forebear]'s [knuckles] being [knurled].

4

Miss Schmidt muffled to the pharynx in a quilted robe, bed-socked, slippered and shawled, half-dozed in her easy chair. When she heard the sounds she had waited for, she jumped up, went to her door, which was ajar, and stood a moment to listen and be sure. Then she tightened her sash, checked the hooks-and-eyes under her chin, tugged her voluminous robe downwards at the hips, and pulled the shawl a little higher on her shoulders. She crossed her arms at the wrists and pressed her hands modestly against her collarbones and scurried silently past the bathroom, down the long hall to the foyer. Bitty was in the kitchen and Sam Bittleman was hanging up a damp trench coat on the hall tree.

'Mr Bittelman – '

'Sam,' he corrected jovially. 'Top of the morning to you, Miss Schmidt. It turned morning, y'know, ten minutes ago.'

'Oh dear, yes, I know it's late,' she whispered. 'And I'm terribly sorry, really I am, I wouldn't for the world trouble you. I mean I *am* sorry, I don't want to be a nuisance. Oh *dear*!' Her perennially frightened face crinkled with her small explosion of distress.

'Now you just tell me what's troubling you, lady, and we'll get it fixed,' he said warmly.

'You're very kind. Very kind. It happens there is something. I mean, something to fix. In . . . in my *room*.' She bent forward with this, as with a deep confidence.

'Well, let's go have a look. Bitty!' Miss Schmidt put a shocked hand over her lips as he raised his voice. 'I'm going to fix something for the lady. Be right with you.' He turned back to Miss Schmidt and made a jocular bow. 'Lead on.'

'We mustn't wake the . . . anybody,' she reproved him, then blushed because she had. He only grinned, and followed her back to her room. She entered, opened the door as wide as it would go, and self-consciously picked up the wastepaper basket and set it to hold the door open. She looked up from this task right into Sam's twinkling eyes, and sent up a prayer that he wouldn't tease her about it. One never knew what Sam was going to say; sometimes he was beyond understanding and sometimes he was just – *awful*. 'The window,' she said. 'The blind.'

He looked at it. 'Oh, that again. Durn things are always getting the cords frayed.' The venetian blind hung askew, the bottom slats almost vertical, leaving a lower corner of the window exposed. Sam tugged at the raising-cord. It was double; one part was jammed tight and the other ran free. He pulled it all the way out and ruefully exhibited the broken end. 'See? That's it, all right. Have to see if I can't put in a new cord for you in the morning, if I can find one.'

'In the morning? But – I mean, well, Mr uh – Sam, what about now? That is, what am I going to *do*?'

'Why, just don't worry your pretty little head about it! Get your beauty-sleep, little lady, and by the time you're back from school tomorrow I'll have it –'

'You don't understand,' she wailed softly, 'I can't go to bed with it like that. That's why I waited up for you. I've tried everything. The drapes won't go across it and there's nothing to hang a towel to and the chair-back isn't high enough to cover it and – and – oh, *dear*!'

'Oh-h-h.'

Struck by something in his single, slow syllable, she looked sharply at him. There was something – what was it? like a hum in the room. But it wasn't a sound. He hadn't changed ... and yet there was something in his eyes she had never seen before. She had never seen it in anyone's eyes. About Sam Bittel-man there had always been a leisurely strength, and it was there now, but easier, stronger, more comforting than ever. To her, with her multiple indecisions, unsurenesses, his friendly certitude was more wondrous than a halo might have been. He said, 'Just what bothers you about that window?'

Her usual self moved quite clearly to indicate, indignantly, that part of the window was uncovered and surely that spoke for itself; yet her usual self was unaccountably silent, and she gave him his answer: 'Somebody might look *in*!'

'You know what's outside that window?'

'Wh – Oh. Oh, the back of the garage.'

'So nobody's going to see in. Well now, suppose there was no garage, and you turned out your lights. Could anybody see in?'

'N-no ...'

'But it still bothers you.'

'Yes, of course it does.' She looked at the triangle of exposed glass, black with night outside, and shuddered. He leaned against the doorpost and scratched his head. 'Let me ask you something,' he said, as if her permission might make a difference. 'S'pose we took away the garage, and you forgot and left your lights on, *and* somebody saw you?'

She squeaked.

'Really bothers you, don't it?' He laughed easily, and instead of infuriating her, the sound flooded her with comfort. 'What exactly is bothersome about that, aside from the fact that it's bothersome?'

'Why ... why,' she said breathlessly, 'I know what *I'd* think of a hussy that would parade around that way with the lights on and – '

'I didn't say parade. Nor "prance", either, which is the other word people use, I don't know why. So what really bothers you is what some peepin' Tom might think, hm? Now, Miss Schmidt, is that really anything to worry about? What do you care what he thinks you are? Don't you know what you are?' He paused, but she had nothing to say. 'You ever sleep naked?'

She gasped, and, round-eyed, shook her head.

'Why not?' he demanded.

'Why I – I – ' She had to answer him; she had to. Fear rose like a thin column of smoke within her, and then a swift glance at his open, friendly face dispelled it completely, it was extraordinary, uncomfortable, exhilarating, disturbing, exciting all at once. He compelled her and comforted her at the same time.

She found her voice and answered him. 'I just couldn't sleep ... like that. Suppose there was a fire?'

'Who said that?' he snapped.

'I beg your – '

'Who said "suppose there's a fire"? Who told you that?'

'Why, I suppose it – yes, it was my mother.'

'Not your idea then. Figured as much. "Thou shalt not kill." Do you believe that?'

'Of course!'

'You do. How old were you when you learned that?'

'I don't – know. All children –'

'Children seven, eight, nine? All right. How old were you when you were taught not to unpin your diapers? Not to let anyone *see* you?'

She did not answer but the answer was there.

'Wouldn't you say you'd learned "thou shalt not expose thy body" earlier, better, more down-deep than "thou shalt not kill"?'

'I – yes.'

'Do you realize it's a deeper commandment with you than any of the Ten? And aside from right-'n'-wrong, isn't it deeper than the deepest, strongest one of all – save thyself? Can't you see yourself dying under a bush rather than walk naked out on the road and flag a car? "Suppose there's a fire?" Can't you see yourself burn to death rather'n jump out of a window without your bathrobe?'

She didn't answer except from her round eyes and her whole heart.

'Does that make any *sense*, to believe a thing like that?'

'I don't know,' she whispered. 'I – have to think.'

Surprisingly, he said, 'Retroactive.' He pointed to the window. 'What can we do about that?' he asked.

Absently she glanced at it. 'Never mind it tonight, Mr Bittelman.'

'Sam. Okay. Good night, little lady.'

She felt herself, abruptly, tottering on the edge of a bottomless pit. He had walked in here and disoriented her, ripped into shreds a whole idea-matrix which had rested undisturbed in the foundations of her thinking, like a cornerstone. Just at this startled second she had not made the admission, but she would have to admit to herself soon that she must think 'retroactive', as he had put it, and that when she did she would find that the clothes convention was not the only one she would have to reappraise. The inescapable, horizonless, unfamiliar task loomed over her like a black cloud – her only comfort, her only handhold was Sam Bittelman, and he was leaving. 'No!' she cried. 'No! No! No!'

He turned back, smiling, and that magic happened again, his sureness and ease. She stood gasping as if she had run up a hill.

'It's all right, little lady.'

'Why did you tell me all this? Why?' she asked pathetically.

'You know something? I didn't tell you a thing,' he said gently. 'I just asked questions. They were all questions you could've asked yourself. And what's got you scared is answers – answers that came from here – ' He put a gentle knuckle against her damp forehead. ' – and not from me. You've lived with it all quite a while; you got nothing to fear from it now.' And before she could answer he had waved one capable hand, winked, and was gone.

For a long time she stood there, trembling and afraid to think. At last she let her open eyes see again, and although they saw nothing but the open door, it was as if some of Sam's comfort slipped in with vision. She turned around, and around again, taking in the whole room and reaping comfort and more comfort from the walls, as if Sam had hung it for her to gather like ripe berries. She put it all in the new empty place within her, not to fill, but at least to be there and to live with until she could get more. Suddenly her gaze met the silly little wastebasket sitting against the door, holding it open, and to her utter astonishment she laughed at it. She picked it up, shook her head at it as if it had been a ridiculous puppy which had been eating her talcum powder; she even spanked it lightly, once, and put it down, and closed the door. She got into bed and put out the light without even looking at the window.

5

'Aw, you shouldn't!' cried Bitty with a joyous sort of chagrin as she pushed open Sue Martin's door. 'Here I've got all your fresh linen and you've went and made the bed!'

Sue Martin, sleep-tousled and lovely in a dark *négligé*, rose from the writing desk. 'I'm sorry, Bitty. I forgot it was Thursday.'

'Well Thursday it is,' the older woman scolded, 'and now I'll have to do it up all over again. Young lady, I've told you and told *you* I'll take care of the room.'

'You have plenty to do,' Sue smiled. 'Here, I'll help. What's Robin up to?'

Together they took down the spread, the light blanket, then the sheets from the big double bed. 'Kidnapped by that young idiot O'Banion again. He's driving out to the new project over Huttonville way and thought Robin might want to see the bulldozers.'

'Robin loves bulldozers. He's not an idiot.'

'He's an idiot,' said Bitty gruffly, apparently needing no translation of the two parts of Sue's statement. 'Time this was turned, since we're both here,' she said, swatting the mattress.

'All right.' Sue Martin loosely folded the spread and blanket and carried them to the chest. 'Robin just loves him.'

'So do you.'

Sue's eyes widened. She shot a look at the other woman, but Bitty's back was turned as she bent over the bed. When she spoke, her voice was perfectly controlled. 'Yes, for some time.' She went to stand beside Bitty and they laid hold of the mattress straps. 'Ready?' Together they heaved and the mattress rose up, teetered for a moment on edge and fell back the other way. They pulled it straight.

'Well, what are you doing about it?' Bitty demanded.

Sue found her eyes captured by Bitty's for a strange moment. She saw herself, in a flash of analogue, walking purposefully away from some tired, dark place towards something she wanted; and as she walked there appeared running softly behind her, around her, something like a moving wall. She had a deep certainty that she could not stop nor turn aside; but that as long as she kept moving at the same speed, in the same direction, the moving wall could not affect her. She – and it – were moving towards what she wanted, just as fast as she cared to go. While this was the case, she was not being restrained or compelled, helped or hindered. So she would not fear this thing, fight it or even question it. It could not possibly change anything. In effect, irresistible as it might be, it need not and therefore did not exist for her. Here and now, some inexplicable something had happened to make it impossible not to answer Bitty's questions – and this compulsion was of no moment at all for her as long as Bitty asked questions she wanted to answer. 'What are you doing about it?' was such a question.

'Everything I should do,' said Sue Martin. 'Nothing at all.'

Bitty grunted non-committally. She took a folded sheet from the top of the highboy and shook it out across the bed. Sue Martin went round to the other side and caught it. She said, 'He has to know why, that's all, and he can't do anything or say anything until he does know.'

'Why what?' Bitty asked bluntly.

'Why he loves me.'

'Oh – you know that, do you?'

This was one question, compulsion or not, that Sue Martin did not bother to answer. It was of the order of 'Is this really a bed?' or 'Is it Thursday?' So Bitty asked another: 'And you're just waiting, like a little edelweiss on an Alp, for him to climb the mountain and pick you?'

'Waiting?' Sue repeated, puzzled.

'You're not doing anything about it, are you?'

'I'm being myself,' said Sue Martin. 'I'm living my life. What I have to give him – anyone who's *right* for me – is all I am, all I do for the rest of my life. As long as he wants something more, or something different, nothing can happen.' She closed her eyes for a moment. 'No, I'm not waiting, exactly. Put it this way: I know how to be content with what I am and what I'm doing. Either Tony will knock down that barrier he's built, or he won't. Either way I know what's going to happen, and it's good.'

'That wall – why don't you take a pickaxe and beat it down?'

She flashed the older woman a smile. 'He'd defend it. Men get very fond of the things they defend, especially when they find themselves defending something stupid.'

Bitty shook out the second sheet. 'And don't you have any of his kind of trouble – wondering *why* you love him?'

Sue Martin laughed. 'Wouldn't we live in a funny world if we had to understand everything that was real, or it wouldn't exist? It's always good to know *why*. It isn't always necessary. Tony'll find that out one day.' She sobered. 'Or he won't. Hand me a pillowslip.'

They finished their task in silence. Bitty bundled up the old linen and trudged out. Sue Martin stood looking after her. 'I hope she wasn't disappointed,' she murmured, and, 'I don't think so . . . and what did I mean by that?'

6

One morning Mary Haunt opened her eyes and refused to believe them. For a moment she lay still looking at the window numbly; there was something wrong with it, and a wrong feeling about the whole room. Then she identified it: there was sunlight streaming in and down through the venetian blind where no sunlight should be at her rising time. She snatched her watch off the night table and squinted at it, and moaned. She reared up in bed and peered at the alarm clock, then turned and punched furiously at the pillow. She bounded out of bed, struggled into her yellow robe, and flew out of the room with her bare feet slapping angrily down the long corridor. Sam Bittelman was sitting at the kitchen table peering at the morning paper over the tops of his black-rimmed reading-glasses. Bitty was at the sink. 'What'm I, the forgotten man or something?' Mary Haunt demanded harshly.

Sam put down his paper and only then began to remove his gaze from it. 'M-m-m? Oh, good morning, gal.' Bitty went on with her business.

'Good *nothing*! Don't you know what time it is?'

'Sure do.'

'What's the big fat idea leaving me to sleep like this? You know I got to get to work in the morning.'

'Who called you four times?' said Bitty without turning

around or raising her voice. 'Who went in and shook you, and got told *get out of my room* for it?'

Mary Haunt poised between pace and pace, between syllables. Now that Bitty mentioned it, she *did* half-remember a vague hammering somewhere, a hand on her shoulder ... but that was a dream, or the middle of the night or – or had she really chased the old lady out? '*Arrgh*,' she growled disgustedly. She stamped out into the foyer and snatched up the phone. She dialled. 'Get me Muller,' she snapped at the voice that answered.

'Muller,' said the phone.

'Mary Haunt here. I'm sick today. I'm not coming in.'

'So with this phone call,' said the telephone, 'I'll notice.'

'Why you lousy Heinie, without me you couldn't run a yo-yo, let alone a radio station!' she shouted, but she had hung up before she started to shout.

She padded back into the kitchen and sat down at the table, 'Got coffee?'

Bitty, still with her back turned, nodded in the appropriate direction and said, 'On the stove,' but Sam folded his paper and got up. He went to the stove, touched the pot briefly with the back of his hand, and carried it back, picking up a cup and saucer on the way. 'You'll want milk.'

'You know better than that,' she said, arching her lean body. While she poured herself a cup, Sam sat down at the other end of the table. He leaned his weight on his elbows, his forearms and worn hands flat on the table. Something like the almost-silent whisper from a high-speed fan made her look up. 'What are you looking at?'

He didn't answer her question. 'Why do you claim to be twenty-two?' he asked instead, and quick as the rebound of billiard ball from cue ball, propelled by hostility, inclusive as buckshot, her reply jetted up: '*What's it to you?*' But it never reached her lips; instead she said 'I have to,' and then sat there astounded. Once she had worn out a favoured phonograph record, knew every note, every beat of it, and she had replaced it; and for once the record company had made a mistake and the record was not what the label said it was. The first half-second of the new record was like this, a moment of expectation and stunned disbelief. This was even more immediate and personal, however; it was like mounting ten steps in the dark and finding, shockingly, that there were only nine in the flight. From this moment until she left the kitchen, she was internally numb and frightened, yet fascinated, as her mind formed one set of words and others came out.

'You have to,' asked Sam mildly, 'the way you have to be in the movies? You just *have* to?'

The snarl, *have I kept it a secret?* came out, 'It's what I want.'

'Is it?'

There didn't seem to be any answer to that, on any level. She waited, tense.

'What you're doing – the job at the radio station – living here in this town instead of someplace else – all of it; is what you're doing the best way to get what you want?'

Why else would I put up with it all – the town, the people – you? But she said, 'I think so.' Then she said, 'I've thought so.'

'Why don't you talk to young Halvorsen? He might be able to find something you'd do even better'n going to Hollywood.'

'I don't *want* to find anything better!' This time there was no confusion.

From the other end of the room, Bitty asked, 'Were you always so all-fired pretty, Mary Haunt? Even when you were a little girl?'

'Everyone always said so.'

'Ever wish you weren't?'

Are you out of your mind? 'I ... don't think so,' she whispered.

Gently, Sam asked her, 'Did they throw you out, gal? Make you leave home?'

Defiantly, defensively, *They treated me like a little princess at home, like a piece of fine glassware. They carried my books and felt good all day if I smiled. They did what I wanted, what they thought I wanted, at home or in town. They acted as if I was too good to walk that ground, breathe that air, they*

*jumped at the chance to take advantage of being at the same
place at the same time; they did everything for me they could
think of doing, as if they had to hurry or I'd be gone. Throw
me out? Why, you old fool!* 'I left home my own self,' she said.
'Because I had to, like – ' But here words failed her, and she
determined not to cry, and she cried.

'Better drink your coffee.'

She did, and then she wanted something to eat with it, but
couldn't bear to sit with these people any longer. She sniffed
angrily. 'I don't know what's the matter with me,' she said. 'I
never overslept before.'

'Long as you know what you want,' said Sam, and whether
that was the stupid, *non-sequitur* remark of a doddering dotard,
or something quite different, she did not know. 'Well,' she
said, rising abruptly; and then felt foolish because there was
nothing else to say. She escaped back to her room and to bed,
and huddled there most of the day dully regarding the two
coddled ends of her life, pampering in the past and pampering
in the future, while trying to ignore today with its empty
stomach and its buzzing head.

7

During Prohibition it had been a restaurant, in that category
which is better than just 'nice' but not as good as 'exclusive';
the town was too small then to have anything exclusive. Now
it was a bar as well, and although there was imitation Carrara
on some walls, and a good deal of cove-lighting, the balcony
had never been altered and still boasted the turned-spoke railing
all the way around, looking like a picket fence that had gone
to heaven. There was a little service bar up there, and a man
could stay all evening watching what went on down below
without being seen. This was what Tony O'Banion was doing,
and he was doing it because he had felt like a drink and had
never been to the club before, and he wanted to see what kind
of place it was and what Sue Martin did there; and everyone of
these reasons were superficial – if he preceded them with 'why',

he felt lost. Within him were the things he believed, about the right sort of people, about background, breeding and blood. Around him was this place, as real as the things he believed in. *Why* he was here, why he wanted a drink just now, why he wanted to see the place and what happened in it – this was a bridge between one reality and the other, and a misty, maddening, nebulous bridge it was. He drank, and waited to see her emerge from the small door by the bandstand, and when she did he watched her move to the piano and help the pianist, a dishevelled young man, stack and restack and shuffle his music, and he drank. He drank, and watched her go to the cashier and spend a time over a ledger and a pile of checks. She disappeared through the swinging doors into the kitchen, and he drank; he drank and she came out talking to a glossy man in a tuxedo, and he winced when they laughed.

At length the lights dimmed and the glossy man introduced her and she sang in a full, pleasant voice something about a boy next door, and someone played an accordion which was the barest shade out of tune with the piano. Then the piano had a solo, and the man sang the last chorus, after which the lights came up again and he asked the folks to stick around for the main show at ten sharp. Then the accordion and the piano began to make dance music. It was all unremarkable, and Tony didn't know why he stayed. He stayed, though: 'Waiter! Do it again.'

'Do it twice.'

Tony spun around. 'Time someone else bought, h'm?' said Sam Bittelman. He sat down.

'Sam! Well, sit down. Oh, you *are*.' Tony laughed embarrassedly. His tongue was thick and he was immeasurably glad to see the old man. He was going to wonder why until he remembered that he's sworn off wondering why just now. He was going to ask what Sam was doing there and then decided Sam would only ask him the same, and it was a question he didn't want to fool with just now. Yes he did.

'I'm down here slumming in the fleshpots and watching the lower orders cavorting and carousing,' he blurted, making an immense effort to be funny. He wasn't funny. He sounded like a little snob, and a tight little snob at that.

Sam regarded him gravely, not disapproving, not approving. 'Sue Martin know you're here?'

'No.'

'Good.'

The waiter came just in time; Sam's single syllable had given him a hard hurt; but for all the pain, it was an impersonal thing, like getting hit by a golfer on his backswing. When the waiter had gone Sam asked quietly, 'Why don't you marry the girl?'

'What're ya – kidding?'

Sam shook his head. O'Banion looked into his eyes and away, then down at Sue Martin where she leaned against the piano, leafing through some music. *Why don't you marry the girl?* 'You mean if she'd have me?' It was not the way he felt, but it was something to say. He glanced at Sam's face which was still waiting for a real answer. All right then. 'It wouldn't be right.'

' "Right"?' Sam repeated.

O'Banion nipped his thick tongue in the hope it might wake his brains up. The rightness of it ... vividly he recalled his mothers' words on the subject: 'Aside from the amount of trouble you'll save yourself, Anthony, you must remember that it's not only your right, it's your *duty* not to marry beneath your class. Fine hounds, fine horses, fine humans, my dear; it's breeding that matters.' That was all very well, but how to say it to this kind old man, himself obviously a manual worker all his life? O'Banion was not a cruel man, and he was well aware that coarse origins did not always mean dull sensibilities. Actually, some of these people were very sensitive. So he made a genuinely noble try at simultaneous truth and kindness: 'I've always felt it's wiser to form relationships like that with – uh – people of one's own kind.'

'You mean, people with as much money as you got?'

'No!' O'Banion was genuinely shocked. 'That's no longer a standard to go by, and it probably never was, not by itself.' He laughed ruefully and added 'Besides, there hasn't been any money in my family since I can remember. Not since 1929.'

'Then what's your kind of people?'

How? How? 'It's . . . a way of life,' he said at length. That pleased him. 'A way of life,' he repeated, and took a drink. He hoped Sam wouldn't pursue the subject any further. Why examine something when you're content with it the way it is?

'Why are you here anyway, boy?' Sam asked. 'I mean, in this town instead of in the city, or New York or some place?'

'I'm good for a junior partnership in another year or so. Then I can transfer as a junior partner to a big firm. If I'd gone straight to the city it would take me twice as long to get up there.'

Sam nodded. 'Pretty cute. Why the law? I always figured lawyer's work was pretty tough and pretty dusty for a young man.'

His mother had said, 'Of course the law field's being invaded by all sorts of riffraff now – but what isn't? However, it's still possible for a gentleman to do a gentleman's part in law.' Well, that wouldn't do. He'd have to go deeper. He averted his eyes from old Sam's casual penetration and said, 'Tough, yes. But there's something about law work . . .' He wondered if the old man would follow this. 'Look, Sam, did it ever occur to you that the law is the biggest thing ever built? It's bigger'n bridges, bigger'n buildings – because they're all built *on* it. A lawyer's a part of the law, and the law is part of everything else – everything we own, the way we run governments, everything we make and carry and use. Ever think of that?'

'Can't say I did,' said Sam, 'Tell me something – the law, is it finished?'

'Finished?'

'What I mean, this rock everything's built on, how solid is it? Is it going to change much? Didn't it change a whole lot to get the way it is?'

'Well sure! Everything changes a lot while it's growing up.'

'Ah. It's grown up.'

'Don't you think it has?' O'Banion asked with sudden truculence.

Sam grinned easily. 'Shucks, boy, I don't think. I just ask questions. You were saying about "your sort of people": you think you-all *belong* in the law?'

'Yes!' said O'Banion, and saw immediately that Sam would not be satisfied with so little. 'We do in this sense,' he said earnestly. 'All through the ages men have worked and built and – owned. And among them there rose a few who were born and bred and trained to – to –' He took another drink, but it and the preceding liquor seemed not to be helping him. He wanted to say *to rule* and he wanted to say *to own*, but he had wit enough about him to recognize that Sam would misunderstand. So he tried again. 'Born and bred to – live that – uh – way of life I mentioned before. It's to the interest of those few people to invest their lives in things as they are, to keep them that way; in other words, to work for and uphold the law.' He leaned back with a flourish that somehow wasn't as eloquent as he had hoped and very nearly upset his glass to boot.

'Don't the law contradict itself once in a while?'

'Naturally!' O'Banion's crystallizing concept of the nobility of his work was beginning to intoxicate him more than anything else. 'But the very nature of our courts is a process of refinement, constant purification.' He leaned forward excitedly. 'Look, laws are dreams, when they're first thought of – inspirations! There's something . . . uh . . . holy about that, something beyond the world of men. And that's why when the world of men comes into contact with it, the wording of the inspiration has to be re-done in the books, or interpreted in the courtroom. That's what we mean by "precedents" – that's what the big dusty books are for, to create and maintain consistency under the law.'

'What about justice?' murmured Sam, and then quickly, as if he hadn't meant to change the subject, 'That's not what I mean by contradiction, counsellor. I meant all laws that all men have dreamed up and lived by and got theirselves killed over. Tell me something, counsellor, is there even one single law so right for men that it shows up in every country that is or was?'

O'Banion made a startled sound, a half a dozen excellent examples flashed into his mind at once, collided, and, under the first examination, faded away.

'Because,' said Sam in a voice which was friendly and almost apologetic, 'if there ain't such a law, you might say every set of laws ever dreamed up, even the sets that were bigger and older and lasted longer than the one you practise, even any set you can imagine for the future – they're all goin' to contradict one another some way or other. So, who's really to say whose set of laws are right – or fit to build anything on, or breed up a handful of folks fit to run it?'

O'Banion stared at his glass without touching it. For an awful moment he was totally disoriented; a churning pit yawned under his feet and he must surely topple into it. He thought wildly, you can't leave me here, old man! You'd better say something else, and fast, or I . . . or I . . .

There was a sort of pressure in his ears, like sound too high-pitched for humans. Sam said softly, 'You really think Sue Martin ain't good enough for you?'

'I didn't say that, I didn't say that!' O'Banion blurted hoarse with indignation, and fright, and relief as well. He shuddered back and away from the lip of this personal precipice and looked redly at the composed old face. 'I said different, too different, that's all. I'm thinking of her as well as – '

For once Sam bluntly interrupted, as if he had no patience with what O'Banion was saying. 'What's different?'

'Background, I told you. Don't you know what that is?'

'You mean the closer a girl's background is to yours, the better chance you'd have bein' happy the rest of your life?'

'Isn't it obvious?' The perfect example popped into his mind, and he speared a finger out and downwards towards the piano. 'Did you hear what she was singing just before you got here? "The boy next door". Don't you understand what that really means, why that song, that idea, hits home to so many people? Everybody understands that; it's the appeal of what's familiar, close by – the similar background I'm talking about!'

'You have to shout?' chuckled Sam. Sobering, he said, 'Well,

counsellor, if you're goin' to think consistently, like you said,
couldn't you dream up a background even more sim'lar than
your next-door neighbour?'

O'Banion stared at him blankly, and old Sam Bittelman
asked, 'Are you an only child, counsellor?'

O'Banion closed his eyes and saw the precipice there waiting;
he snapped them open in sheer self-defence. His hands hurt
and he looked down, and slowly released them from the edge
of the table. He whispered, 'What are you trying to tell me?'

His bland face the very portrait of candour, Sam said,
'Shucks, son, I couldn't tell you a thing, not a blessed thing.
Why, I don't know anything you don't know to tell you! I
ain't asked you a single question you couldn't've asked yourself,
and the answers were all yours, not mine. Hey . . .' he breathed,
'you better come along home. You wouldn't want Miz Martin
to see you looking the way you do right now.'

Numbly, Anthony Dunglass O'Banion followed him out.

8

It was hot, so hot that apparently even Bitty felt it, and after
supper went to sit on the verandah. It was very late when at
last she came in to do the dishes, but she went ahead without
hurrying, doing her usual steady, thorough job. Sam had gone
to bed, Mary Haunt was sulking in her room after yet another
of these brief, violent brushes with Miss Schmidt. O'Banion
was crouching sweatily over some law-books in the parlour,
and Halvorsen –

Halvorsen was standing behind her, just inside the kitchen.
On his face was a mixture of expressions far too complicated
to analyse, but simple in sum – a sort of anxious wistfulness.
In his hands was a paper sack, the mouth of which he held as
if it were full of tarantulas. His stance was peculiar, strained
and off-balance, one foot advanced, his shoulders askew; his
resolution had equated with his diffidence and immobilized
him, and there he stayed like a bee in amber.

Bitty did not turn. She went right on working steadily, her

back to him, until she had finished the pot she was scouring. Still without turning, she reached for another and said, 'Well, come on in, Philip.'

Halvorsen literally sagged as her flat, matter-of-fact voice reached him, shattering with its exterior touch his interior deadlock. He grinned, or just bared his teeth, and approached her. 'You *do* have eyes in the back of your head.'

'Nup.' She rapped once with her knuckle on the window-pane over the sink. Night had turned it to black glass. Halvorsen watched the little cone of suds her hands had left, then refocused his eys on the image in the glass – vivid, the kitchen and everything in it. Hoarsely, he said, 'I'm disappointed.'

'I don't keep things I don't need,' she said bluntly, as if they'd been talking about apple-corers. 'What's on your mind? Hungry?'

'No.' He looked down at his hands, tightened them still more on the bag. 'No,' he said again, 'I have, I wanted . . .' He noticed that she had stopped working and was standing still, inhumanly still, with her hands in the dishwater and her eyes on the window-pane. 'Turn around, Bitty.'

When she would not, he supported the bottom of the paper bag with one hand and with the other scrabbled it open. He put his hand down inside it. 'Please,' he tried to say, but it was only a hiss.

She calmly shook water off her hands, wiped them on a paper towel. When she turned around her face was eloquent – as always, and only because it always was. Its lines were eloquent, and the shape of her penetrating eyes, and the light in them. As a photograph or a painting such a face is eloquent. It is a frightening thing to look into one and realize for the first time that behind it nothing need be moving. Behind the lines of wisdom and experience and the curved spoor of laughter, something utterly immobile could be waiting. Only waiting.

Halvorsen said, 'I think all the time.' He wet his lips. 'I never stop thinking, I don't know how. It's ... there's something wrong.'

Flatly, 'What's wrong?'

'You, Sam,' said Halvorsen with difficulty. He looked down at the bag over his hand. She did not. 'I've had the ... feeling ... for a long time now. I didn't know what it was. Just something wrong. So I talked to O'Banion. Miss Schmidt too. Just, you know, talk.' He swallowed. 'I found out. What's wrong, I mean. It's the way you and Sam talk to us, all of us.' He gestured with the paper bag. '*You never say anything!* You only ask questions!'

'Is that all?' asked Bitty good-humouredly.

'No,' he said, his eyes fixed on hers. He stepped back a pace.

'Aren't you afraid that paper bag'll spoil your aim, Philip?'

He shook his head. His face turned the colour of putty.

'You didn't go out and buy a gun just for me, did you?'

'You see?' he breathed. 'Questions. You see?'

'You already had it, didn't you, Philip? Bought it for something else?'

'Stay away from me,' he whispered, but she had not moved. He said, 'Who are you? What are you after?'

'Philip,' she said gently – and now she smiled. 'Philip – *why do you want to be dead?*'

9

Phil Halvorsen stood gaping at the old woman, and the gun, still shrouded in its silly paper bag, began whispering softly as he trembled. The butt fitted his hand as his hand fitted the butt; *It's holding me*, he thought hysterically, knowing clearly that his hysteria was a cloud, a cloak, a defence against that which he was not equipped to think about ... well, maybe not ready to think about; but how had she known?

For nearly two days he had been worrying and gnawing at this sense of wrongness about him. Back and back he would come to it, only to reach bafflement and kick it away angrily; not eating enough, hardly sleeping at all; *let me sleep first!* something wailed within him, and as he sensed it he kicked it away again: more hysteria, not letting him think. And then a word from O'Banion, a phrase from Miss Schmidt, and his own ragbag memory: The Bittelmans never said – they always asked. It was as if they could reach into a man's mind, piece together questions from the unused lumber stored there, and from it build shapes he couldn't bear to look at. *How many terrible questions have I locked away?* And has she broken the lock? He said, 'Don't ... ask me that ... why did you ask me that ... why did you ask me that?'

'Well, why ever not?'

'You're a ... you can read my mind.'

'Can I?'

'*Say* something!' he shouted. The paper bag stopped whispering. He thought she noticed it.

'Am I reading your mind,' she asked reasonably, 'if I see you walk in here the way you did looking like the wrath o' God, holding that thing out in front of you and shying away from it at the same time, and then tell you that if you accidentally pull the trigger you might have to die for it? Read minds? Isn't it enough to read the papers?'

Oh, he thought ... Oh-h. He looked at her sharply. She was quite calm, waiting, leaving it to him. He knew, suddenly and certainly, that this woman could out-think him, out-talk him, seven ways from Sunday without turning a hair. This meant either that he was completely and embarrassingly wrong, or that her easy explanations weren't true ones – which was the thing that had been bothering him in the first place. 'Why did you say I bought the gun for something else?' he snapped.

She gave him that brief, very warm smile. 'Didn't say; I asked you, right? How could I really know?'

For one further moment he hesitated, and it came to him that if this flickering doubt about her was justified, the chances were that a gun would be as ineffective as an argument. And besides ... it was like a silent current in the room, a sort of almost-sound, or the aural pressure he could feel sometimes when a car was braking near him; but here it came out feeling like comfort.

He let the bag fall until it swung from its mouth. He twisted it closed. 'Will you – I mean,' he mumbled, 'I don't want it.'

'Now what would I do with a gun?' she asked.

'I don't know. I just don't want it around. I can't throw it away. I don't want to have anything to do with it. I thought maybe you could put it away somewhere.'

'You know, you'd better sit down,' said Bitty. She didn't exactly push him but he had to move back to get out of her way as she approached, and when the back of his knees hit a chair he had to sit down or fall down. Bitty continued across the kitchen, opened a high cupboard and put the bag on the topmost shelf. 'Only place in the house Robin can't climb into.'

'Robin. Oh yes,' he said, seeing the possibilities. 'I'm sorry. I'm sorry.'

'You'd better talk it out, Philip,' she said in her flat, kind way. 'You're fixing to bust wide open. I won't have you messing up my kitchen.'

'There's nothing to talk about.'

She paused on her way back to the sink, in a strange hesitation, like one listening. Suddenly she turned and sat down at the table with him. 'What did you want with a gun, Philip?' she demanded; and just as abruptly, he answered her, as if she had hurled something at him and it had bounced straight back into her waiting hands, 'I was thinking about killing myself.'

If he thought this would elicit surprise, or an exclamation, or any more questions, he was disappointed. She seemed only to be waiting, so he said, with considerably more care, 'I don't know why I told you that but it came right out. I said I was thinking about doing it. I didn't say I was going to do it.' He looked at her. Not enough? Okay then: 'I couldn't be sure exactly what I was thinking until I bought a gun. Does that make any sense to you?'

'Why not?'

'I don't ever know exactly what I think unless I try it out. Or get all the pieces laid out ready to try.'

'Or tell somebody?'

'I couldn't tell anybody about this.'

'Did you try?'

'*Damn* it!' It was a whisper, but it emerged under frightening pressure. Then normally, 'I'm sorry, Bitty, I'm real sorry. I suddenly got mad at the language, you know what I mean? You say something in words of one syllable and it comes out meaning something you never meant. I told you, "I couldn't tell anybody about this." That sounds as if I knew all about it and was just shy or something. So you ask me, "Did you try?" But what I really mean was that this whole thing, everything about it, is a bunch of – of feelings and – well, crazy ideas *that I couldn't tell anyone about.*'

Bitty's rare smile flicked. 'Did you try?'

'Well I'll be – . You're worse than ever,' he said, this time without anger. 'You *do* know what I'm thinking.'

'So what were you thinking?'

He sobered immediately. 'Things . . . all crazy. I think all the time, Bitty, like a radio was playing all day, all night, and I can't turn it off. Wouldn't want to; wouldn't know how to live without it. Ask me is it going to rain and off I go, thinking about rain, where it comes from, about clouds, how many different kinds there are; about air-currents and jet-streams and everything else you pick up reading those little paragraphs at the bottom of newspaper columns; about –'

'About why you bought a gun?'

'Huh? Oh . . . all right, all right, I won't ramble.' He closed his eyes to hear his thoughts, and frowned at them. 'Anyway, at the tail end of these run-downs is always some single thing that stops the chain – for the time. It might be the answer to some question I asked myself, or someone asks me, or it might just be as far as the things I know will take me.

'So one day a few weeks ago I got to thinking about guns, and never mind the way I went, but what I arrived at was the idea of a gun killing me, and then just the idea of being dead. And the more I thought, the more scared I got.'

After waiting what seemed to be long enough, Bitty said, 'Scared.'

'It wasn't kill – being dead that scared me. It was the feeling

I had about it. I was glad about it. I wanted it. That's what scared me.'

'Why do you want to be dead?'

'That's what I don't know.' His voice fell. 'Don't know, I just don't know,' he mumbled. 'So I couldn't get it out of my head and I couldn't make any sense out of it, and I thought the only thing I could do was to get a gun and load it and – get everything ready, to see how I felt then.' He looked up at her. 'That sounds real crazy, I bet.'

Bitty shrugged. Either she denied the statement or it didn't matter. Halvorsen looked down again and said to his clenched hands, 'I sat there in my room with the muzzle in my mouth and all the safeties off, and hooked my thumb around the trigger.'

'Learn anything?'

His mouth moved but he couldn't find words to fit the movement. 'Well,' said Bitty sharply, 'why didn't you pull it?'

'I just – ' He closed his eyes in one of these long, inward-reading pauses. ' – couldn't. I mean, *didn't*. I wasn't afraid, if that's what you want to know.' He glanced at her and couldn't tell what she wanted to know. 'Sitting there, that way, I came to realize that this wasn't the way it should happen,' he said with some difficulty.

'What is the way?'

'Like this: if ever there was an earthquake, or I looked up and saw a safe falling on me, or some other thing like that, something from outside myself – I wouldn't move aside. I'd let it happen.'

'Is there a difference between that and shooting yourself?'

'Yes!' he said, with more animation than he had shown so far. 'Put it like this: there's part of me that's dead, and wants the rest of me dead. There's part of me that's alive, and wants all of me alive.' He looked that over and nodded at it. 'My hand, my arm, my thumb on the trigger – they're alive. All the live parts of me want to help me go on living, d'you see? No live part should help the dead part get what it wants. The way it'll happen, the way it should happen, is not when I do something to make it happen. It'll be when I don't do something. I won't get out of the way, and that's it, and thanks for keeping the gun for me, it's no use to me.' He stood up and found his eyes locked with hers, and sat right down again, breathing hard.

'Why do you want to be dead?' she asked flatly.

He put his head down on his hands and began to rock it slowly to and fro.

'Don't you want to know?'

Muffled, his voice came up from the edge of the table. 'No.' Abruptly he sat up, staring. 'No? What made me say no, Bitty?' he demanded, 'what made me say that?'

She shrugged. He jumped up and began pacing swiftly up and down the kitchen. 'I'll be dogged,' he murmured once, and 'Well, what d'ye kn –'

Bitty watched him, and catching him on a turn when their eyes could meet, she asked, 'Well – why do you want to –'

'Shut up,' he said. He said it, not to her, but to any interruption. His figmentary signal-light, which indicated dissatisfaction, unrightness, was casting its glow all over his interior landscape. To be hounded half to death by something like this, then to discover that basically he didn't want to investigate it. . . . He sat down and faced her, his eyes alight. 'I don't know yet,' he said, 'but I will, I will.' He took a deep breath. 'It's like being chased by something that's gaining on you, and you duck into an alley, and then you find it's blind, there's only a brick wall; so you sit down to wait, it's all you can do. And all of a sudden you find a door in the wall. Been there all the time. Just didn't look.'

'Why do you want to be dead?'

'B-because I – I shouldn't be alive. Because the average guy – Different, that's what I am, different, unfit.'

'Different, unfit.' Bitty's eyebrows raised slightly. 'They the same thing, Philip?'

'Well, sure.'

'You can't jump like a kangaroo, you can't eat grass raw like a cow – different. You unfit because you can't do those things?'

He made an annoyed laugh. 'Not that, not that. People, I mean.'

'You can't fly a plane. You can't sing like Sue Martin. You can't spout law like Tony O'Banion. That kind of different?'

'No,' he said, and in a surge of anguish, 'No, no! I can't talk about it, Bitty!' He looked at her and again saw that rare, deep smile. He answered it in kind, but weakly, remembering that he had said that to her before. 'This time I mean I can't talk about such things to you. To a lady,' he said in abrupt, unbearable confusion.

'I'm no lady,' said Bitty with conviction. Suddenly she punched his forearm; he thought it was the first time she had ever touched him. 'To you I'm not even a human being. Not even another person. I mean it,' she said warmly. 'Have I asked you a single question you couldn't've asked yourself? Have I told you anything you didn't know?'

His peculiar linear mind cast rapidly back and up again. He felt an odd instant of disorientation. It was not unpleasant. Bitty said gently, 'Go on talking to yourself, boy. Who knows – you might find yourself in good company.'

'Aw ... thanks, Bitty,' he mumbled. His eyes stung and he shook his head. 'All right, all *right*, then ... it just came to me, one big flash, and I guess I couldn't sit here – here,' he said, waving his arm to include the scrubbed, friendly kitchen, 'and look at you, and think about these – uh this – all at once.' He swallowed heavily. 'Well, that time I told you about, that day I found out I wanted to be dead, it was like getting hit on the head. Right after that, only a couple of minutes, I got hit on the head just as hard by something else. I didn't know – want to know till now that they were connected, some way.' He closed his eyes. 'It was a theatre, that rathole down across the Circle. You know. It – it hit out at me when I wasn't looking. It was all covered with ... pictures and – and it said SEE this and SEE that and SEE some dirty other thing, adults only, you know what I mean.' He opened his eyes to see what Bitty was doing, but Bitty was doing nothing at all. Waiting. He turned his face away from her, and said indistinctly into his shoulder,

'All my life those things meant nothing to me. *There!*' he shouted, 'you see? Different, different!'

But she wouldn't see. Or she wouldn't see until he did, himself, more clearly. She still waited.

He said, 'Down at work, there's a fellow, Scodie. This Scodie, he's a good man, really can turn out a day's work. I mean, he likes what he's doing, he cares. Except every time a girl goes by, everything stops. He snaps up out of what he's doing, he watches her. I mean, *every* time. It's like he can't help himself. He does it the way a cadet salutes an officer on the street. He does it like that crossing-guard on the toy train, that pops out of his little house every time his little light goes on. He watches until the girl's gone by, and then he says "mmm*yuh!*" and looks over at me and winks.'

'What do you do, every time?'

'Well, I – ' He laughed uncertainly. 'I guess I wink back at him and say, mm-*hm!* But I know why I do it, it's because he expects me to; he'd think it was sort of peculiar if I didn't. But he doesn't do it for me; I don't expect anything of him one way or the other. He does it – ' Words failed him, and he tried again. 'Doing that, he's part of – everybody. What he does is the same thing every song on every radio says every minute. Every ad. in every magazine does it if it possibly can, even if it means a girl in her underwear with stillson wrenches for sale.' He leapt to his feet and began to pace excitedly. 'You got to back off a little to see it,' he told Bitty, who smiled behind his back. 'You got to look at the whole thing all at once, to see how *much* there is of it, the jokes people tell – yeah, you got to laugh at them, whatever, you even have to know a couple, or they'll ... The window displays, the television, the movies ... somebody's writing an article about transistors or termites or something, and every once in a while he figures he's been away from it long enough and he has to say something about the birds and the bees and "Gentlemen prefer". Everywhere you turn the whole world's at it, chipping and chipping away at it – '

He stamped back to the table and looked into Bitty's face

intently. 'You got to back away and look at it all at once,' he cautioned again. 'I'm not in kindergarten, I know what it's all about. I'm not a woman-hater. I've been in love. I'll get married, some say. Go ahead and tell me I'm talking about one of the biggest, strongest, down-deep urges we have – I'll buy that. That's what I *mean*, that's what I'm *talking* about.' His forehead was pink and shiny; he took out a crumpled handkerchief and batted at it. 'So *much* of it, all around you, all the time, filling a big hungry need in average people. I don't mean the urge itself; I mean all this *reminding*, this, what do you call it, indoctrination. It's a need or folks wouldn't stand for so much of it, comic books, lipstick, that air-jet in the floor at the funny-house at the Fair.' He thumped into his chair, panting. 'Do you begin to see what I mean about "*different*"?'

'Do you?' asked Bitty, but Halvorsen didn't hear her; he was talking again. 'Different, because I don't feel that hunger to be reminded, I don't need all that high-pressure salesmanship, I don't want it. Every time I tell one of my jokes, every time I wink back at old Scobie, I feel like a fool, like some sort of a liar. But you got to protect yourself; you can't ever let anyone find out. You know why? Because the average guy, the guy-by-the-millions that needs all that noise so much, he'll let you be the way he is, or he'll let you be ... I'm sorry, Bitty. Don't make me go into a lot of dirty details. You see what I mean, don't you?'

'What do you mean?'

Irritated, he blew a single sharp blast from his nostrils. 'Well, what I mean is, they'll let you be the way they are, or you have to be ... sick, crippled. You can't be anything else! You can't be Phil Halvorsen who isn't sick and who isn't crippled but who just doesn't naturally go around banging his antlers against the rocks so the whole world can hear it.'

'So – that's what you mean by unfit?'

'That's why I wanted to be dead. I just don't think the way other people do; if I act the way other people do I feel ... feel guilty. I guess I had this piling up in me for years, and that day with the guns, when I found out what I wanted to do ... and then that theatre-front, yawping over me like a wet mouth full of dirty teeth ...' He giggled foolishly. 'Listen to me, will you ... Bitty, I'm sorry.'

She utterly ignored this. 'High-pressure salesmanship,' she said.

'What?'

'You said it, I didn't. ... Isn't hunger one of those big deep needs, Philip? Suppose you had a bunch of folks starving on an island and dropped them a ton of food – would they need high-pressure salesmanship?'

It was as if he stood at the edge of a bottomless hole – more, the very outer edge of the world, so close his very toes projected over the emptiness. It filled him with wonder; he was startled, but not really afraid, because it might well be that to fall down and down into that endless place might be a very peaceful thing. He closed his eyes and slowly, very slowly, came back to reality, the kitchen, Bitty, Bitty's words. 'You mean ... the av– the ordin– you mean, people aren't really interested?'

'Not that interested.'

He blinked; he felt as if he had ceased to exist in his world and had been plunked down in a very similar, but totally new one. It was far less lonely here.

He hit the table and laughed into Bitty's calm face. 'I'm going to sleep,' he said, and got up; and he knew she had caught his exact shade of meaning when she said gently, 'Sure you can.'

EXCERPT FROM FIELD EXPEDITION [NOTEBOOK] [I] had thought up to now that in [Smith]'s [immorally] excessive enthusiasm and [bull-headedness] [I] had encountered the utmost in [irritants]. [I] was in [error]; [he] now surpasses these, and without effort. In the first place, having placated and outwitted the alerted specimen, [he] has destroyed [my] preliminary detailed [report] on him; this is [irritat]ing not only because it was done without consulting [me], not only because of the trouble [I] went to to [write] it all up, but mostly because [he] is technically within [his] [ethics-rights]—the emergency created by [his] [bumbling mismanagement] no longer exists. [I] have [force]fully pointed out to [him] that it was only by the application of [my] kind of

cautious resourcefulness that [he] succeeded, but [he] just [gloats]. [I]
[most strongly affirm-and-bind-myself], the instant [we] get back home
and are released from Expeditionary [ethic-discipline], [I] shall [bend]
[his] [   ]s over [his] [   ] and [tie a knot in] them.

[We] have now, no [credit-thanks] to [Smith], reached a point where all
our specimens are in a state of [heavy] preconditioning of their unaccountably random Synapse Beta sub Sixteen. Being a synapse, it will
of course come into full operation only on a reflexive level and in an
extreme emergency, which [we] are now setting up.

Unless [Smith] produces yet more [stupidities], the specimens should
live through this.

10

It had become improbably hot, and very still. Leaves drooped
at impossible angles, and still the dust lay on them. Sounds
seemed too enervated to travel very far. The sky was brass all
day, and at night, for want of ambition, the overcast was no
more than a gauzy hood of haze.

It was the Bittelmans' 'day off' again, and without them the
spine had been snatched out of the household. The boarders
ate pokily, lightly, at random, and somehow got through the
time when there was nothing to do but sit up late enough to
get tired enough to get whatever rest the temperature would
permit. It was too hot, even, to talk, and no one attempted it.
They drifted to their rooms to wait for sleep; they slumped
in front of fans and took cold showers which generated more
heat than they dissipated. When at last darkness came, it was
a relief only to the eyes. The household pulse beat slowly and
slower; by eight o'clock it was library-quiet, by nine quite
silent, so that the soft brushing of knuckles on Miss Schmidt's
door struck her like a shout.

'Wh-who is it?' she quavered, when she recovered her breath.

'Sue.'

'Oh – oh. Oh, do come in.' She pulled the damp sheet tight
up against her throat.

'Oh, you're in bed already. I'm sorry.'

'*I'm* sorry. It's all right.'

Sue Martin swung the door shut and came all the way in. She was wearing an off-the-shoulder peasant blouse and a pleated skirt with three times more filmy nylon in it than one would guess until she turned, when it drifted like smoke. 'My,' said Miss Schmidt enviously. 'You look cool.'

'State of mind,' Sue smiled. 'I'm about to go to work and I wish I didn't have to.'

'And Bitty's out. I'm honorary baby-sitter again.'

'You're an angel.'

'No, oh, no!' cried Miss Schmidt. 'I wish everything I had to do was that easy. Why, in all the time I've known you, every time I've done it, I – I've had nothing to do!'

'He sleeps pretty soundly. Clear conscience, I guess.'

'I think it's because he's happy. He smiles when he sleeps.'

'Smiles? Sometimes he laughs out loud,' said Sue Martin. 'I was a little worried tonight, for a while. He was so flushed and wide-awake – '

'Well, it's *hot*.'

'It wasn't that.' Sue chuckled. 'His precious Boff was all over the place, "fixin' things", Robin said. What he was fixing all over the walls and ceiling, Robin didn't say. Whatever it was, it's finished now, though, and Robin's sound asleep. I'm sure you won't even have to go in. And Bitty ought to be home soon.'

'You'll leave your door open?'

Sue Martin nodded and glanced up at the large open transom over Miss Schmidt's door. 'You'll hear him if he so much as blinks. . . . I've got to run. Thanks *so* much.'

'Oh, really, Mrs M – uh, Sue. Don't thank me. Just run along.'

'Good night.'

Sue Martin slipped out, silently closing the door behind her. Miss Schmidt sighed and looked up at the transom. After Sue's light footsteps had faded away, she listened, listened as hard as she could, trying to pour part of herself through the transom, across the hall, through Sue Martin's open door. A light sleeper at any time, she knew confidently that she was on guard now and would wake if anything happened. If she slept at all in this sticky heat.

She might sleep, at that, she thought after a while. She shifted herself luxuriously, and edged to a slightly cooler spot on the bed. 'That wicked Sam,' she murmured, and blushed in the dark. But he had been right. A *nightgown* in weather like this?

Suddenly, she slept.

In O'Banion's room, there was a soft sound. He had put off taking a shower until suddenly he had used up his energy, and could hardly stir. I'll just rest my eyes, he thought, and bowed his head. The soft sound was made by his forehead striking the book.

Halvorsen lay rigid on his bed staring at the ceiling. There, almost as if it was projected, was the image of a flimsy cylinder vomiting smoke. Go ahead, he thought, detachedly. Or go away. I don't care which. Before I talked to Bitty, I wanted you. Now, I don't care. Is that better? He closed his eyes, but the image was still there. He lay very quietly, watching the insides of his eyelids. It was like being asleep. When he was asleep the thing was there too.

Mary Haunt sat by her window, pretending it was cooler there than in bed. There was no anger in her, just now as she lay back and dreamed. The Big Break, the pillars of light at her première, her name two storeys tall over a Broadway marquee – these had no place in this particular favourite dream. I'll do over Mom's room, she thought, dimity, this time, and full, full skirts on the vanity and the night table. She closed her eyes, putting herself in Mom's room with such vividness that she could almost smell the cool faint odour of lavender sachets and the special freshness of sheets dried in the sun. Yes, and something else, outside the room, barely, just barely she knew bread was baking, so that the kitchen would be heavenly with it; the bread would dominate the spice-shelf for a while, until it was out of the oven and cooled. 'Oh, Mom . . .' she whispered. She lay still in her easy-chair, holding and holding to the vision until this room, this house, this town didn't matter any more.

Some hours went by.

Robin floated in a luminous ocean of sleep where there was nothing to fear and where, if he just turned to look, there were love and laughter waiting for him. His left hand uncurled and he thrust the second and third fingers together into his mouth. Somehow he was a big bulldozer with a motor that sounded like Mitster and tracks that clattered along like Coffee-pot, and Boff and Googie were riding along with him and laughing. Then without effort he was a glittery ferris-wheel, but he could watch himself too in one of the cars, screaming his delight and leaning against Tonio's hard arm. All this, yet he was still afloat in that deep bright place where there was no fear, where love and laughter hid around some indescribable corner, waiting. Bright, brighter. Warm, warm, warmer . . . oh, hot, *hot!*

11

Miss Schmidt opened her eyes to an impossible orange glare and a roar like the end of the world. For one full second she lay still, paralysed by an utter disbelief; no light could have become so bright, no sound could have risen to this volume, without waking her as it began. Then she found a way to focus her eyes against that radiance, and saw the flames, and in what was left to her of her immobile second, she explained the whole thing to herself and said relievedly, of course, of course: it's only a nightmare and *suppose there's a fire?* – and that's so *silly*, Sam –

And then she was out of bed in a single bound, standing in the centre of the room, face to flaming face with reality. Everything was burning – everything! The drapes had already gone and the slats of the venetian blind, their cords gone, were heaped on the floor, going like a campfire. Even as she watched the screen sagged and crumpled, its pine frame glaring and spitting pitch through blistering paint. It fell outside.

Outside, outside! The window's open, you're on the ground floor; yes, and there on the chair, not burning yet, your bathrobe; take the robe and jump, quick!

Then, beyond belief, there was a sound louder than the

earth-filling roar, and different; fine hot powder and a hot hail
of plaster showered on her shoulders; she looked up to see the
main beam, right over her head, sag towards her and hang
groaning, one part reaching to the other with broken flat fingers
of splintered wood which gloved themselves in flame as she
saw them. She cowered, and just then the handle of the door
turned and a gout of smoke slammed it open and whisked out
of sight in the up-draught; and there in the hall stood Robin,
grinding a fat little fist into one abruptly wakened eye. She
could see his lips move, though she could hear nothing in this
mighty bellow of sound. She knew it, though, and heard it
clearly in her mind: 'What's 'at noice?'

The beam overhead grumbled and again she was showered
with plaster. She batted it off her shoulders, and whimpered.
A great flame must have burst from the roof above her just
then, for through the window she saw a brilliant glare reflected
from the white clapboards of the garage wall outside. The glare
tugged at her – *jump!* – and besides, her robe . . .

The beam thundered and began to fall. Now she must make
a choice, in microseconds. The swiftest thought would not be
fast enough to weigh and consider and decide; all that could
matter now was what was inside her, throwing switches (some
so worn and easy to move!). A giant was throwing them, and
he was strong; his strength was a conditioning deeper than
thou shalt not kill; he was a lesson learned before she had
learned to love God, or to walk, or to talk. He was her mother's
authority and the fear of all the hairy, sweaty, dangerous
mysteries from which she had shielded herself all her life;
and his name and title were Cover Thyself! With him, helping
him, was the reflexive Save Thyself! and against these – Robin,
whom she loved (but love is what she felt, once, for a canary,
and once for a Raggedy Ann doll) and her sense of duty to Sue
Martin (but so lightly promised, and at the time such a meaningless formality). There could be no choice in such a battle,
though she must live with the consequences for all her years.

Then –

– it was as if a mighty voice called *Stop!* and the very flames

froze. Half a foot above her hung the jagged end of the burning
beam, and chunks of plaster, splinters and scraps of shattered
lath and glowing joist stopped in mid-air. Yet during this sliver
of a fraction of time, she knew that the phenomenon was
a mental something, a figment, and the idea of time-cessation
only a clumsy effort of her mind's to account for what was
happening.

Save Thyself was still there, hysterical hands clutching for
the controls, but *Cover Thyself* disappeared into the background. Save herself she would, but it would be on new terms.
She was in the grip of a reflex of reflexes, one which took into
consideration all the factors a normal reflex would, to the end
goal of survival. But along with these, it called up everything
Reta Schmidt had ever done, everything she had been. In a single
soundless flash, a new kind of light was thrown into every
crevice and cranny of her existence. It was her total self now,
reacting to a total situation far wider than that which obtained
here in this burning room. It illuminated even the future – that
much of it which depended upon these events, between them
and the next probable major 'cross-roads'. It cancelled past
mis-judgements and illogics and replaced them with rightness,
even for the times she had known what was right and had done
otherwise. It came and was gone even while she leaped, while
she took two bounding steps across the floor and the beam
crashed and crushed and showered sparks where she had been
standing.

She scooped up the child and ran down the hall, through the
foyer, into the kitchen. It was dark there, thick with swirling
smoke, but the glass panels on the kitchen door glared with
some unfamiliar light from outdoors. She began to cough
violently, but grimly aimed at the light and drove ahead. It was
eclipsed suddenly by a monstrous shadow, and suddenly it
exploded inwards. There were lights out there she had never
seen before, and half-silhouetted in the broken doorway was a
big man with a gleaming helmet and an axe. She tried to call, or
perhaps it was only a scream, but instead she went into a spasm
of coughing.

'Somebody in here?' asked the man. A beam of light, apparently from the street, lit up the shield on the front of his helmet as he leaned forward. He stepped inside. 'Whew! Where are you?'

She went blindly to him and pushed Robin against his coat. 'The baby,' she croaked. 'Get him out of this smoke.'

He grunted and suddenly Robin was gone from her arms. 'You all right?' He was peering into the black and the smoke.

'Take him out,' she said. 'Then I'll want your coat.'

He went out. Miss Schmidt could hear Robin's clear voice: 'You a fireman?'

'I sure am,' rumbled the man. 'Want to see my fire engine? Then sit right there on the grass and wait one second. Okay?'

'Okay.'

The coat flew through the doorway.

'Got it?'

'Thank you.' She put the huge garment on and went out. The fireman waited there, again holding Robin in his arms. 'You all right, ma'am?'

Her lungs were an agony and she had burns on her feet and shoulders. Her hair was singed and one of her hands was flayed across its back. 'I'm just fine,' she said.

They began to walk up the road. Robin squirmed around in the man's arms and popped his head out to look back at the brightly burning house.

' 'Bye, Boff,' he said happily, and then gave his heart to the fire engine.

12

'*Mother, the bread's burning!*'

Mary Haunt opened her eyes to an impossible glare and a great roaring. She shrieked and flailed out blindly, as if she could frighten it away, whatever it was; and then she came enough to her senses to realize that she still sat in her chair by the window, and that the house was on fire. She leaped to her feet, sending the heavy chair skittering across the room where it toppled over against the clothes-press. As it always did when it was bumped, the clothes-press calmly opened its doors.

But Mary Haunt didn't wait for that or anything else. She struck the screen with the flat of her hand. It popped out easily, and she hit the ground almost at the same time as it did. She ran off a few steps, and then, like Lot's wife, curiosity overtook her and she stopped. She turned around in fascination.

Great wavering flames leapt fifty and sixty feet in the air and all the windows were alight. From the town side she could hear the shriek and clang of fire engines, and windows and doors opening, and running feet. But the biggest sound of all was the roar of the fire, like a giant's blow-torch.

She looked back at her own window. She could see into the room easily, the chair on its side, the bed with its chenille top-spread sprouting measles of spark and char, and the gaping doors of the – 'My clothes! My clothes!'

Furiously she ran back to the window, paused a moment in horror to see fire run along the picture-moulding of the inside wall like a nightmare caterpillar. 'My clothes,' she whispered. She didn't make much money at her job, but every cent that wasn't used in bed and board went on her back. She mouthed something, and from her throat came that animal growl of hers; she put both hands on the sill and leaped, and tumbled back into the house.

She was prepared for the heat but not for that intensity of light, and the noise was worst of all. She recoiled from it and stood for a moment with her hands over her eyes, swaying with the impact of it. Then she ground her teeth and made her way across to the clothes-press. She swept open the bottom drawer and turned out the neatly folded clothes. Down at the bottom was a cotton print dress, wrapped carefully around a picture frame. She lifted it out and hugged it, and ran across to the window with it. She leaned far out and dropped it gently on the grass, then turned back in again.

The far wall, by the door, began to buckle high up, and sud-denly there was fire up there. The corner near the ceiling toppled into the room with a crash and a cloud of white dust and greasy-looking smoke, and then the whole wall fell, not towards her, but away, so that her room now included a section of the corridor outside. As the dust settled somebody, a man, came roaring inarticulately and battering through the rubble. She could not know who it was. He apparently meant to travel the corridor whether it was all there or not, and he did, disappearing again into the inferno.

She staggered back towards the clothes-press. She felt mad, drunk, crazy. Maybe it was the de-oxygenated atmosphere and maybe it was fear and reaction, but it was sort of wonderful, too; she felt her face writhing and part of her was numb with astonishment at what the rest of her was doing: she was laughing. She slammed into the clothes-press, gasping for breath, filled her lungs and delivered up a shrill peal of laughter. Almost helpless from it, she fumbled down a dull satin evening gown with a long silver sash. She held it up in front of her and laughed again, doubling over it, and then straightened up, rolling the dress up into a ball as she did so. With all her might she hurled it into the rubble of the hallway. Next was a simple black dress with no back and a little bolero; with an expression on her face that can only be described as cheerful, she threw it after the evening gown. Then the blue, and the organdie with the taffeta underskirt, and the black and orange one she used to call her Hallowe'en dress; each one she dragged out, held up, and hurled: 'You,' she growled between her convulsions of laughter, 'you, and you, and *you*.' When the press was empty, she ran to the bureau and snatched open her scarf drawer, uncovering a flowerbed of dainty, filmy silk and nylon and satin shawls, scarves, and kerchiefs. She whipped out an oversized babushka, barely heavier than the air that floated it, and ran with it to the flaming mass where her door once was. She dipped and turned like a dancer, fluttering it through flame, and when it was burning she bounded back to the bureau and put it in the drawer with the others. Fire streamed out of the drawer and she laughed and laughed. . . .

And something nipped her sharply on the calves; she yelped and turned and found the lace of her black *négligé* was on fire.

She twisted back and gathered the cloth and ripped it away. The pain had sobered her and she was bewildered now, weak and beginning to be frightened. She started for the window and tripped and fell heavily, and when she got up the smoke was suddenly like a scalding blanket over her head and shoulders and she didn't know which way to go. She knelt and peered and found the window in an unexpected direction, and made for it. As she tumbled through, the ceiling behind her fell and the roof after it.

On her belly she clawed away from the house, sobbing, and at last rose to her knees. She smelt of smoke and burned hair and all her lovely fingernails were broken. She squatted on the ground, staring at the flaming shell of the house, and cried like a little girl. But when her swollen eyes rested on that square patch on the grass, she stopped crying and got up and limped over to it. Her cotton print, and the picture ... she picked the tidy package up and went tiredly away with it into the shadows where the hedge met the garage.

13

O'Banion raised his head groggily from the flyleaf of his *Blackstone* and the neat inscription written there:

> The law doth punish man or woman
> That steals the goose from off the common,
> But lets the greater felon loose,
> That steals the common from the goose,

– a piece of Eighteenth Century japery which O'Banion deplored. However, it had been written there by Opdycke when he was in law school, and the Opdyckes were a darn fine family. Princeton people, of course, but nobody minded.

All this flickered through his mind as he swam up out of sleep, along with 'What's the matter with my head?' because any roaring that loud must be in his ears; it would be too incredible anywhere else, and 'What's the matter with the light?' Then he was fully awake, and on his feet. 'My *God!*'

He ran to the door and snatched it open. Flame squirted at him as if from a hose; in a split second he felt his eyebrows disappear. He yelled and staggered back from it, and it pursued him. He turned and dived out of the window, landing clumsily on his stomach with his fists clenched over his solar plexus. His own weight drove the fists deep, and for a full minute he lay groaning for air. At last he got up, shook himself, and pelted around the house to the front. One fire engine was already standing by the kerb. There was a police car and the knot of bug-eyed spectators who spring apparently out of the ground at the scene of any accident anywhere at any hour. At the far end of the Bittelman lot there was a sharp scream of rubber and a glare of lights as a taxicab pulled in as close to the police barrier as it could get. The door was already open; a figure left it, half running, half thrown out by the sudden stop.

'Sue!' But no one heard him – everyone else was yelling too: 'Look!' 'Somebody stop her!' 'Hey!' 'Hey, you!'

O'Banion backed off a little to cup his hands and yell again, when directly over his head a cheerful small voice said, 'Mommy runs fast!'

'Robin! You're all right –' He was perched on top of the fire engine with one arm around the shining brass bell, looking like a Botticelli seraph. Someone beside him – good heavens, it was Miss Schmidt, dishevelled and bright-eyed, wrapped up in some tent-like garment – Miss Schmidt screamed, 'Stop her, stop her, I've got the baby here!'

Robin said to Miss Schmidt, 'Tonio runs fast too, shall we?'

Now they were all yelling at O'Banion, but in four paces he could hear nothing but the roar ahead of him. He had never seen a house burn like this, all over, all at once. He took the porch steps in one bound and had just time to turn his shoulder to the door. It was ajar, but couldn't swing fast enough under such an impact. It went down flat and solid, and for one crazy moment O'Banion was riding it like an aquaplane in a sea of fire, for the foyer floor was ablaze. Then the leading edge of the door caught on something and spilled him off. He rolled over twice in fuming debris and then got his feet under him.

It was like a particularly bad dream, so familiar, so confusing. He turned completely around to orient himself, found the corridor, and started up it, yelling for Sue at the top of his voice. He saw a left-hand wall lean down towards him and had to scamper back out of the way. It had barely poured its rubble down when he was on, in, and through it. Over the crash and roar, over his own hoarse bellowing, he thought he heard a crazy woman laughing somewhere in the fire. Even in his near-hysteria, he could say, 'Not Sue, that's not Sue Martin. . . .' And he was, before he knew it, at and past Sue Martin's room. He flung out a hand and caught the door-jamb, which immediately came off in his hand. He bounced off the end wall and turned as he did so, like a sprint swimmer, and swung into Sue Martin's room. 'Sue! Sue!'

Was he mistaken? Did someone call. 'Robin – Robin honey . . .'?

He dropped to his knees, where he could see in relatively clearer air. 'Sue, oh Sue!'

She lay half buried in rubble from the fallen ceiling. He threw off scorched and broken two-by-fours and burning lath, took her by the shoulders and lifted her out of the heap of broken plaster – thank the powers for that! it had protected her to some degree. 'Sue?'

'Robin,' she croaked.

He shook her. 'He's all right, he's outside, I saw him.'

She opened her eyes and frowned at him. Not at him; at what he had said. 'He's here somewhere.'

'I saw him. Come on!' He lifted her to her feet, and as she dragged, 'It's the truth; do you think I would lie to you?'

He felt strength surge into her body. 'You forgot to say, "I, an O'Banion",' she said, but it didn't hurt. They stumbled to the window and he pushed her through it and leaped after her. For two painful breaths they lay gulping clean air, and then O'Banion got to his feet. His head was spinning and he almost lay down again. He set his jaw and helped Sue Martin up. 'Too close!' he shouted. Holding her up, he half-dragged her no more than a step when she suddenly straightened, and with unexpected and irresistible strength leapt back towards the burning wall, pulling him with her. He caught at her to regain his balance, and she put her arms tight around him. 'The wall!' he screamed, as it leaned out over them. She said nothing, but her arms tightened even more, and he could have moved more easily if he had been bound to a post with steel chains. The wall came down then, thunder and sparks, like the end of the world; madly, it occurred to him just then that he could solve one of his problem cases by defining the unorthodox contract under suit as a stock certificate.

But instead of dying he took a stinging blow on his right shoulder, and that was all. He opened his eyes. He and Sue Martin still stood locked together, and all around them was flame like a flower-bed with the rough outline of the house wall and its peaked roof. Around their feet was the four-foot circular frame of the attic vent, which had ringed them like a quoit.

The woman slumped in his arms, and he lifted her and picked his way, staggering, into the friendly dark and the welcome hands of the firemen. But when they tried to lift her away from him she held his arm and would not let go. 'Put me down, just put me down,' she said. 'I'm all right. Put me down.'

They did and she leaned against O'Banion. He said, 'We're okay now. We'll go up to the road. Don't mind about us.' The firemen hesitated, but when they began to walk, they were apparently reassured, and ran back to their work. Hopeless work, O'Banion amended. But for a few sagging studs and the two chimneys, the house was little more than a pit of flames.

'Is Robin really – '

'Shh. He's really. Miss Schmidt got him out, I think. Anyway, he's sitting on the fire engine enjoying every minute. He watched you going in. He approves of your speed.'

'You – '

'I saw you too. I yelled.'

'And then you came after me.' They walked a slow pace or so. 'Why?'

Robin was safe, of course, he was about to say, so you didn't have to – and then there was within him a soundless white flash that lit up all he had ever done and been, everything he had read, people and places and ideas. Where he had acted right, he felt the right proven; where he had been wrong, he could see now the right in full force, even when for years he had justified his wrong. He saw fully now what old Sam Bittelman had almost convinced him of intellectually with his searching questions. He had fought away Sam's suggestion that there was something ludicrous, contradictory about the law and its pretensions to permanence. Now he saw that the law, as he knew it, was not under attack at all. As long as a man treated the body of law like a great stone buttress, based in bedrock and propping up civilization, he was fortifying a dead thing which could only kill the thing it was built to uphold. But if he saw civilization as an intricate, *moving* entity, the function of law changed. It was governor, stabilizer, inhibitor, *control* of something dynamic and progressive, subject to the punishments and privileges of evolution like a living thing. His whole idea of the hair-splitting search for 'precedent' as a refining process in law was wrong. It was an adaptive process instead. The suggestion that not one single law is common to all human cultures, past and present, was suddenly no insult to law at all, but a living compliment; to nail a culture to permanent laws now seemed as ridiculous a concept as man conventionally refusing to shed his scales and his gills.

And with this revelation of the viability of man and his works, O'Banion experienced a profound realignment in his (or was it really his) attitude towards himself, his effortful preoccupation to defend and justify his blood and breeding and his gentleman's place in the world. It came to him now that although the law may say here that men are born equal, and there that they must receive equal treatment before the law, no one but a complete fool would insist that men *are* equal. Men, wherever they came from, whatever they claim for themselves, are only what's in their heads and what's in their hearts. The purest royal blood that yields a weak king will yield a failure; a strong peasant can rise higher and accomplish more, and if what he accomplishes is compatible with human good, he is surely no worse than a beneficent king. Over and above anything else, however, shone the fact that a good man needs least of all to prove it by claiming that he comes from a line of good men. And for him to assume the privileges and postures of the landed gentry after the land is gone is pure buffoonery. Time enough for sharp vertical differentiations between men when the differences become so great that the highest may not cross-breed with the lowest; until then, in the broad view, differences are so subtle as to be negligible, and the concept 'to marry out of one's class' belongs with the genesis of hippogriffs and gryphons – in mythology.

All this, and a thousand times more, unfolded and was clear to O'Banion in this illuminated instant, so short it took virtually no time at all, so bright it lit up all the days of his past and part of his future as well. And it happened between pace and pace, when Sue Martin said, 'You followed me. Why?'

'I love you,' he said instantly.

'Why?' she whispered.

He laughed joyously. 'It doesn't matter.'

Sue Martin – *Sue Martin!* – began to cry.

14

Phil Halvorsen opened his eyes and saw that the house was on fire. He lay still, watching the flames feed, and thought, isn't this what I was waiting for?

Now there can be an end to it, he thought peacefully. Now I never need worry again that I'm wrong to be as I am, and other people's needs, the appetites and rituals of the great Average will no longer accuse me. I cannot be excluded unless I exist, so here's an end to being excluded. I cannot be looked down on when I can no longer be seen.

The ceiling began to develop a tan patch, and hot white powder fell from it to his face. He covered it with the pillow. He was resigned to later, final agonies because they would be final, but he saw no reason to put up with the preliminaries. Just then most of the plaster came down on him. It didn't hurt much, and it meant the thing would be over sooner than he had thought.

He heard faintly, over the colossal roaring, a woman scream. He lay still. As much as anyone – perhaps more – he would ordinarily be concerned about the others. But not now. Not now. Such concern is for a man who expects to live with a conscience afterwards.

Something – it sounded like an inside wall – went down very near. It jolted the foot of his bed and he felt its hot exhalation and the taste of its soot, but otherwise it did not reach him. 'So come on,' he said tightly, 'get it over with, will you?' and hurled the pillow away.

As if in direct and obedient answer the ceiling over him opened up – *up*; apparently a beam had broken and was ripping down into an adjoining room, upwards here. Then the tangle of stringers it carried fell away and started down. High above was blackness, suddenly rent by smoky orange light – the inside of the roof, a section of which was falling in with the stringers.

'All right,' said Halvorsen, as if someone had asked him a question. He closed his eyes.

He closed his eyes on a flash of something like an inner and unearthly light, and time stood still ... or perhaps it was only that subjectively he had all the time in the world to examine this shadowless internal cosmos.

Most immediately, it laid out before him the sequence of events which had brought him here, awaiting death on a burning bed. In this sequence a single term smote him with that 'well, of *course*!' revelation that rewarded his plodding, directive thoughts when they were successful for him. The term was 'Average', and his revelation came like a burst of laughter: for anyone else this would have been a truism, an unarguable axiom; like a fool he had let his convoluted thinking breeze past 'Average', use 'Average', worry about 'Average' without ever looking at it.

But 'Average' – Average Appetite – was here for him to see, a line drawn from side to side on a huge graph. And all over the graph were spots – millions of them. (He was in a place where he could actually see and comprehend 'millions'.) On that line lived this creation, this demi-god, to whom he had felt subservient for so long, whose hungers and whose sense of fitness ought to have been – *had* been – Halvorsen's benchmark, his reference point. Halvorsen had always felt himself a member of a minority – a minority which shrank as he examined it, and he was always examining it. All the world catered to Average Man and his 'normal' urges, and this must be proper, for he was aware of the reciprocities: Average Man got these things because these things were what Average Man wanted and needed.

Want and need ... and there was the extraordinary discovery he had made when Bitty asked him : if people really needed it, would there have to be so much high-pressure salesmanship?

This he threw on the graph like a transparent overlay; it too bore a line from side to side, but much lower down, indicating with much more accuracy just how interested Average Man was in the specific appetite about which he made so much noise. Now bend close and look at those millions of spots – individual people all, each with his true need for the kind of cultural pressure which was driving a man, here, to his death from guilt.

The first thing Halvorsen saw was that the dots were scattered so widely that the actual number falling on the line Average Man was negligible: there were countless millions more un-average people. It came to him that those who obey the gospel of Average Man are, in their efforts to be like the mass of humanity, obeying the dictates of one of the smallest minorities of all. The next thing to strike him was that it took the presence of *all* these dots to place that line just where it was; there was no question of better, or worse, or more or less fit. Except for the few down here and their opposite numbers up there, the handful of sick, insane, incomplete or distorted individuals whose sexual appetites were non-existent or extreme, the vast majority above and below the true average were basically 'normal'. And here where he, Halvorsen, might appear on the graph – he had plenty of company.

He'd never known that! The magazine covers, the advertisements, the dirty jokes – they hadn't let him know it.

He understood, now, the mechanism of this cultural preoccupation; it came to him in the recollection that he had appeared at work for three hundred consecutive working days and nobody noticed his ears. And then one day a sebaceous cyst in his left lobe had become infected, and the doctor removed it and he showed up at work with a bandage covering his ear. *Everybody began to think about Halvorsen's ear!* Every interview had to begin with an explanation of his ear or the applicant would keep straying his attention to it. And he'd noticed, too, that after he explained about the cyst, the interviewee would always glance at Halvorsen's other ear before he got back to business. Now, in this silver place where all inter-relationships were true ones, he could equate his covered and noticeable ear with a Bikini bathing suit, and see clearly how normal interest-disinterest – acceptance – can be put under forced draught.

It came to him also *why* this particular cultural matrix did this to itself. In its large subconscious, it probably knew quite clearly the true status of its sensual appetites. It must reason, then, that unless it kept these appetites whipped up to a froth at all times, it might not increase itself, and it felt it must increase. This was not a pretty thought, but neither is the pounce of a cat on a baby bird; yet one cannot argue with the drive behind it.

So it was that Halvorsen's reasons for not living ceased to be reasons; with the purest of truth he could say I am not unmanned; I am not unfit; I am not abnormal . . . I am not alone.

All this in no-time, as he closed his eyes to await the mass even now falling on him. And the reflex of reflexes acted just as eyelids met; he spun off the bed, bounced out of the near-by window, and was on the grass outside as the ceiling and walls together met the floor in a gout of flame.

15

The girl climbed up to the front seat of the fire engine. 'Move over.'

Miss Schmidt swung her worried gaze away from the burning house, and said in a preoccupied tone, 'I don't think you'd be allowed to, little girl. We're from that hou– why, it's Mary Haunt!'

'Didn't recognize me, huh?' said Mary Haunt. She swung a hip and shunted Miss Schmidt over. 'Can't say I blame you. What a mess!' she said, indicating the house.

'Mr O'Banion is in there; he went after Mrs Martin. And have you seen Mr Halvorsen?'

'No.'

'Tonio! Tonio!' Robin suddenly cried.

'Shh, dear. He'll be along.'

'Dare he *iss*! Dare he *iss*! Mom*ee*!' he shrieked, 'come see my fire engine, shall we?'

'Oh, thank God, thank God they're safe,' said Miss Schmidt. She hugged Robin until he grunted.

'I'm all choked up,' growled Mary Haunt. Again she made the angry gesture at the house. '*What* a mess. Everything I own – the warpaint, the clothes, all my magazines – everything, gone. You know what that means. I – '

I've got to go home now. And it was here, on the slightest matter of phrasing that the strange flash of silver suffused Mary Haunt; not under the descending scythe of Death, nor under the impact of soul found, heart found: just for the nudge of a word, she had her timeless instant.

All her life and the meaning of her life and all the things in it: the dimity curtains and home-baked bread, Jackie and Seth whamming away at each other for the privilege of carrying her books, the spice-shelf and the daffodils under the parlour windows. She'd loved it so, and reigned over it; and, mostly, she'd been a gentle princess and ruled kindly.

Did they throw you out, gal?

She'd never know where it started, how it came about, until now. Now, with astonishment, she did. Daddy started it, before she was old enough to walk, Daddy one of the millions who had applauded a child actress called Shirley Temple, one of the thousands who had idolized her, one of the hundreds who had deified her. 'Little Mary Hollywood', he'd called his daughter, and it had been 'When you're in pictures, honey – ' Every morning was a fountain to empty the reservoir of his dreams; every night he filled again from the depthless well of his ambition for her.

And everyone believed him. Mom came to believe him, and her kid brother, and finally everyone in town. They had to; Daddy's unswerving, undoubting conviction overrode any alternatives, and she herself clinched it, just by being what she was, an exquisite child exquisitely groomed, who grew more beautiful (by Hollywood standards) every year. She wanted what every child wants: loving attention. She got it in fullest measure. She wanted to do what every child wants to do: gain the approval of her elders. She tried; and indeed, no other course was open to her.

Did they throw you out, gal?

Perhaps Daddy might have outgrown it; or if not, perhaps he'd have known, or found out, how to accomplish his dream in a real world. But Daddy died when she was six, and Mom took over his dream as if it had been a flower from his dead hand. She did not nourish it; she pressed it between the leaves of her treasured memories of him. It was a live thing, true, but arrested at the intensity and the formlessness of his hopes for her when she was six. She encouraged the child only to want to be in pictures, and to be sure she would be; it never occurred to her that there might be things for the child to learn. Her career was coming; it was coming like Christmas.

But no one knew when.

And when she cleaned house, they all thought it was sweet, so pretty to watch, but they'd rather take the broom away from her; and when she baked, it was pretty too but not what she was really *for;* and when she read the diet sections in the grocery magazines, that was all right, but the other features – how to make tangerine gravy for duck, how to remove spots from synthetic fibres – 'Why, Mary, you'll have a little army worrying about those things for you!'

Movie magazines then, and movies, and waiting, until the day she left.

Did they throw you out, gal?

Screen Society had a feature on Hollywood High School, and it mentioned how many stars and starlets had come from there, and the ages some of them had been when they signed contracts. And suddenly she wasn't the Shirley Temple girl at all, she was older, years older than two girls in the article, the same age as five of them. Yet here she was still, while the whole town waited ... suppose she never made it? Suppose nothing happened here? And she began to interpret this remark, that look, the other silence, in ways that troubled her, until she wanted to hide, or to drop dead, or leave.

Just like that, leaving was the answer. She told no one, she took what clothes she had that were good, she bought a ticket for just anywhere and wrote thrilling, imaginative, untrue letters at wider and wider intervals. Naïvely she got a job which might mean her Big Break and which actually never would. And at last she reached a point where she would not look back, for wanting home so much; she would not look forward, for knowing there was nothing there; she held herself in a present of futility and purposive refusal to further the ambition she insisted she had; and she had no pleasure and no outlet but anger. She took refuge in her furies; she scorned people and what they did and what they wanted, and told them all so. And she took the picture of Mom standing in front of the house in the spring, with the jonquils all about and the tulips coming, and she wrapped it up in the cotton print Mom had made for her fourteenth birthday and never given her because *Screen Society* had said princess-style for teenagers was corny.

Did they throw you out, gal?

Old Sam had asked her that; he knew, even when she didn't. But now, in this strange silver moment, she knew; she knew it all. Yes, they had thrown her out. They had let her be a dead man's dream until she was nearly dead herself. They never let her be Mary Haunt who wanted to fix the new curtains and bake a berry pie, and have a square hedge along the Elm Street side and go to meeting on Sundays. They had marked her destiny on her face and body and on the clothes she wore, and stamped it into her speech and fixed her hair the way they wanted it, and to the bottom of her heart she was angry.

And now, all of a sudden, and for the very first time, it occurred to her that she could, if she wanted, be Mary Haunt her own self, and be it right there at home; that home was the best place to be that very good thing, and she could replace their disappointment with a very real pride. She could be home before the Strawberry Festival at the church; she would wear an apron and get suds on her forehead when she pushed her hair back, the way Bitty did sometimes.

So Mary Haunt sat on a fire engine, next to the high-school librarian who was enveloped in a tremendous raincoat, saying that everything was burned up, lost; and about to say, 'I've got to go home now.' But she said, 'I can go home now.' She looked into Miss Schmidt's eyes and smiled a smile the older woman had never seen before. 'I can, I can! I can go home now!' Mary Haunt sang. Impulsively she took Miss Schmidt's hand and squeezed it. She looked into her face and laughed, 'I'm not mad any more, not at you or anybody ... and I've been a little stinker and I'm sorry; I'm going *home*!' And Miss Schmidt looked at the smudged face, the scorched hair drawn back into a childish pony-tail and held by a rubber band, the spotless princess dress. 'Why,' said Miss Schmidt, 'you're beautiful, just beautiful!' 'I'm not. I'm seventeen, only seventeen,' Mary Haunt said out of a wild happiness, 'and I'm going home and bake a cake.' And she hugged her mother's picture and smiled; even the ruined house did not glow quite this way.

EXCERPT FROM FIELD EXPEDITION [NOTEBOOK] [! ! !] Did it ever work! [You'd] think these specimens had used Synapse Beta sub Sixteen all their lives! If [we] had a [tenth] as much stamina [we] could [lie down] in a [bed] of paradoxes and go to [sleep].

[We] will observe for a [short period] longer, and then pack up and leave. This is a [fascinating] place to visit, but [I] wouldn't want to [live] here.

16

It was October, and possibly the last chance they'd have for a picnic, and the day agreed and was beautiful for them. They found a fine spot where a stand of birch grew on both sides of an old split-rail fence, and a brook went by just out of sight. After they were finished O'Banion lay on his stomach in the sun, and thoughtfully scratched his upper lip with a bit of straw.

His wife laughed softly.

'Hm?'

'You're thinking about the Bittelmans again.'

'How'd you know?'

'Just used to it. When you go off into yourself and look astonished and mystified and annoyed all at once, it's the Bittelmans again.'

'Harmless hobby,' said Halvorsen, and smiled.

'Is it? Tonio, how would you like me to go all pouty and coy and complain that you've spent more time thinking about them than about me?'

'Do by all means go all pouty and coy. I'll divorce you.'

'Tony!'

'Well,' he said lazily, 'I had so much fun marrying you in the first place that it might be worth doing again. Where's Robin?'

'Right h– Oh dear. *Robin!*'

Down in the cleft, where the brook gurgled, Robin's voice answered instantly. 'Frogs here, Mommy. Deelicious!'

'Does he eat 'em raw?' asked Halvorsen mildly.

Sue laughed. 'That just means "pretty" or "desirable" or even "bright green". Robin, don't you dare get wet, you promise me?'

'I promise me,' said the voice.

'And don't go away!'

'I don't.'

'Why don't they show up?' demanded O'Banion. 'Just once, that's all I'd ever want. Just show their faces and answer two questions.'

'Why don't who – oh, Sam and Bitty. What two questions?'

'What they did to us, how and why.'

'That's one question, counsellor?' asked Halvorsen.

'Yes. Two: What they are.'

'Now, why'd you say "what" instead of "who"?'

'It comes to that.' He rolled over and sat up. 'Honey, would you mind if I ran down everything we've found out so far, just once more?'

'Summarize and rest your case?'

'I don't know about resting it . . . reviewing the brief.'

'I often wonder why you call it a brief,' Halvorsen chuckled.

O'Banion rose and went to the fence. Putting one hand on a slender birch trunk, he hopped upwards, turning, to come to rest sitting on the top rail. 'Well, one thing I'm sure of: Sam and Bitty could *do* things to people, and they did it to all of us. And I refuse to believe that they did it with logic and persuasion.'

'They could be pretty persuasive.'

'It was more than that,' O'Banion said impatiently. 'What they did to me changed everything about me.'

'How very intriguing.'

'Everything about the way I *think*, hussy. I can look back on that now and realize that I was roped, thrown and notched. When he wanted me to answer questions I had to answer them, no matter what I was thinking. When he was through with me he turned me loose and made me go back to my business as if nothing had happened. Miss Schmidt told me the same thing.' He shifted his weight on the rail and said excitedly. 'Now there's our prize exhibit. All of us were – changed – by this thing, but Reta – she's a *really* different person.'

'She wasn't more changed than the others,' said Sue soberly. 'She's thirty-eight years old. It's an interesting age because when you're there and look five years older, and then spruce up the way she did and look five years younger, it looks like twenty years' difference, not ten. That's all cosmetics and clothes, though. The real difference is as quiet and deep as – well, Phil here.'

Again Halvorsen found a smile. 'Perhaps you're right. She shifted from the library to teaching. It was a shift from surrounding herself with other people's knowledge to surrounding other people with hers. She's alive.'

'I'll say. Boy friend too.'

'Quiet and deep,' said O'Banion thoughtfully, swinging his feet. 'That's right. All you get out of Halvorsen when you ask him about it is a smile, like a light going on and, "Now it's right for me to be me." '

'That's it – all of it,' chuckled Halvorsen happily.

'And Mary Haunt, bless her. Second happiest child I ever saw. *Robin! Are you all right?*'

'Yis!' came the voice.

'I'm still not satisfied,' said O'Banion. 'I have the feeling we're staring at very petty and incidental results of some very important cause. In a moment of acute stress I made a decision which affected my whole life.'

'*Our.*'

He blew her a kiss. 'Reta Schmidt says the same thing, though she wouldn't go into detail. And maybe that's what Halvorsen means when he says. "*Now* it's right for me ..." *You* annoy me.'

'Sir!' she cried with mock horror.

He laughed. 'You know what I mean. Only you got exposed to the Bittelmans and didn't change. Everybody else got wonderful,' he smiled. 'You just stayed wonderful. Now what's so special about you?'

'Must I sit here and be – '

'Shush. Think back. Was there any *different* kind of thing that happened to you that night, some kind of emergency thinking you did that was above and beyond anything you thought you could do?'

'Not that I remember.'

Suddenly he brought his fist down on his thigh. 'There *was*! Remember right after we got out of the house, the wall fell on us? You dragged me back and held me still and that attic vent dropped right around us?'

'That. Yes, I remember. But it wasn't special. It just made sense.'

'*Sense?* I'd like to put a computer on that job – after scorching it half through and kicking it around a while. Somehow you calculated how fast that thing was falling and how much ground it would cover when it hit. You computed that against our speed outwards. You located the attic vent opening and figured where it would land, and whether or not it could contain us both. Then you estimated our speed *if* we went towards the safe spot and concluded that we could make it. *Then* you went into action, more or less over my dead body to boot. All that in – ' he closed his eyes to relive the moment. ' – all of one and a half seconds absolute tops. It wasn't *special?*'

'No, it wasn't,' she said positively. 'It was an emergency, don't you see? A real emergency, not only because we might get hurt, but in terms of all we were to each other and all we could be if only you –'

'Well, I did,' he smiled. 'But I still don't understand you. You mean you think more, not less – widen your scope instead of narrowing your focus when it's that kind of emergency? You can think of all those things at once, better and faster and more accurately?'

Halvorsen suddenly lunged and caught O'Banion's foot, pulling it sharply upwards. He shouted '*Yoop!*' His right hand whipped up and back and scrabbled at the tree-trunk; his torso twisted and his left hand shot straight down. His legs flailed and straightened; for a moment he seesawed on the rail on his kidneys. At last he got his left hand on the rail and pulled himself upwards to sit again. 'Hey! What do you think you're –'

'Proving a point,' said Halvorsen. 'Look, Tony: without warning you were thrown off balance. What did you do? You reached out for that tree-trunk without looking – got it, too;

you knew just how fast and how far to go. But at the same time you put your left hand straight down, ready to catch your weight if you went down to the ground. Meantime you banged around with your legs and shifted your weight this way just enough to make a new balance on top. Now tell me: did you sit there after I pushed you and figure all those things out, one by one?'

'By golly no. Snop – snap – synapses.'

'What?'

'Synapses. Sort of pathways in the brain that get paved better and better as you do something over and over. After a while they happen without conscious thought. Keeping your balance is that kind of thing, on the motor level. But don't tell me you have a sort of ... personal-cultural inner ear – something that makes you react reflexively in terms of your past and your future and ... but that's what happened to me that night!' He stared at Halvorsen. 'You figured that out long ago, you and your IBM head!'

'It always happens if the emergency's a bad one,' Sue said composedly. 'Sometimes when you don't even know it is an emergency. But what's remarkable? Aren't drowning men supposed to see their whole lives pass before them?'

'Did you say that always happens with your emergencies?'

'Well, doesn't it?'

Suddenly he began to chuckle softly, and at her questioning look he said, 'You remind me of something a psychologist told me once. A man was asked to describe his exact sensations on getting drunk. "Just like anybody else," he says. "Well, describe it," says the doctor. The man says, "Well, first your face gets a little flushed and your tongue gets thick, and after a while your ears begin to wiggle – " Sue, honey, I've got news for you. Maybe you react like that in important moments, a great big shiny flash of truth and proportional relationships, but believe me, other people don't. I never did until that night. *That's it!*' he yelled at the top of his voice.

From down the slope came a clear little voice, 'Wash 'at noice?'

Sue and Halvorsen smiled at one another and then O'Banion said earnestly, 'That's what Bitty and Sam gave us – a synaptic reflex like the equilibrium mechanisms, but bigger – much bigger. A human being is an element in a whole culture, and the culture itself is alive ... I suppose the species could be called, as a whole, a living thing. And when we found ourselves in a stress situation which was going to affect us signally – dangerously, or just importantly – we reacted to it in the way I did just now when you pushed me – only on a cultural level. It's as if Sam and Bitty had found a way to install or develop that "balancing" mechanism in us. It resolved some deep personal conflict of Halvorsen's; it snapped Mary out of a dangerous delusion and Miss Schmidt out of a dangerous retreat. And, well, you know about me.'

'I can't believe people don't think that way in emergencies!' she said, dazed.

'Maybe some do,' said Halvorsen. 'Come to think of it, people do some remarkable things under sudden stress; they make not obvious but very right choices under pressure, like the man who cracks a joke and averts a panic or the boy who throws himself on a grenade to save his squad. They've surveyed themselves in terms of all they are and measured that against their surroundings and all it is – all in a split fraction of a second. I guess everyone has it. Some of it.'

'Whatever this synapse is, the Bittelmans gave it to us ... yes, and maybe set the house on fire too ... why? Testing? Testing what – just us, or human beings? *What are they?*' demanded the lawyer.

'Gone, that's what,' said Halvorsen.

For a very brief time, he was wrong to say that.

EXCERPT FROM FIELD EXPEDITION [NOTEBOOK] [Our] last [hour] here, so [we] [induced] three of the test specimens to [locus B] for final informal observation. [Smith] pretends to a certain [chagrin]. After all, [he] [says] all [we] did was to come [sizable abstract number] of [terrestrially immeasurable distance unit]s, forgoing absolutely the company of [our] [   ] and the pleasures of the [   ]; strain [our] ingenuity and our [technical equipment] to the [break]ing point, even

getting trapped into using that [miserable impractical] power supply and
[charge]ing it up every [month] – all to detect and analyse the incidence
of Synapse Beta sub Sixteen. And here these specimens sit, locating
and defining the Synapse during a brief and idle conversation!
Actually, [I] [think] [Smith] is [pleased] with them for it.
We shall now [dismantle] the [widget] and the [wadget] and [take off].

Robin was watching a trout.

'Tsst! Tsst!'

He was watching more than a trout, really; he was watching
its shadow. It had occurred to him that perhaps the shadow
wasn't a shadow, but another and fuzzier kind of fish which
wouldn't let the more clear-cut one get away from over it,
so maybe that was why the trout kept hanging into the current, hanging and *zoom!* darting forward. But he never was
fast enough for the fuzzy one, which stayed directly under
him no matter what.

'Tss! Robin!'

He looked up, and the trout was forgotten. He filled his powerful young lungs with air and his face with joy, and then made
a heroic effort and stifled his noisy delight in obedience to that
familiar finger-on-lips and its explosive '*Shh!*'

Barely able to contain himself, he splashed straight across
the brook, shoes and all, and threw himself into Bitty's arms.
'Ah Robin!' said the woman, 'wicked little boy. Are you a
wicked little boy?'

'Yis. Bitty-bitty-BITTY!'

'Shh. Look who's with me.' She put him down, and there
stood old Sam. 'Hey-y-y-y, boy?'

'Ah Sam!' Robin clasped his hands together and got them
between his knees, bending almost double in delight. 'Ware
you *been*, Sam?'

'Around,' said Sam. 'Listen, Robin, we came to say good-
bye. We're going away now.'

'Don't go 'way.'

'We have to,' said Bitty. She knelt and hugged him. 'Good-
bye, darling.'

'Shake,' said Sam gravely.

'Shake, rattle an' roll, 'said Robin with equal sobriety.

'Ready, Sam?'

'All set.'

Swiftly they took off their bodies, folded them neatly and put them in two small green plastic cases. On one was lettered [WIDGET] and on the other [WADGET], but of course Robin was too young to read. Besides, he had something else to astonish him. 'Boff!' he cried. 'Googie!'

Boff and Googie [waved] at him and he waved back. They picked up the plastic cases and threw them into a sort of bubble that was somehow there, and [walked] in after them. Then they [went].

Robin turned away and without once looking back, climbed the slope and ran to Sue. He flung himself into her lap and uttered the long, whistle-like wail that preceded his rare bouts with bitter tears.

'Why *darling*, whatever happened? What *is* it? Did you bump your –'

He raised a flushed and contorted face to her. 'Boff gone,' he said wetly. 'Oh, oh-h-h, Boff an' Googie gone.'

He cried most of the way home, and never mentioned Boff again.

INCIDENTAL [NOTES] ON FIELD REPORT: The discovery of total incidence and random use of Synapse Beta sub Sixteen in a species is unique in the known [cosmos]; yet introduction of the mass of data taken on the Field Expedition into the [master] [computer] alters its original [dictum] not at all: the presence of this Synapse in a species ensures its survival. In the particular case at hand, the species undoubtedly bears, and will always bear, the [curse] of interpersonal and intercultural frictions, due to the amount of paradox possible. Where so many actions, decisions, and organizational activities can occur uncontrolled by the Synapse and its [universal-interrelational] modifying effect, paradox must result. On the other [hand], any species with such a concentration of the Synapse, even in partial use, will not destroy itself and very probably cannot be destroyed by anything.

Prognosis positive.

Their young are delightful. [I] [feel good]. [Smith], [I] [forgive] [you].

Another S F Penguin by Theodore Sturgeon

More than Human

Awarded First Prize by the International Fantasy and Science Fiction Committee

'We're not a group of freaks. We're *Homo Gestalt*, you understand? We're a single entity, a new kind of human being. We weren't invented. We evolved. We're the next step up. We're alone; there are no more like us.'

More Than Human, a vision of man's future evolution, intriguingly echoes current research into human relationships. It is also an outstanding novel in its own right – compelling and acute.

'The only brilliant newcomer lately . . . Sturgeon is a talented writer . . . and the book is alive with pathos and exhilaration' – *Time and Tide*

Not for sale in the U.S.A. or Canada